Mrs Winterbottom
takes a
Gap Year

Also by Joanna Nell

The Single Ladies of Jacaranda Retirement Village
The Last Voyage of Mrs Henry Parker
The Great Escape from Woodlands Nursing Home
The Tea Ladies of St Jude's Hospital

Mrs Winterbottom
takes a
Gap Year

JOANNA NELL

HODDER &
STOUGHTON

First published in Great Britain in 2023 by Hodder & Stoughton
An Hachette UK company

1

A CIP catalogue record for this title is available from the British Library

Hardback ISBN 978 1 399 70595 0
Trade Paperback ISBN 978 1 399 70596 7
ebook ISBN 978 1 399 70597 4

Typeset in Sabon LT Std by Bookhouse, Sydney

Printed and bound in Great Britain by Clays Ltd, Elcograf S.p.A.

Hodder & Stoughton policy is to use papers that are natural, renewable and recyclable
products and made from wood grown in sustainable forests. The logging and
manufacturing processes are expected to conform to the environmental regulations of
the country of origin.

Hodder & Stoughton Ltd
Carmelite House
50 Victoria Embankment
London EC4Y 0DZ

www.hodder.co.uk

For Peter

The use of travelling is to regulate imagination by reality, and instead of thinking how things may be, to see them as they are.

SAMUEL JOHNSON

1

Sorry, not sorry

DR HEATHER WINTERBOTTOM OFTEN JOKED THAT SHE'D fallen half an hour behind on her first day, and forty years later, she was still trying to catch up. She always apologised for keeping her patients waiting, even on the rare occasions her appointments ran to time. What's more, her face, with its harried arrangement of frown lines and down-turned mouth, had taken on an expression of permanent contrition. All that was about to change. Today, on her last ever day as a doctor, she would take back those thirty precious minutes and add them to the rest of her life. There was an entire world beyond Netherwood Medical Centre, so many things she wanted to do and see. This day marked the beginning of a whole new chapter in her life, if not a whole new life. But first, she had to remove a cotton bud from Mr Clifton's left ear.

Mrs Clifton had never trusted her husband to be an effective advocate for his own body and always accompanied him to his appointments. Between them, they'd clocked up enough hours in Heather's waiting room for it to qualify as a second residence. Ever the pragmatist, Mrs Clifton had packed sandwiches and a thermos of tea.

The Cliftons were the kind of couple who scraped mud off the bottom of each other's boots before getting into the car. They wore matching fleeces and finished each other's sentences. Unlike Heather and her husband, Alan, who lived in the same house and worked at the same practice but were rarely seen together, the Cliftons were rarely seen apart.

Heather brought up Mr Clifton's file on the computer while the couple debated who should sit in which chair.

'You're the patient, Bob,' Cynthia Clifton insisted, her tone failing to match her smile.

'But you're the one who does all the talking.' Bob's strained smile mirrored his wife's.

'How long have you two been married again?' Heather asked as she squinted into the otoscope, forceps at the ready.

'Fifty years,' they chimed in synchrony.

'And never a cross word,' said Cynthia.

'That's because we spend so much time not speaking to each other.' Bob laughed and his wife punched him playfully on the arm.

Heather held up the cotton bud tip on the end of the forceps for inspection. 'Remember, Bob, nothing smaller than your elbow in your ear.'

'I don't know how many times I've told him, doctor, but he never listens to me.'

Bob stretched his jaw and rubbed his ear. 'Why do you think I stuffed my ears with cotton wool in the first place?'

Heather smiled. The contraction of the muscles around her eyes and mouth felt strained and unfamiliar. One of her goals for retirement, as well as getting her body into shape, was to exercise her 'sorry' face back into something less apologetic.

'This is for you, Dr Winterbottom,' Cynthia said, producing a candy-striped gift bag.

'We're going to miss you,' Bob added. 'You're the best doctor we've ever had.'

The only doctor they'd had, Heather almost pointed out, since the Cliftons refused to see any of the other doctors in the practice. On the rare occasion she and Alan managed a holiday, Bob and Cynthia would store up their collective ailments and await her return. Still, it made a change to receive a compliment rather than a complaint.

Heather opened the gift bag. At first she wasn't sure what to make of the large padded rectangle decorated in colourful William Morris print.

'It's a kneeling pad,' Cynthia added helpfully, 'for weeding your borders.'

'Thank you, that's very thoughtful of you.' Heather tried to remember if she even had any borders, herbaceous or otherwise.

'We couldn't imagine life without our garden, could we, Bob?'

'It certainly gives us a reason to get out of bed every morning.'

Heather hoped she and Alan weren't heading for the same afterlife of potting mix and not-so-dynamic lifter.

Following a teary farewell hug from Cynthia, and a stoic handshake from Bob, Heather added the kneeling pad to the growing pile of farewell cards and gardening implements under her desk. One of her patients had given her a mug featuring a cartoon couple standing next to a blue caravan with the words 'Living the Dream', while one of her more insightful regulars had gifted her a bottle of sherry.

There was just time to swig a mouthful of cold coffee and spit it out again before she called in the next patient. It wasn't even nine and she was already running three quarters of an hour behind, a personal best. Tomorrow, however, she would drink her coffee while it was still hot. Over a leisurely alfresco breakfast on the patio, she and Alan would plan the rest of their lives. She was looking forward to having a normal conversation with her husband, rather than discussing their patients, or using words like 'framework' or 'stakeholders', things that belonged in a boardroom rather than a medical practice. Another world lay just beyond her fingertips. All she had to do was get through the rest of today's appointments and return seventy-three phone calls.

To steel herself, Heather snuck a peek at the holiday brochure she kept hidden under her stack of unread copies of the *British Medical Journal*. She hadn't had time to read the *BMJ* in years and certainly wouldn't be wasting a second of her retirement catching up. No, *Treasures of the Greek Islands*, which she'd picked up a few weeks ago from the travel agent opposite her regular hairdresser, was the only reading matter that mattered now. She flicked through, ogling the deserted beaches, olive trees and whitewashed buildings before stuffing it away out of sight.

Seeing the next name on her list, she contemplated opening the sherry. In the waiting room, Jaxon Smith was running up and down between the crowded rows of seats, pistol-whipping the knees of the other waiting patients with a plastic

AK-47. A slug trail of silvery mucus ran from each nostril, drying in a thick green crust on his top lip. When Heather called his name, Mrs Smith, sporting sausage-skin leggings, dragged him by the rat's tail on the back of his mostly shaved head towards the consulting room.

Seven minutes later, they left again, Mrs Smith shouting over her shoulder, 'Don't forget, I pay your wages!'

Heather didn't bother pointing out that the only tax the Smiths had ever paid was the unavoidable duty on booze and ciggies. She was more focused on how she was going to clean up her ravaged consulting room. An entire paper bed roll lay in ticker-tape ribbons, every cupboard had been ransacked and the curtain rail around the couch, no match for the weight of a hefty four-year-old, lay on the floor like a collapsed tent at the end of Glastonbury. Heather was almost grateful to the young hooligan and his odious mother. In the future, whenever she looked back and felt guilty about abandoning the Cliftons and the hundreds of other patients she'd come to think of as family, she would think of Jaxon Smith.

By mid-morning, the jaws of Heather's plastic hairclip were biting into her scalp, and she marvelled at how she could be simultaneously dehydrated and yet dying for the loo. She often quipped to medical students that to be a successful GP you needed a soft heart, a thick skin and a ten-gallon bladder. Unfortunately, her storage capacity wasn't what it used to be, and the next patient would have to wait. Hurrying along the corridor to the bathroom she nearly collided with Alan as he emerged from his consulting room.

'How's your last day going?' he asked.

'The usual war zone,' said Heather. 'But I did manage to clear my own printer jam for a change, so it hasn't been all bad.'

Alan glanced at his watch. 'Don't forget the girls are throwing us a surprise party at half past.'

The not-so-surprise party. A pair of 'Happy Retirement' helium balloons had been drifting around the surgery all morning, the garish foil blimps making a dash for freedom every time the waiting room door opened, only to be hauled back inside again by their trailing strings. Heather longed to open the front door and watch them float away for good. One of the balloons was already deflating while the other remained taut and bouncy on the ceiling. Wrinkled and flaccid, the first balloon was barely at head height. She couldn't help but see it as a metaphor. Energised by what lay ahead, Heather was sprinting for the finish line while Alan was fading fast, looking as if he'd barely make it to lunchtime.

'Are you okay with all this?' Heather asked, searching Alan's wan face. This was a big day for him. It was more than walking away from a job, and however grateful she was to have made it this far relatively unscathed, she knew Alan processed things differently.

'I'm fine,' he replied. 'Absolutely fine.'

She believed the fine. Not so much the absolutely. 'Sure?'

He pulled himself up straight, gaining another couple of inches. Stiffened his already stiff upper lip. 'Never better. I'm off to do battle one last time with the Netherwood Medical Centre Patient Participation Group,' he said, referring to the group of volunteers who met monthly to tell him how to run the practice he and Heather had been successfully running for the past forty years.

~

'Surprise!'

Someone let off a party popper. The smell of gunpowder had barely reached Heather's nose and the coloured strands hardly touched the floor before Rita, the scarily efficient head receptionist, had removed all traces with the dustpan and brush.

'Oh, my goodness,' said Heather, clutching her chest in a touch of BAFTA-winning melodrama. 'I wasn't expecting . . .'

All this. She really hadn't been expecting the Lilliputian spread of tiny finger sandwiches and miniature wraps, mini frittatas and mini muffins; a welcome departure from the usual catering by Mr Kipling. The only nod towards tradition was a plate of Alan's favourite sausage rolls.

'Lovely spread,' said Alan, licking his fingers in anticipation as he approached the buffet.

Somebody handed Heather a specimen container's worth of warm prosecco and she helped herself to a sandwich. She sipped and looked around the smiling faces. In addition to the receptionists, practice nurses and the current medical student on attachment, the party also boasted the Big Five of endangered community professionals: district nurses, health visitors, physiotherapists, more midwives than there were currently pregnant mothers in the village, and even a psychiatric nurse, a species rarely spotted in the wild. They might all work independently, but they were one big family.

Her heart swelled as she took in all the familiar faces, these people who always went above and beyond their contracted duties, day in, day out. It wasn't the building, the elegant Georgian facade with its modern glass extension, she was going to miss – it was the staff who made Netherwood Medical

Centre so special. The thought of saying goodbye made the egg and cress sandwich she'd just eaten feel like a sandbag. All this – the balloons, the cake, the speech Alan would have been working on – was so final. There was no room for second thoughts. No coming back from mini frittatas.

She'd been so ready to call it a day, certain she was doing the right thing. Now she wasn't so sure, her vision of the future less clear, as if the perfect watercolour picture she'd painted had been left out in the rain. She mustn't let Alan see her doubt. Instead, she mingled, smiled a lot, and helped herself to another glass of the rapidly disappearing prosecco.

After ten minutes of identical exchanges with different people, all permutations on the theme that, yes, she was looking forward to retirement, and, no, neither of them would be taking up golf, Heather looked for Alan. He'd cornered a trainee midwife who was pretending to laugh at his jokes. Luckily Pauline, the practice manager, saved her by tapping the side of her glass with a cake fork.

'Ladies and gentlemen,' she began. 'On behalf of the staff and friends of Netherwood Medical Centre, I'd like to present Alan and Heather with a farewell gift to thank them for all their hard work and dedication. I'm sure you'll all join me in wishing them the best of luck in their well-earned retirement.'

Pauline stepped forward with two identical packages, one each for Heather and Alan, both wrapped in tissue paper. *Please, not more gardening equipment.* Heather tore at the packaging, breath hitching when she saw what was inside. The rectangular name plaque that had been mounted on the wall outside the practice was cold and surprisingly heavy in her hands.

Dr Heather Winterbottom BM BCh DCH DRCOG MRCGP

All those letters after her name. The once-shiny surface had weathered over the years, but someone had polished the brass until it shone like new, the engraved letters now as clear and precise as the epitaph on a freshly carved tombstone. She and Alan had been officially unscrewed, permanently removed from the building.

Knowing Rita, she would have already overseen the re-grouting of the holes in the two-hundred-year-old masonry. Heather didn't blame them. In general practice, there was no time to breathe or take stock, let alone grieve. It was impossible to outrun the growing mountain of bureaucracy. And there were always more patients than appointments.

'There's a lump in my throat,' Alan croaked.

It was reassuring to know he was only human, choked up with poignancy and nostalgia.

'Mine too, darling,' said Heather, touching his back.

'No,' he shook his head and coughed, pointing to his throat. 'Sausage.'

He tried to dislodge it with some exaggerated swallowing, while a room full of qualified medical professionals silently panicked. In the end, Alan took matters into his own hands, and chased the sausage roll down with a slice of cake.

While relieved to see her husband's face return to a more normal colour, Heather's own throat remained stubbornly clogged with anguish, uncertainty, and the beginnings of regret, like lingering catarrh after a cold. This was it, the end of an era. The end of her professional career. She couldn't wait to escape and yet, how could she leave all this behind?

There was no washing the enormity of it down with fresh cream sponge.

Pauline hadn't finished. 'We have another very special gift for you both,' she said, handing over an envelope.

Still coughing, Alan tore open the envelope.

'It's a joint membership of the National Trust! This is very special indeed,' he said, as if he couldn't wait to dive into the world of rose gardens and orangeries, plant sales and gift shops.

Heather murmured her thanks. Inside, a tiny piece of her died. Forget the olive groves and rustic tavernas of Greece, from now on it would be sensible shoes and flasks of lukewarm tea on gloomy Tuesday afternoons. Alan's idea of a perfect retirement was heritage listed and served with clotted cream.

Holding the envelope to his heart, Alan stepped forward. 'Thank you everyone. I'm lost for words,' he said. Never one to resist a captive audience, he soon found them again. Here it came. *The Speech*. All the exits were sealed. There was no escape. Heather eyed the empty prosecco bottle, remembering too late the sherry.

'As some of you may know, my father, Gordon Winterbottom, founded this practice back in 1948. That was the same year the NHS was born, the first health service anywhere in the world completely free at the point of delivery. Let me set the scene for you.'

No, Alan, no scene setting.

'It was also the year of the first hip replacement. Polio was rife and penicillin, the first antibiotic, still in its infancy. The life expectancy for a man was sixty-five years, and for a woman, seventy.'

Several pairs of eyes had already glazed over, but Alan was in his element; the most animated Heather had seen him in weeks.

'Things have changed a lot since then. Thanks to childhood vaccination, something my father passionately advocated for, polio has been all but eradicated. Men can expect to live to almost eighty nowadays, and women eighty-three.'

'Don't count on it,' Heather hiss-whispered through smiling teeth.

'Did you know that there are ten times the number of doctors today compared to 1948, but only a quarter of the hospital beds?'

Apparently, nobody knew. Nor, Heather suspected, did they particularly care given that it was a Friday afternoon. It was beginning to sound like a party political broadcast. She cleared her throat.

Alan glanced in her direction.

'Here's another fact you may not be aware of. Research has shown that, on average, doctors interrupt their patients after only ninety seconds. Apparently, wives only give their husbands sixty.' The married men in the room nodded in recognition. 'Back to my father. He was a generous man, and I'm sure you're all too young to remember that he was admired in the village as much for his impressive vegetables as for his bedside manner.'

Alan's voice cracked. Heather moved to his side in comfort and solidarity, and to subtly remind him of the time.

'I like to think of us all as one big, happy family,' he said. 'Heather and I have done our best to build this practice and move it forward into a new century, but now is the time to hand over the reins to the younger generation. Only the

11

knowledge that we are leaving the Netherwood community in such excellent hands has made it easier for Heather and me to hang up our stethoscopes for good. It's time for us to enjoy getting to know each other again.' He turned to Heather. 'Sorry, have we met?'

Cue the obligatory polite laughter. Heather released a breath she hadn't realised she was holding. Thank goodness that was over. Except that Alan hadn't finished. He unfolded a piece of paper and found his reading glasses. Heather tried miming a sawing action across her own throat, hoping he'd notice out of the corner of his eye. Apparently blinkered, he began to read aloud.

'In his much-lauded funeral oration commemorating the dead who lost their lives in the Peloponnesian War, the Greek statesman Pericles said, "What you leave behind is not what is engraved in stone monuments, but what is woven into the lives of others."'

'I think that's an excellent note to end on, don't you?' Heather interrupted, drawing the bewildered audience into what she hoped was a final round of applause.

'But I hadn't finished my speech,' said Alan, looking crestfallen as the crowd thinned. His unuttered words filled both sides of the crumpled paper in his hands.

'People are busy, Alan. They need to get back to work, not listen to you pontificating about dead Greeks.'

'But Pericles's Funeral Oration is one of the greatest speeches in history.'

'When was this exactly?'

'431 BC.'

She softened, imagining him as a small boy desperate to share his knowledge with a father who was always too busy to listen. She pictured him as a seven-year-old who'd been dropped off at boarding school and told how lucky he was. Lucky to suffer within the same grim yet hallowed halls as his father and grandfather. Alan rarely talked about his schooldays, describing them only as miserable, character-building years, preferring to share stories of how, on exeat weekends, he'd been allowed to carry his father's battered leather Gladstone bag as he accompanied him on his rounds.

'Look, I'm all for a trip to Greece, Alan, but how about the twenty-first century version?'

Sun, sea, sand, thousands of years of history, and only three and a half hours from Gatwick airport. She just had to pick the right moment to show him the brochure.

2

Felicity Kendal's bottom

HEATHER SAT UP SO QUICKLY THAT SHE HAD TO BLINK AWAY the stars. Heat spilled from her adrenal glands and raced to her scalp, her fingers and toes.

She'd slept through the alarm.

The first time in forty years.

The patients would be waiting.

It took seconds for her brain to catch up and rein in her stampeding heart. As of this morning there were no more alarm clocks, no appointments, schedules or deadlines. From now on, she and Alan could do things because they wanted to, not because they had to. This was the first day of the rest of their lives. The sun had set on their old world and risen on a new one. Only the sun wasn't shining. Between the parted curtains, the day looked dull and overcast. And for some reason, she could smell fish.

The brand-new waffle robe, one of a matching pair she'd ordered online weeks ago, was still folded neatly inside its plastic wrapper. She'd been saving it for this moment, the sharp creases in the white woven cotton testament to just how long she'd been looking forward to it. When she finally put it on, the fabric was disappointingly stiff and scratchy against her skin. Heather secured the belt with a knot and set out to trace the mysterious fishy odour to its source.

Someone who looked like Alan, a man who rarely lifted a finger in the kitchen and stuck religiously to toast with his favourite Tiptree orange marmalade for breakfast, was standing over a frying pan at the stove. At his feet, Stan watched on, stiff as a sphinx, with stalactites of drool hanging from his loose jowls. Stan's intense concentration, and the occasional licking of his lips, comically mirrored the man's actions. From behind, the man's morning hair even resembled Stan's wiry deerhound fur. Did dogs turn into their owners, or vice versa?

'Would you like one, love?' Alan called cheerfully.

'No, thank you.' Heather scooped coffee into the glass coffee plunger and flicked the switch on the kettle. 'I think I'll stick to muesli.'

'Go on, they're fresh from Craster. Best kippers in the world.' She wasn't sure how he could claim that preserved fish were fresh, but she let it go. Heather had waited patiently for this morning and nothing was going to spoil it.

Alan showed her the pan where the brown fish, eyes glazed in their bisected heads, were floating in butter. She recoiled as he slid the glistening fillets onto two slices of hot buttered toast then kissed his fingers like a Michelin chef. Stan shadowed Alan from the stove to the sink, and then to the kitchen table, his eyes never once leaving the plate.

'I thought we could eat outside,' said Heather. She'd arranged cups, saucers and a jug of milk on a tray next to the pot of coffee.

Knife and fork poised, Alan said feebly, 'But we always have breakfast in the kitchen,' as if his resolve wouldn't last another dozen steps out to the patio furniture.

'Come on, live a little, Alan. Where's your sense of adventure?'

He thought about it, then, not bothering to hide his reluctance, picked up his plate and followed her outside. Stan trotted after them.

The sky was blanketed in dull, grey cloud that, unlike a real blanket, was doing a good job of keeping the heat out rather than in. The chill crept through the thin cotton of her new robe and Heather pretended not to shiver. She couldn't remember the last time they'd used the patio. The weather hadn't been great this year. Even the wisteria, usually heavy with chandeliers of purple blossom at this time of year, was looking spindly and virtually flowerless against the wall. The teak table and chairs had grown dark and mossy in the damp winter shadow at the back of the house and the wooden slats were starting to splinter. Despite promising to do so on numerous occasions, Alan still hadn't got around to jet-washing the mildewed pavers.

It wasn't quite the *Homes & Gardens* scene she'd imagined, but they were at least having breakfast together. For years, their marriage had felt like a relay race, each day a sprint in which their only interaction was handing over the baton of responsibility for their children or patients or a list of jobs that needed to be done at home. They'd finally crossed the finish line, and they could move forward at their own pace, side by side.

'We really need to buy new outdoor furniture,' said Heather as she lowered herself cautiously onto the slimy seat.

'No point when we barely use it. I'll give this lot a good clean and oil,' Alan said.

Alan was clearly not planning to incorporate anything *alfresco* into his daily ritual. Persuading him to change the habits of a lifetime was always going to be a challenge. And yet the kippers had taken Heather by surprise. Rather than dwell on the smelly, greasy pan he'd left in the sink, she chose to see it as a sign that maybe, just maybe, he was open to trying new things.

'You don't know what you're missing,' said Alan through a mouthful of grey fish. When the knife and fork couldn't keep up with his appetite, he resorted to shovelling the toast into his mouth with his fingers, accompanied by such groans of pleasure that Heather feared he was going to climax at the table. It was a long time since he'd made those sounds in bed. She couldn't remember the last time they'd made love. She tried to remember the last time they had even held hands. These days they barely touched or made physical contact of any kind, aside from the accidental brush of elbows or shoulders as they turned over in bed or reached for the same kitchen cupboard. Like the gradual fading of a once vivid photograph, it had happened so slowly neither of them had noticed.

It was easy to blame the job. They were both busy all day, and exhausted by the time they got home. They still loved each other even if they didn't show it. It went without saying, didn't it?

The time had come to wipe the slate clean and start again, not as colleagues or business partners, but as husband and wife. But they'd been colleagues longer than they'd been a married couple. What if their relationship only worked as Dr and Dr Winterbottom, and not as Mr and Mrs?

Heather tried to look away from the molten butter dripping down Alan's unshaven chin, and onto the front of his putrid old dressing gown where it formed a dark puddle in the company of several other unidentified stains.

'Why aren't you wearing the new robe I bought you?'

'I prefer this one. It's always been my favourite. I thought I'd lost it until I found it at the bottom of Stan's basket. I can't think how it got there.' He eyed Heather. She looked away.

'At least let me wash it,' said Heather, catching a whiff of dog, and now fish.

'Don't go upsetting Mrs Gee.'

'I am quite capable of doing a load of washing without Mrs Gee's assistance, thank you very much.' Heather poured the dregs of her coffee, which to her disappointment had already gone cold, onto the meadow-length grass that hugged the patio. 'Just as I'm sure you're quite capable of mowing this lawn.'

'You know how Mr Gee gets if anyone touches the lawnmower,' said Alan defensively.

'The trouble is he can barely make it from one end of the lawn to the other these days. And you can hear Mrs Gee's knees creaking from the next room. They must both be eighty if they're a day.'

Alan had the decency to look uncomfortable as he mopped the fishy butter from his empty plate. Mr and Mrs Gee had come with the house, and their presence had been, along with Alan's elderly mother Gwen, and the giant wisteria that held the blown bricks on the back wall together like a woody skeleton, non-negotiable.

At first, the awkwardness of having a housekeeper and a gardener – although Heather preferred to think of them as helpers she tipped generously, rather than paid employees – had outweighed the undeniable benefits. Heather's working-class mother hadn't lived long enough to see her handing over the shameful brown envelope of cash every Friday afternoon in exchange for a spotless house and equally spotless children, nor her father to tell her never to trust a man who didn't cut his own grass. But there simply weren't enough hours in the day to be a mother to two girls, a housewife, Gwen's full-time carer, and Netherwood's only female doctor.

'We need to talk about the Gees, Alan. They are number one on the agenda.'

'Agenda? I was looking forward to a life without meetings.'

'There are things we need to discuss. Important things we need to agree on. Like when to give notice to Mr and Mrs Gee. Now we're retired, there's no reason we can't do all these things for ourselves. I mean, I'm not completely incapable of squirting Harpic around a toilet bowl.' She was sure that even Alan could successfully trim the hedge without a trip to Accident & Emergency.

'We can't make them redundant after all these years,' he said. 'They've been so good to us. I gave Mrs Gee my word that there would be a job for them here at The Elms for as long as they wanted. A promise is –'

'I know, a promise.'

The conversation was hardly worth having. Heather would raise the issue. Alan would set out his position on the issue. Heather would offer objections. Alan would counter the objections. They would literally bore each other into a stalemate. The status quo would prevail. The Gees were staying.

'What else is on your *agenda*?' Alan asked, not bothering to hide his disdain.

'Item two is money.'

At this, he sat up. She knew how to play him, knew that when she was trying to make a point, he stopped listening until he heard something he agreed with, at which he was all ears again.

'You're right,' he said. 'We need to be more careful now we're pensioners.'

Heather hadn't thought of herself as a pensioner, certainly not like her blue-rinsed grandmother who used to queue up at the post office counter on a Friday to collect her measly allowance. 'We've planned for this, Alan. We didn't work all those hours, missing precious time with the girls so we could merely subsist in our dotage. The new cars we never bought, the kitchen extension we never built, the holidays we never took. I went along with all those sacrifices so we could build up our nest egg. Why do you think I put up with Parsimonious Pauline, all these years?'

Pauline, Alan's fiscal soulmate, had instigated the rationing of jellybeans to 'one per brave child' and had been known to send emails with subject lines such as 'Toilet paper consumption: Can we improve?'

'It's thanks to Pauline that we can enjoy a comfortable retirement, Heather.'

'Let's enjoy it then. I've seen too many elderly patients moulder away while amassing a small fortune so their ungrateful kids could buy a holiday home in France. I want to start living while I still have life left to live.'

'It was your idea to retire early, Heather.'

'Early? What are you talking about? We've both reached the state pension age. I only suggested selling up because I thought it was what you wanted, Alan.'

'I only went along with it because I thought it was what *you* wanted.'

The offer to buy Netherwood Medical Centre had come out of the blue but they both saw it was too good to refuse. The centre needed new blood, she'd told him. Someone with the energy and vision to take it to the next level. Someone with the fortitude to meet the demands of a growing and rapidly ageing population. Someone fluent in the gibberish nonsense of twenty-first century healthcare.

'I feel like I'm giving up,' he'd said quietly. 'My father never quit. He thrived on hard work.'

Until he dropped dead on the job, Heather had wanted to point out.

Now, they sat in uncompanionable silence. With hindsight, this was a conversation they probably should have had before they agreed to sell the practice. But once they'd set the wheels in motion, there had been no stopping the retirement juggernaut. The deal was done, the papers signed and, for better or worse, here they were sitting on mossy garden furniture contemplating their ever-shrinking futures under a sky that threatened rain any second.

'It's too late now. There's no going back so we might as well get on with it,' Heather said. 'I suggest we draw up a plan of action.'

'It's retirement,' Alan said. 'We're talking about not going to work every day, not management consultancy.'

Heather was fast losing patience. 'Surely it's a good idea to have a few goals?'

'If it's the World Cup final, then yes. For once I'm looking forward to not having any goals.'

On the other side of the village, the church clock chimed the hour. It sounded more like a death knell.

'All right then, you go first.' Alan leaned back, one of the wooden struts in his chair fracturing under his weight.

Tempting as it was to produce the holiday brochure, Heather knew her husband better than to spring it on him. She'd need to bring him around to the idea more slowly, use all her wit and wiles to reel him in. Of all the tactics she'd tried in their marriage, the one that yielded the most consistent results was to offer him two options – never more than two – one of which she knew he'd reject out of hand, the other being the very thing she really wanted.

'We could go on a diet and get fit. Or we could go on holiday.'

He narrowed his eyes, suspiciously.

'I presume the getting fit part is directed at me.'

'Both of us. And Stan. Look at him. He's supposed to be chasing deer through the Scottish Highlands.'

Through the kitchen door she could see the dog licking the floor under the stove. For all Mrs Gee's insistence that she never fed him treats, he was possibly the only flabby deerhound registered with the Kennel Club.

Alan looked smug. 'Well, Dr Winterbottom, I am one step ahead of you. As you may know, the humble kipper is high in Omega-3, vitamin A and vitamin D, calcium and protein. Positively a superfood.'

'Wouldn't you like to get more . . . in shape?'

'What are you talking about? I'm not in bad shape for a man of my age.' Alan caressed his paunch as though it were an unborn baby.

'That's because most men of your age are sedentary and eat too much fruitcake.'

'I couldn't disappoint the fan club.'

He smiled a little at the mention of the band of faithful followers who saw Alan as the village's answer to Tom Jones. They were all women of a certain age who consulted Heather for their 'tears and smears' while being sure to remind her that they saw Alan for 'anything more important'. He'd let it slip some years ago that he was partial to a slice of fruitcake. Heather dubbed what followed 'The Great Netherwood Bake Off'. Alan's waistline had expanded as the fans vied for his attentions. When she'd reminded him of the Heart Foundation's guidelines for optimal waist measurement, he'd protested that he could still fit into his thirty-six-inch-waist jeans. Of course he could. As long as they sat at the level of his thirty-six-inch pubic bone.

'It's your own fault, Alan. You encouraged them.'

Alan made a *pfft* sound, but he was smiling. She was gaining ground.

'Isn't it a bit late to start worrying about it at this stage of life? By my age, my father had been dead eight years.'

'My point exactly. If you started looking after yourself, you could live another twenty or thirty years.'

After a few moments of stunned silence, Alan said, 'Okay, but please don't expect me to do anything that requires sweating in front of strangers.'

'Pilates then.'

'Why Pilates?'

'So that you can get up off the floor on your own when you start falling over,' Heather muttered, pushing away an image of her husband at ninety. Coping with Alan at sixty-seven was hard enough.

He let out a sigh, the meaning of which was as plain as if illuminated in neon above his head. Heather sighed too. They knew each other's sighs. Unlike the couples who yelled and threw things, she and Alan could communicate entirely in the tones of their expired air.

'Look, Heather, I'm exhausted. The stress of the last few weeks has taken it out of me. I want to slow down, to relax and unwind.'

'In that case, you need to get away,' said Heather, trying not to sound too pleased with herself.

Alan harrumphed. He had his legs crossed now as well as his arms. He looked like a contortionist trying to escape from a terry-towelling straitjacket. His body language was deafening. 'We're already going away this year. To visit Tilly in New Zealand at Christmas, remember?'

'That's months away. How about something a little closer to home? Like Greece. Just think about it. Sun, sea and sailing. We can see the sights, explore the history, then eat dinner at one of those quaint little tavernas.'

Judging by the pained look on his face, she may as well have suggested they watch back-to-back *Carry On* films for a fortnight.

'I've done Greece, Heather.'

'You've *done* Greece? When?'

'I studied Ancient Greece at school, then on my year off before university, I bought a rail ticket, headed down through Europe and caught the ferry across from Brindisi to Corfu and on to the other islands.'

'Which ones?' Heather asked out of curiosity.

Alan tapped his forehead. 'Do you know, I can't remember exactly. I do recall waking up on several different beaches with a hangover. I couldn't tell you which ones though.'

'Come on, Alan. You must have seen more than the inside of a bar on each island.'

He tapped his chin cleft, then shook his head. 'No, pretty much all I was interested in back then was beer. And chasing girls.'

Alan didn't notice the tightening of her jaw. At an age when she was at home caring for her mother, who was dying from the slowest progressive neurological condition that medicine had ever given an unpronounceable name to, her future husband was shagging his way around the Greek archipelago and having the time of his life.

Not bothering to disguise the sarcasm in her retort, Heather said, 'Well, I can see why you wouldn't want to go back.'

'I'm not saying I never want to go again, Heather. But why the rush? Think of retirement as a marathon, not a sprint. We've got all the time in the world. Let's go next year. Or the year after.'

'And in the meantime?' She pictured shapeless days, watching *Homes Under the Hammer* every afternoon, the passage of hours marked only in the boiling and cooling of the kettle.

Alan uncurled his limbs.

'Since you asked, there is something I'd like to do. A project I can really get my teeth into. It's something I've always wanted to do but somehow never got round to. Now there's nothing to stop me turning my fantasy into reality.'

She nodded. 'Okay, tell me. What does your dream retirement look like?' Learning to skydive? Renovating an abandoned villa in Tuscany? Writing a novel? Really, she had no idea. She was so out of touch with Alan's fantasies that nothing would surprise her. Heather only hoped it was something she could get excited about too.

Another wooden slat splintered under Alan's weight as he leaned forward and rubbed his hands together conspiratorially. 'I'm going to build a vegetable garden.'

All credit to Alan, who she'd always considered predictable. This really was a surprise. Inside her brain's left hemisphere, however, the synapses were sparking but refusing to co-ordinate a suitable response.

Alan's triumphant smile wilted. 'Well?'

'I hate to point out the obvious flaw in the plan, Alan, but you hate gardening.'

'I hate mowing the lawn and weeding.' She was about to remind him that Mr Gee did those jobs, but Alan held up his wait-a-minute finger. 'Think about it, Heather – growing our own organic produce. Potatoes, runner beans, carrots, lettuce. The lot!'

This wasn't something he'd conjured up on the spur of the moment. There would have been spreadsheets involved.

'You want us to become Netherwood's version of Tom and Barbara from *The Good Life*?'

'Now that you mention it, I've always had a thing for Felicity Kendal's bottom,' he said dreamily.

Heather rolled her eyes.

'I'm still trying to get my head around this.'

'I've already been sketching out some plans.' Securing his dressing gown belt, Alan began pacing the lawn, waving his arms about. It was the most energetic she'd seen him in months. Perhaps he wouldn't need Pilates after all. Breathless, he leaned on the slimy wooden table at Heather's eye level. 'And the best bit is I've worked out that we could chop our Tesco bill by three quarters,' he announced, a huge grin subtracting a decade from his weary face.

Now wasn't the time to remind him that the nearest Tesco had closed down five years ago.

3

Close encounter in the third aisle

FORTUNATELY, BY THE END OF THE FIRST WEEK OF THE REST of his life, Alan was back to toast and marmalade for breakfast. The novelty of the kippers had worn off, he'd confessed, although Heather suspected it was more the novelty of having to scrub his own fishy pan each morning when even the stoic Mrs Gee refused to touch it. Unfortunately, by the end of the week they had not only run out of marmalade, but just about everything else too. The fridge and pantry were empty, Heather's weekly grocery shop having failed to cater for two adults eating three meals a day at home. It was time to go shopping.

The regular supermarket shop was one task she'd never ceded to Mrs Gee, relishing the time to herself as she browsed the shelves for the same items she bought every week.

Heather freshened her make-up in the hall mirror and collected the reusable shopping bags from the cupboard under the stairs. To her surprise, Alan was waiting for her with a list.

'I've conducted a detailed inventory and drawn up an itemised shopping list,' he said, instantly complicating the task that Heather had performed without fanfare or ceremony their entire marriage. When she protested that she carried an equally detailed inventory in her head and didn't need a list, he produced two identical mustard jars.

'Two French,' he said, as if presenting evidence to a jury, 'but no English.'

'You don't like English mustard, Alan.'

'It's called patriotism, Heather. Besides, what if we have visitors?'

Heather tried to remember the last time they'd entertained any visitors. An echo of the loneliness she'd felt after losing her parents resonated in her chest.

'Add friends and a social life to that list while you're at it,' she replied, only half-joking.

'From now on we only buy the things we really need,' he said. 'Generic medicines work just as well as branded ones since they contain the same active ingredient, the same molecules. Therefore, it stands to reason that home brand foodstuffs will meet our nutritional needs as adequately as those with a well-known name or fancy packaging.'

'Does that mean you're willing to spread marmalade that doesn't have a Royal warrant on your generic toast?'

He ignored her.

She reached for the scrap of paper in Alan's hand, but he was in no hurry to relinquish it.

'It's *my* list,' he said.

'*I'm* the one who does the shopping.'

'From now on, we both do the shopping,' he said.

'But you're dressed for the garden.' Or was it, *by* the garden? She pointed to the grass-stained trousers that barely skimmed his ankles, the thin, collared shirt with fraying cuffs, and the scuffed deck shoes she was sure she'd thrown away eons ago.

Alan gave Heather's outfit equal scrutiny. 'It's the supermarket, not tea at Buckingham Palace,' he said.

She considered her lipstick in the mirror. How much Plum Passion was too much for Sainsbury's? She'd never worn much make-up for work, but since this was the first official outing of the week – of her retirement – she'd decided to make an effort. Now she worried Alan was right, and her one good summer dress was too formal, her handbag too 'footballer's wife' for a trip to the supermarket. With limited outfits on strict rotation, Heather had always felt secure in her choices of professional attire. She checked herself in the mirror again. There wasn't time to change. Alan was growing restless, jingling his car keys.

'We can take my car,' she said.

'My car is easier to reverse out.'

'But mine has a full tank of petrol.'

Short of suggesting that they drove separately to the supermarket, they agreed on a compromise. They would take Heather's car, but Alan would drive. It reminded her of squabbles between their girls, Sarah and Tilly, over who got to sit in the front seat. Alan appeased her by promising she could drive on the way back.

A little way down the road, while retuning the radio away from her favourite station, Alan remarked that they didn't really need two cars now that they were retired.

'One car? It's totally impractical, living in a village like Netherwood. We're ten miles from Darlingford.'

'What's the big deal? We'll be going everywhere together from now on.'

'But what if I want to go somewhere on my own?'

'I thought the whole idea of us retiring at the same time was so we could do things together.'

'The problem is that, so far, it appears we don't want to do the same things, Alan.'

His bottom lip jutted as it had done after she'd interrupted Pericles's funeral oration and he drove deliberately slowly, even for Alan.

Ten minutes later, Alan refused to believe that Tesco had gone. After two entire circuits of the Darlingford ring-road, he finally conceded, and they turned in to the carpark at Sainsbury's. Ignoring all the empty spaces Heather so helpfully pointed out, he squeezed into a tiny space between two four-wheel drives. She could barely conceal her amusement as he tried to extricate himself from the driver's door in the narrow gap that was half the width he was.

'The trolleys are all chained together,' Alan said after struggling to free one. Perplexed, he watched another shopper insert a pound coin, and release her trolley. 'A pound?' he blurted. 'For a trolley?'

'It's a deposit, Alan. You get it back at the end.'

The woman waiting behind them was fidgeting. 'Here you go,' she said impatiently, handing over a coin from her wallet. 'You can keep it.' Seeing Alan, the woman exclaimed, 'Oh! I didn't recognise you, Dr Winterbottom!' She looked at Heather. 'And Dr Winterbottom. Or is it plain old Mr and Mrs now? How are you both enjoying retirement?'

'So far, so good, Sandra,' said Heather, reaching into her own wallet and handing over a pound coin. 'There you go.' The last person Heather wanted to owe money to was Sandra Miller, who would consider it a down payment on any number of future kerbside consultations.

Sandra recoiled from the coin. 'No, no. I won't hear of it. After all you've done for my family over the years, please keep it.'

One pound.

The irony was that Heather had never charged a single patient for her skill and expertise. In forty years, not a penny. How could you put a price on caring for families? Yet here it was: the final reckoning for steering three generations of Millers through life's ups and downs amounted to a pound. Sandra Miller alone had gone through at least a pound's worth of Kleenex in Heather's consulting room, sharing her grief at losing her mother too soon, and her father not soon enough. Heather had secretly helped her teenage daughter avert an unwanted pregnancy too, meaning Sandra Miller would never know how close she'd come to being Netherwood's youngest grandmother, nor what value her husband got for the pound when Heather had treated that nasty little discharge after his business trip to Thailand. And all in the strictest confidence.

Alan wrestled a trolley loose from the stack and strode ahead. It went without saying that he ended up with the wobbly one, and Heather couldn't help but smile as three out of the four wheels behaved normally while the fourth stubbornly clung to the scuffed supermarket floor like a toddler in a tantrum. He refused to go back and swap it for another, his valiant efforts to keep the thing on track soon attracting the attention of the other shoppers. Inevitably, the first collision was into a fully laden trolley belonging to Victoria Dankworth, the sergeant-at-arms of Alan's fan club.

'Dr Winterbottom,' she said, breathily, pawing Alan's arm. 'You're looking so well.' Noticing Heather standing nearby, she nodded deferentially. 'And here's the other Dr Winterbottom.'

The other Dr Winterbottom. Forty years after giving up her last name to become Alan's wife, Heather was used to her moniker.

'How are you both enjoying retirement?'

'Marvellous,' said Alan.

'Marvellous,' Heather repeated flatly. She left him to fend for himself and pushed the juddering trolley towards the salad section. A bag of mixed leaves had barely touched the wire bottom of the trolley when Alan, having escaped Victoria Dankworth's hungry clutches, swooped.

'Home grown is so much healthier,' he said, trying to return the bag to the chiller cabinet.

'Alan, unless you've found a handful of magic seeds somewhere, we'll need to actually buy some pre-grown fruit and veg for a while.'

'But –'

The salad was wrestled back and forth until it ended up in the trolley at last.

'It's salad, Alan. You win some, you lose some.'

He trailed behind to the next display where he began palpating an avocado with such concentration Heather thought he was about to order it a mammogram. To distract him, she held up two punnets of tomatoes for his verdict.

'Cherry or vine?'

Alan trotted to her side. 'I remember when tomatoes used to come in a paper bag,' he said with a sigh. 'The greengrocer would pick the ripest and then spin the bag over and over to twist the corners closed. They even tasted like tomatoes.'

This was worse than shopping with two under-fives. When Sarah and Tilly were little, Heather used to send them off to find things for her: three red apples, one green cucumber, four yellow bananas. The girls told her they loved to play 'being helpful'. While the eldest, Sarah, really was helpful, more often than not little Tilly would get side-tracked, on one occasion returning with a six-pack of boys' underwear saying she didn't want to be a girl anymore. She sparked so many missing child announcements that, after a while, Heather used Tilly's convenient disappearance to finish her shopping in peace before raising the alarm, confident in the knowledge that if her youngest daughter were abducted, she would be returned very quickly. Unfortunately, men in their sixties were harder to lose, no matter how hard you tried.

She watched Alan examine a butternut squash as if he'd never seen one before. A security guard was hovering, perhaps thinking Alan was about to pocket the innocent vegetable. The next time she looked, Heather found Alan reminiscing in the citrus fruit section.

'Remember when we used to only get mandarins at Christmas? One in the stocking along with a shiny new penny and a handful of walnuts.' He was talking to the small orange fruit in the palm of his hand. This was taking forever.

'If we want to be out of here before they close, best do a U-turn out of memory lane.'

He wandered to the next display, wide-eyed. 'There's so much more choice than I remember. What do you think, Heather? Should we get Spanish navels or easy-peelers?'

What if this was all there was, once a week, every week? Discussing the relative merits of imported fruit for the next twenty or thirty years.

'I don't care. For crying out loud, just choose one,' Heather shouted, her sharp tone stunning the screaming toddler in a nearby trolley into silence.

By the time they'd reached the dairy aisle, they were communicating in tight voices, lips pursed like two ventriloquists, mindful that they could be recognised again at any moment. Alan pushed the trolley with undisguised petulance while Heather filled it with her usual weekly grocery items. She'd always felt sorry for the grey-haired couples who silently traipsed the aisles with faraway looks in their dull eyes. Now she understood. They were wondering what on earth they'd seen in each other all those years ago.

Once upon a time, Alan Winterbottom had been quite a catch. He'd been a tall, lean and handsome young man with a first-class medical degree. At school he'd played county cricket, then rowed for the university. This morning Heather had walked in on him shaving his ears. If only they could go back to who they were when they'd first met. Sometimes, she thought she caught a glimpse of those two young people: Alan, smart and interesting, with nice thighs; she, playful, affectionate and quick to laugh at anything he said. It was easy to fall in love. But promising to love someone forever – was that realistic?

There was only one checkout in use and a queue of trolleys had formed. Straight away, Alan fell into conversation with Mrs Robichaux, who recognised him and was anxious to know where he stood on chiropractors. Heather thought she'd got away lightly until she felt a tap on the shoulder. It was Bridget, a patient Heather had always liked. She arrived early for all her appointments, and never failed to follow Heather's medical advice to the letter.

'Excuse me, Dr Winterbottom,' Bridget said, pulling her notebook and pen from her handbag. 'I hope I'm not overstepping the mark here, but I've heard it's possible to cure osteoporosis by jumping up and down on the spot two hundred times a day. Do you think I should try it?'

'Look, I can't see it would do any harm,' Heather said, smiling kindly. She tried to catch Alan's eye so he could rescue her but he was deep in conversation with a man about whether fresh pomegranate would shrink his prostate faster than the bottled juice.

Bridget grabbed Heather by the arm. 'Does it matter what kind of shoes I'm wearing?'

'Whatever's comfortable,' said Heather, forcing another smile.

'Does it make a difference what surface I jump on? Would you recommend concrete, grass or carpet?'

'Look, I'm sorry, Bridget, I'm in a bit of a hurry.' Since this was patently untrue and the queue had not budged in minutes, Heather softened and added, 'Can I have a think about it and get back to you?'

Ten excruciating minutes later, another cashier arrived and opened a second checkout. Heather was busy unloading the items from the trolley onto the conveyor belt, hindered by Alan's attempts to assist, when she caught the eye of yet another ex-patient who was leaning over the confectionary display to scrutinise the Winterbottoms' weekly shop. The excitable woman, whose thyroid was clearly overactive again, offered a running commentary, as if trying to memorise prizes on *The Generation Game.*

'Washing-up liquid. Bread. Tinned tomatoes. Shampoo. Toilet paper.'

She laughed nervously and announced to the world in general, 'Funny, I mean you never imagine doctors needing toilet paper, do you?'

Heather couldn't hand over her credit card fast enough. She didn't even wait for the receipt, pushing the laden trolley towards the exit as if she were competing in the Olympic bobsleigh.

When Alan ran into a distraught-looking man he recognised in the carpark, Heather pushed the trolley back to the car alone. The men were still deep in conversation when, having unloaded all the bags into the boot, Heather returned the trolley and reclaimed both the pound coin and the driver's seat. While she waited, she re-adjusted the seat, mirrors and radio station to their previous settings. Her settings.

'That was Jim Fielder,' said Alan when he eventually extricated himself and climbed into the passenger seat beside her. 'I almost didn't recognise him. He's really gone downhill since his wife left him. Terribly sad.'

Heather started the engine. 'What happened?'

'He came home from golf one day to find she'd packed her bags. She left him a note on the kitchen table. Apparently, she'd run off to Spain with a waiter she met on a girls' trip to Benidorm. Completely out of the blue. Poor chap never saw it coming. And the worst part is she's still entitled to half his pension. Imagine that.'

On the way out they passed Jim Fielder's forlorn figure, folding his trouser legs beneath a pair of bicycle clips. Alan patted Heather's knee.

'Makes me realise what a lucky man I am to have a woman like you,' he said.

A woman like her? What kind of woman was Heather Winterbottom? What had happened to Heather Wilson, that young woman who'd been so full of dreams and plans? Heather wondered if she'd even recognise her if she passed her in the street.

4

Tibia, or not tibia?

Cambridge, 1975

WHEN THE STAINED SHEET WAS PEELED BACK TO REVEAL the cadaver, Heather's breakfast threatened an encore. A pair of ground-glass eyes stared straight into her from between their shrunken lids. Her own eyes were already smarting from the formalin fumes, and she wondered if she was the only one in the dissection room needing to grab the sides of the metal table for support. The cadaver's sunken yellow skin made it look like a waxwork model and yet there was no getting away from the fact that this was a real human being.

Heather had never seen a dead body before, aside from her mother's, an image she'd refused to turn into a memory, and had never seen a man naked. She'd had no brothers and her father had been a discreet man. If she was going to be a doctor, she was going to have to get used to bodies of all kinds. She resisted the urge to pull the sheet up to the cadaver's waist, for modesty.

'Did you know that a dead body still grows hair and stubble?'

Heather was grateful that someone had broken the ice. It was a sandy-haired boy who had yet to grow into his pristine lab coat.

An impossibly sophisticated young woman called Wendy Wallace contradicted him, flicking her sleek ponytail defiantly over her shoulder.

'That's a myth. The scalp and facial skin desiccate and shrink back, leaving the illusion that the hair has grown.'

Around them, nervous chatter echoed off the sterile walls as a bunch of pustular adolescents, most of them straight out of school, found themselves in a room filled with dead bodies, feigning nonchalance with small talk and light-hearted quips. It was, Heather realised, the first step in desensitising these future doctors to the horrors they would one day face, an early lesson in how to balance personal attachment with professional detachment.

'I think he needs a name,' said Heather, clinging to her humanity like a life raft.

Up until that point the fourth student at the table had said nothing beyond introducing himself as Alan.

'I imagine he already has one,' he said. 'I mean, he must have been baptised as a baby, mustn't he?'

Heather pictured the rosy-cheeked baby, head wet from the christening font, who would one day become these withered remains. She wondered about the story behind the rose tattoo on his left arm and the missing finger on his right hand. What had happened in his life that his body had ended up here?

'He looks like a Fred, don't you think?' She held Alan's blue-green gaze, little knowing that she would one day see those North Sea eyes again in her daughters. The Cary Grant cleft in his chin, which looked so charming on his face, luckily bypassed the delicate features of their girls.

Fred.

The name seemed to suit him, and the group agreed. Fred was her first ever patient, her silent teacher. Alan watched her as she unrolled her dissection kit and tested the weight of the shiny new scalpel. The sudden image of her mother scoring the fat on the Sunday joint before she put it into the oven made her catch her breath. Only Alan noticed, his eyebrows lifting enquiringly until Heather turned her attention to the waxen skin of Fred's upper arm. With an unsteady hand, she made her first incision.

An anatomy demonstrator told them what to look for. There were few surprises, few variations from the anatomical norm. The anatomy textbooks had been written long ago. But Heather was searching for something else. She wanted to know who Fred was. What loves and losses had left their invisible marks on him?

As the weeks passed, Fred's six students stripped his body, layer by layer. Skin, fascia, muscle, bone. Archaeologists discovering the wonders of two hundred thousand years of human evolution. Some students approached the task diligently, with reverence and earnest expressions. Elsewhere in the cold, stark dissecting room, others larked around, making jokes to cover their awkwardness and immaturity. One ran out of the first class and was never seen again. Alan Winterbottom was one of those who took great care in each task. Heather remembered his steady hands and the way his tongue traced his top lip as he concentrated. Once, when she noticed a lump of pale fat resting in his thick fringe where he'd swept the hair out of his eyes, without thinking she reached over and brushed it away. He looked up, startled.

'Sorry,' she said, 'you had a bit of Fred in your hair.'

After that, she would often find him watching her intently. A few weeks into Fred's right arm, they began to smile at each other. By the time they'd moved onto his leg, Alan had asked her out for a drink.

Heather's experience with men was essentially non-existent but she'd formed the impression that the way to snag a man you found attractive was to play hard to get. She turned him down, secretly hoping he'd pursue her. He didn't.

And then, on the night after graduation, Alan Winterbottom gate-crashed a party at Heather's college. He made a beeline for her, carrying two glasses of Pimm's and, ignoring the rather gorgeous rugby player she'd been making steady progress with all evening, led her to an empty sofa. After the third glass, his arm was around her shoulders, her breast aching for his hand, while her right index finger traced the outline of the muscles in his left thigh.

Rectus femoris, vastus medialis, vastus intermedius, vastus lateralis.

But these weren't Fred's yellow stringy muscles that they'd dissected together. These were impressive specimens, hard and warm. Rower's legs. When they tensed beneath her touch, she could feel the blood surging through the muscle fibres. The next part of Alan she explored were his lips as he leaned in to kiss her. Soon, blood was surging through her own muscles to her skin, heightening every nerve ending to his hands. Lust fogged her vision and she couldn't have stood up if she tried. While the sensory part of her brain was on overdrive, her motor cortex was punch-drunk on desire.

Then, completely unbidden, a diagram of a human brain popped into her head. She tried to ignore it, focusing instead on Alan's hungry kisses. There were more nerve endings in the lips than anywhere else in the body, she recalled. She wondered if he remembered the slide the lecturer had projected, a diagram showing a brain next to a grotesquely distorted person with enormous lips and hands, supposedly representing the relative area devoted to sensory nerve endings in each part of the body. What was it called again? That image, it had a name.

'*Homunculus*!' she murmured. Thank goodness. At last she could relax.

The pre-synaptic terminals of Heather's trigeminal nerve connected most pleasingly to the lips of a beautiful, warm body. The turgid textbooks and waxy cadavers melted away into the most delicious human anatomy lesson of all.

5

Hobnobbing

'I SEE BILL WOODFORD DIED,' ALAN SAID. HE WAS SITTING at the kitchen table, obscured by the discoloured newspaper he was reading. 'What a shame. That private robotic surgery cost him a fortune.'

'You already knew that,' Heather said. 'You signed his death certificate.'

'I know but seeing it in black and white really brings it home.'

And checking Bill's lifeless body for a pulse didn't?

Having for years been too busy to read more than the newspaper headlines each morning, Alan had announced that his second goal of retirement was to catch up on the past two years' worth of news, and was steadily working his way through the fire hazard of back issues piled up in the utility room. Arguing that he'd only got three per cent of his money's worth, he insisted on reading every single paper in full, cover to cover.

He'd soon settled into a routine. Breakfast at eight followed by newspaper reading until ten, when he would disappear outside to play with bits of wood and power tools. Without fail, at 12.01 pm he returned to the kitchen to listen to the Shipping Forecast on the radio, after which he based the rest of the day's activities – either more gardening or more newspaper reading – on the likelihood of strong winds and rough seas in Viking or North Utsire. Heather often heard him humming to himself as he pottered about, barely registering her presence at all. At first this had been a relief. At least he wasn't pestering her to drink endless cups of coffee or tea with him. After a while, however, she'd begun to feel invisible. As a woman of a certain age she was used to being ignored in public. But it was unsettling when the person who was ignoring her was her own husband.

'I've been having an affair with Colin Firth,' she announced to the top of Alan's head. A murmur of acknowledgement followed by the rustle of a turning page. Heather folded her arms. 'And I'm pregnant with his love child.'

'Incredible,' said Alan, lowering his paper. 'Look at that! England are leading Australia by sixty-nine runs in the second Test.'

She could so easily ruin his day by telling him the final score. She decided to ruin Stan's instead, by insisting he get out of his basket and walk with her. He stood mulishly, paws planted, staring at his lead as if he'd never seen it before.

Hearing a key in the front door, Heather rushed to open it. Mrs Gee nearly fell into her, clutching her heart.

'Dr Winterbottom. You nearly scared me to death!'

'Sorry, Mrs Gee.' *I do live here*, she wanted to add. It would take a while for everyone to adjust to the new situation:

Mrs Gee to having her employers at home during the day, and Alan and Heather to being at home.

'I've done the colours and pegged them out, Mrs Gee,' Heather called over her shoulder as she dragged Stan out. 'And there isn't a full load of whites yet, so don't bother putting them on.'

If the look on her face was anything to go by, Mrs Gee didn't take kindly to any interference. She made a point of grumbling out loud that 'someone' had left streaks when they mopped the hall tiles. Heather decided to leave any difficult conversations regarding the future to Alan.

It was a Hay Wain sort of day in Netherwood, and Heather stopped on the stone bridge to look at the sky reflected in the slow-moving water below. She closed her eyes and inhaled the smell of freshly mown grass, warm tarmac and something else not quite as pleasant. When she opened her eyes, Stan was sniffing at something another dog owner had failed to put in a plastic bag.

The three-hundred-year-old stone bridge that appeared in the foreground of every postcard of the village had been sprayed with graffiti, and she noticed a rusty supermarket trolley under the bridge, which had clogged up with enough rubbish to divert the flow of water. She only ever drove past here, flying over the top of the tiny bridge in her perpetual haste, never noticing that in the epicentre of the bucolic filmset-perfect village of thatched cottages and rose gardens was a filthy, litter-strewn cesspit. Even Stan made his disappointment known, cocking his leg up a spindly ragweed growing through a crack in the pavement.

They skirted the village green, following Stan's nose, one lamppost at a time. Unlike the rest of the sleepy village, the village shop was buzzing as usual, selling newspapers, chocolate, ice creams and whatever its customers couldn't put off buying until their next trip to Darlingford. Villagers trailed in and out like ants raiding a picnic, and Heather could almost hear the owner, a chatty woman with non-insulin dependent diabetes and an unexplained low platelet count, rubbing her palms together at the till. It was comforting to know that, although life might have come grinding to a halt for her and Alan, it was business as usual for the rest of the world.

Heather left Stan tied up outside the shop where he sank into a grateful heap. Parked halfway up the kerb was a delivery van, its engine still running. Luckily, the shop owner had waylaid the harried-looking driver, giving Heather a clear shot at the biscuit aisle, then the counter where she picked up the nearest magazine from the rack and paid a gormless teen who was serving. She was in and out before the owner cornered her for an impromptu consultation.

Bending to untie Stan's lead, she nearly clashed heads with Deidre Banks, who was reaching for an empty ice-cream wrapper that had escaped the bin. Deidre was a classic heart-sink patient with chronic everything, who'd worked her way around all the doctors in the practice looking for a miracle. She gave Heather a look as if to say, 'Where do I know you from?' In the end it seemed Deidre only saw a generic-looking older woman with her generic-looking older dog and failed to join the dots. Heather felt strangely relieved.

Stan's nose led them up Bridgestone Lane, a route Heather knew well, from behind the wheel of her car at least. Every Monday lunchtime she visited patients at The Willows. She'd always thought the sign amusing, gold lettering on the Hunter green background describing the place as an 'exclusive retirement destination for discerning seniors', as if there were other places for the less discriminating kind. Most of the residents could only afford their place courtesy of the rise in house prices that had conveniently coincided with their decision to downsize. Once a sleepy little village, Netherwood was now 'highly desirable' and the housing boom had been driven in part by Netherwood Primary's outstanding Ofsted report. Which meant that no one deserved their place at The Willows more than Esme Clark, the school's retired headmistress. She was the only reason Heather looked forward to Mondays.

Miss Clark had remained Miss Clark even when, to everyone's surprise, she'd married Aubrey, a bank manager from Darlingford. They were both in their fifties by then, and neither had been married before. It was as if they had simply taken a long time to find each other.

Heather had met Miss Clark at a parent–teacher evening almost thirty years ago when Sarah was in her third year at Netherwood Primary and Tilly had just started kindergarten. Despite her no-nonsense demeanour, courtesy of imposing spectacles that made her grey eyes appear owlish, and her over-engineered hairdo, Esme Clark was the most instantly likeable person Heather had ever met. It had helped that Miss Clark had been especially fond of Heather's two daughters, and had come to know them well, as regular visitors to her office.

In Sarah's case this was to collect gold stars for good work, being helpful, polite or neat or any of the many things that Sarah Winterbottom excelled at. Tilly, on the other hand, was never sent to collect a gold star. She was neither neat, nor particularly helpful to her teacher. Her visits were generally to explain why she'd misbehaved in class, usually daydreaming and interrupting the lesson to question something the teacher had said. The problem was that Tilly couldn't explain her disruptive behaviour because she didn't see it as such. And luckily, neither had Miss Clark.

'Tilly thinks differently to most children,' she'd told Heather. 'That doesn't mean there's anything wrong with her. I happen to like the way she thinks. She knows her own mind. Mark my words, Dr Winterbottom, Tilly will go far.'

And she'd been right about that. Tilly had ended up about as far as it was possible to go without leaving the planet's atmosphere. Bored with the Northern Hemisphere, geologist Dr Matilda Winterbottom PhD had accepted a postdoctoral fellowship at the University of Otago in search of more interesting rocks.

When Stan stopped to sniff the green and gold sign outside The Willows, Heather remembered the chocolate Hobnobs she'd bought at the shop. They were Esme's favourite. It was also a Monday, and although it had only been a fortnight since she'd seen Esme, she was missing her favourite patient. After the girls left Netherwood Primary, Miss Clark had registered with Heather as a patient. Not that she'd ever really needed a doctor. In her ninetieth year, she was the only resident at The Willows without an account at the local pharmacy, and she could boast that she'd never been into hospital. Consultations with Esme tended to be more pastoral than medical.

The Willows was set in two acres of manicured gardens. An avenue of weeping willows led to the handsome Edwardian facade that disguised the more modern accommodation of the retirement complex. Heather had never noticed the ornamental pond on the right that was all but obscured by lily pads and the trailing willow branches that kissed the surface of the water.

The receptionist appeared unfazed to see the home's regular doctor walk in with a large dog in tow instead of her medical bag. She was on the phone but smiled as Heather headed towards the courtyard garden. Luckily for Stan, The Willows advertised itself as a pet-friendly establishment, a hilariously ambiguous sign reminding dog owners to promptly dispose of their own waste. It was that kind of place. Esme was sitting in her customary spot, on the bench outside her ground floor unit, knitting. At the approach of the wiry hound, Esme dropped her knitting bundle and clapped her hands in delight.

'Stan, how lovely to meet you at last! I've heard so much about you.' Most people were wary of such a large dog, especially one who was panting like a steam train, but Esme let Stan explore her fingers as he searched her for anything edible.

'You'll never get rid of him now,' said Heather, taking her customary place on the bench beside Esme. The weather always seemed fine when Heather visited, and most of their consultations had taken place on this bench. It was as though this enclosed garden had its own microclimate. She'd also read that statistically Tuesdays were the rainiest day of the week. That meant Mondays at The Willows were always sunny.

Today Esme's pure white hair was loosely coiled on top of her head, Brigitte Bardot style, a more relaxed version of the heavily pinned bun she'd favoured as a headmistress. She wore a crisp linen shirt, and her signature shade of Estée Lauder lipstick, mostly on her lips. In spite of her age, Esme Clark was still an elegant woman.

'What are you knitting?' Heather asked, although she already knew the answer.

'A baby blanket,' said Esme.

'Whose turn is it this time?'

'Your grandson or granddaughter.'

Heather was taken aback. 'I'd slow down a bit if I were you. I'm still a long way off becoming a grandmother.'

'But you told me last time that Sarah and Ravi are having a test-tube baby.'

'They're having another round of IVF,' said Heather. 'Nothing is guaranteed.'

Just as it wasn't guaranteed last time, or the time before, or the other times that were now too numerous to keep track of. As a mother and a doctor, Heather was trying to remain pragmatic. After the last miscarriage, which she realised she'd also told Esme about, she vowed she wouldn't get her hopes up again. Everything had come so easily for Sarah: school prizes, a career in finance, and the perfect man in the shape of Ravishing Ravi. All except for motherhood.

The white stitches growing from the extra-long knitting needles were testament to how invested Esme already was in this potential grandchild. Having never had children of her own, she lived vicariously through other people's experiences of parenthood and grandparenthood. At one time, there was hardly a baby born in Netherwood who hadn't been wrapped in one of Esme Clark's knitted creations.

Esme was always quite sanguine about not having had children. 'I love children, but surprisingly, I didn't miss having my own. People with children always assume that childless couples must be lost and lonely. If anything, the opposite is true. Aubrey and I had each other. It was more than enough for both of us. Besides, I got to enjoy two hundred of the little darlings every day, then hand them back to their parents at three o'clock.'

The age gap – more befitting a mother–daughter relationship – had never overshadowed their friendship. Heather would far rather sit on a bench sharing a packet of chocolate biscuits with Esme than get dolled up to listen as a tipsy girlfriend spilled her woes over a fancy lunch. Esme was thoughtful and listened. Unfortunately, not enough people listened to Esme.

Once, she'd said to Heather, 'It's so good to have a proper conversation that doesn't involve either the weather or gossip about the other residents.'

Heather opened the Hobnobs and offered the packet to Esme.

'So, tell me,' Esme said, taking a bite, 'how is –'

'If you ask me how I'm enjoying retirement, I will snatch that biscuit right out of your hand and put it back in the packet.'

'I was going to ask how Alan is.'

'Oh, sorry, I'm a bit touchy.' Heather rolled her shoulders to release the muscles. 'Alan is fine, thank you.'

Esme licked her fingers and helped herself to another biscuit. Stan sat to attention, letting her know he was on hand if needed.

'I didn't expect to see you back here so soon,' she said. 'I thought you'd be off on some big adventure by now.'

'The furthest I've been since I retired is Sainsbury's.' The sigh fell out of her.

'In my day people went on a world cruise to mark their retirement.'

'I'm not sure that's our kind of thing,' said Heather. 'I doubt Alan would fit into his dinner suit anymore.' The current version of Alan looked as if he'd been tipped out of a green wheelie bin. 'I'd love to go away, somewhere warm and sunny like Greece, but he isn't the slightest bit interested.'

'I'm sure he'll come round to the idea,' said Esme. They exchanged doubtful glances.

Heather pursed her lips and examined her nails. 'I don't know what's got into him. There's a man living in my house who occasionally answers to the name of Alan, but it's like living with a stranger. He still looks like Alan and sounds like Alan but it's as though something is missing. It's as if I'm trying to reassemble the retired version of my husband, only there's a vital component missing from the box, and I don't know what it is.'

Esme patted her knee.

'You don't need to say any more. You're both going through a period of readjustment, that's all. Just as marriage is more than a wedding day, retirement isn't a single day, it's a process, something you must work at.'

'I thought the idea was that we didn't have to work anymore.'

'It'll take time to get to know one another again and adjust to having each other around all the time, living your lives side by side in symbiosis.'

'Symbiosis? Gosh, I haven't heard that word since medical school.'

'As you would know, it comes from the Greek *sym*, meaning together, and *biosis*, meaning a way of living.'

Heather still remembered the definition she'd memorised for her exam. An ecological interaction between two different organisms living in close physical association, typically, but not always, to the advantage of both.

What had happened to them? Heather had hoped that without the stress of work she and Alan would be closer than ever. If anything, the opposite was true. They were drifting further and further apart. It was as if there was an age difference she hadn't noticed before. Alan was only a year older, but he seemed to have aged a decade since he'd retired, while Heather felt ten years younger. He carried himself like an older man, as if he were lugging around the accumulated years like concrete in his bone marrow. Their conversations felt as if they were happening via satellite, always half a sentence behind. His very presence had become wearying.

Esme helped herself to her third Hobnob and nibbled thoughtfully.

'Let me ask you something, Heather. *What is it you plan to do with your one wild and precious life?*' She tapped a book that had been sitting next to her on the bench. 'Mary Oliver. I've been sorting through my poetry collection.'

Heather had to think about it. She was the one who usually asked the searching questions. Having watched so many lives ebb away, she recognised the preciousness of her own. But wild? The wildest thing Heather had done recently was to go to work with bare legs the morning she laddered her last pair of 15 denier tights.

'Well,' said Heather sheepishly, 'I threw caution to the wind and bought this.' She showed Esme the glossy magazine she'd bought at the shop. The last time she'd flicked through a magazine, it had been late one night at the surgery, while she was waiting for a patient to arrive for an urgent after-hours consultation. The women's magazine had advertised a four-page pull-out entitled 'Crochet your own Noah's Ark!' To her horror, Heather had noticed that the magazine was at least a decade old, and the pull-out had long since been pulled out. Luckily, smartphones and tablets had since replaced outdated magazines in doctors' waiting rooms, and nowadays patients conducted business meetings, paid bills, or streamed movies while they waited.

'It's a start,' Esme said, raising her eyebrows at the magazine. 'But I know you. You can do better than that.'

While Esme finished off her Hobnob, Heather flicked through the magazine she'd bought like an impatient child rushing to turn the pages of a picture book, looking at the glossy photos without taking in any of the context.

'Slow down, my dear.'

Heather laughed. 'You see, I'm so used to chasing my tail all day, I've even forgotten how to read a magazine.'

She put the magazine aside and gazed at the garden. 'I thought I was ready to leave,' she said. 'I'm the right age – not too early that it feels like a cop-out and not so late I'd be too frail to enjoy myself. Having said that, whatever age I retired it would still feel like giving up, abandoning the sinking ship.

'Looking back, I think Alan and I enjoyed the best years of medicine, when we could really get to know our patients and make a difference. Now the entire profession has been taken over by call centres and Dr Google. All those years of training and the government thinks we can be replaced by an automated message. My main worry is that my whole identity is wrapped up in being a doctor. Without my job, who am I?'

'I thought that about my teaching career,' said Esme, picking up her knitting again, spacing out the loops on her long grey needles and freeing up a strand of white wool from the ball. 'I thought that was the end of my useful life. It's natural to fear getting older. But take it from me, there's nothing to it, really. In fact, it's quite easy when you get the hang of it. Take my advice, pause, and take a breath. Pace yourself.'

'The problem is everyone's full of advice. It's important to have hobbies. Keep yourself busy. Establish a routine. Blah, blah. I know it'll take time to adjust, only I'm ashamed to say, so far, the whole thing has been such an anticlimax. What is it they say – retire in haste, repent at leisure?'

'I think it's marry in haste, not retire.'

'Whatever. I thought it would be the beginning of something but right now it feels more like an ending, as though I'm on the opposite of a honeymoon. I'm sure every marriage had dull days. It's just that ours seem to be all strung together.'

'Give it time. You're going through a kind of bereavement. You need to grieve the loss of your old life before you can move on and start a new one.'

Perhaps Alan hadn't been so far off the mark with his funeral oration.

6

You can call me Al

WHEN HEATHER ARRIVED HOME, ALAN WAS FILLING AN empty icetray at the kitchen sink. She watched a man she'd never seen before pour the contents of a cocktail shaker into a glass.

'You must be Heather. Care for a mojito?'

Too stunned to reply, Heather accepted the proffered drink.

'By the way, we've used up the last of the white rum,' said Alan, inspecting an empty bottle.

Heather didn't even know they had any white rum. What was her husband doing drinking at this time of day? She'd been warned that retirement could turn into one long happy hour, but the Shipping Forecast hadn't even started yet. And more importantly, who was this stranger mixing cocktails in her kitchen?

'Excuse me, but who are you?' Heather asked.

'This is Kevin,' Alan said, as if that explained everything.

Heather guessed the man was around forty. He was medium height, medium build, and would have been quite unremarkable but for an impressive handlebar moustache that made him look like a time traveller from the nineteenth century.

'The mojitos were my idea,' said Kevin. 'I noticed a huge clump of mint growing behind the garage. I told Alan it would be a shame to waste it, and we'd worked up quite a thirst, hadn't we, Al?'

Al? No one ever called her husband that. Heather wondered if this was one of those weird dreams in which you were convinced you were awake. Only worse. Like turning up to an exam you hadn't studied for. Naked.

Stan inspected Kevin for treats but finding nothing of interest, loped to his basket and collapsed.

'Cheers!' Alan raised his glass to Kevin's, then Heather's.

'Would someone mind telling me what's going on?' said Heather.

'I found Kevin on Facebook Marketplace,' Alan began.

'In which section?' Heather asked, amused.

'Greenhouses. He's upgrading and was selling off his old one.'

'I live in the village so I offered to drop it round,' Kevin explained. 'Actually, when we met face to face, I realised Al used to be my GP.'

'And now you're drinking lunchtime mojitos together.' Heather smiled. It was no less ethical than sharing a packet of Hobnobs with Esme, she supposed.

'Kevin's a NOGGIN,' said Alan. 'Actually, he's chief NOGGIN.'

Kevin pulled down the front of his t-shirt to reveal the words, NOGGINS *like to get down and dirty*.

'I'm going to need more to go on, I'm afraid.'

'Netherwood Organic Gardening Group,' said Alan proudly as if he'd founded the organisation himself. 'They're looking for like-minded people to join. Kevin's invited me to their next meeting.'

The look on his face reminded Heather of how the girls used to look when they'd made a new friend. *And you both like My Little Pony! I'm so pleased for you.*

'And in the meantime,' said Kevin, 'I've offered to help reassemble the greenhouse. We just needed a little livener before we started.'

It was obviously working. Alan was the liveliest Heather had seen him in weeks. She kept to herself her misgivings about the two of them operating power tools after finishing the bottle of white rum.

'Don't let me hold you up,' said Heather.

She made a point of placing her untouched mojito next to the sink and priggishly filling the kettle instead.

'Are you sure you won't join us?' Kevin looked almost offended.

'Another time,' Heather replied. Like six o'clock in the evening. 'Please excuse me, I need to get on.'

Get on with what, exactly? Thanks to Mrs Gee, the house was spotless, and the laundry neatly folded. Stan had been walked and *Escape to the Country* didn't start for another hour. The only pressing task was to sort out the dining room that was allegedly home to a long wooden table and eight matching chairs. The kind of arrangement a more civilised family would use at mealtimes. Unfortunately, the mahogany table that had belonged to Alan's parents had gained a sedimentary layer of paperwork, journals and other miscellaneous items, while the matching Edwardian sideboard was currently serving as a mausoleum for obsolete laptops, mobile phones and other electronic devices. In addition, the dining room now doubled as a halfway house for everything they'd brought home on their last day at the practice. The brass name plaques, still wrapped in their tissue paper shrouds, were lying in state on top of a box containing framed black-and-white photos of the village from the turn of the previous century, and children's toys from the waiting room that surely broke every modern health and safety guideline.

Alan had refused to throw anything away, saying it might come in useful one day. Quite what he planned to do with the dusty plastic palm that had tripped up many a walking stick was a mystery. With all the old medical equipment he'd held onto – the leather examination couch with turned wooden legs, an ancient spirometer that resembled a hookah, and the suction cups of the primitive ECG machine that left twelve tiny love bites across the patient's chest – Alan could always open his own museum.

Then there was the human skull on the bookshelf, part of the skeleton he'd owned at medical school. What was once a learning aid and a whimsical student decoration now seemed decidedly macabre. Mrs Gee refused to enter the room, though not because it contained human remains. She complained she couldn't manoeuvre the vacuum cleaner around the boxes.

Heather and Alan had assured each other they would get round to the dining room soon, although the more time they had on their hands, the less inclined either of them were to do the things they were previously too busy to do. Heather felt as if she had lost her multi-tasking superpower on the day she left work. The luxury of doing one thing at a time had morphed into a reluctance to do anything. Perhaps she should go back and enjoy that cocktail after all. She'd never been a big drinker, especially in the middle of the day. But wasn't retirement all about trying new things?

As Heather dithered at the kitchen door, she overheard Kevin say, 'Cyril has a henhouse he wants to sell, Al. It's light and airy, with four good-sized nesting boxes. Clean lines, stripped floorboards and a lovely aspect. No point wasting good money on a brand-new one.'

'Do you think he would sell it to me? It sounds perfect.'

'Of course. One NOGGIN to another. It's all about community, you see. We're one big happy family.'

Which was more than could be said for the Winterbottoms.

Heather took her tea to the living room, where she sat watching Alan and Kevin through the window while she tried to muster the enthusiasm to start on the dining room. It was hard to tell what they were saying, and which of them was the foreman, but much head-scratching, pacing, measuring and re-measuring later, a greenhouse appeared, and they both looked very pleased with themselves. This was followed by more pacing, measuring and head-scratching over what Heather recognised were plans Alan had drawn onto graph paper. He'd been collecting wood for years, dozens of offcuts, saying he was going to build a vegetable patch. He'd stored the wood in the garage, leaving their poor cars to fend off the elements in the driveway. Now she was suspicious. He'd accumulated an awful lot of materials for a simple raised garden bed. She wondered if the Trojans had been suspicious when they'd seen the delivery truck backing up to the Greek camp loaded with seasoned timber and reclaimed sleepers.

He'd alluded to a project he wanted to complete once he retired, something his father had started. But Heather had taken it all with a pinch of salt. Alan talked about a lot of things he never got around to doing. For weeks, Heather had been keeping a note of things around the house that needed Alan's attention. All the jobs that he'd promised he'd get round to when he had a spare minute: cupboard doors hanging off their hinges, the leaking tap in the bathroom, the mirror she'd bought two years ago still waiting to be hung and, of course, the patio furniture that needed sanding and oiling. She'd entertained a fantasy of him running around with his toolkit fixing everything in the first few days of his retirement.

More likely, he would shake his head and say, 'That's not a five-minute job, Heather,' even about the jobs that would literally take five minutes. Like moving a pot plant. It was as though, after dividing his entire working life into five- or ten-minute appointments, he never wanted to be constrained again. He had more pressing matters now, such as dredging the recesses of his wardrobe for his oldest, tattiest items of clothing, or expressing outrage at Tory cabinet ministers he already knew had been thrown out of parliament. Or erecting a second-hand greenhouse.

It looked as though at least one project was well under way. She'd always wanted to build an orangery overlooking the garden. Thanks to chief NOGGIN Kevin, they were the proud new owners of a glasshouse to rival anything at Kew. Except that, instead of somewhere to sit and enjoy a cup of tea, it looked as if the new addition would be used for growing actual oranges. It was the sheer scale of Alan's plans that worried her. Judging by the length of yellow builder's twine they'd unravelled around the rest of the garden, Alan would be planting more than a row of lettuce. Her garden, such as it was, would soon be unrecognisable. Other wives might have put their foot down at the very thought of losing the view from their living room window. But for Heather, a view of her husband, happy and engaged and, more importantly, not moping about under her feet, beat a pristine green lawn. Besides, it wasn't as though they had grandchildren to run barefoot on the grass.

The Elms had been her home for forty years, but Heather still thought of it as Alan's house. It was so much grander than her childhood home: a modest red brick semi on a housing estate of identical red brick semis. Bathed in that first flush of romantic love, it had been easy to overlook the fact that the house would come with an additional feature: her future mother-in-law. Even years after Gwen died, Heather had never felt completely at ease in the house. It was as though her mother-in-law was still there, haunting her. She popped up again and again, in a piece of furniture that Alan refused to part with, or a tree or shrub she'd planted that threatened to take over the garden. When the last of the majestic trees the house was named after succumbed to Dutch elm disease in the eighties, Heather had half-jokingly suggested they change the name to Wisteria House, after the indestructible climber Gwen had planted, but Alan wouldn't hear of it. It was bad enough having the ghost of Alan's father looking over her shoulder at work, always feeling as though she had an uninvited and moderately inappropriate chaperone. Much as she loved the Gees and acknowledged them for everything they'd done for the family, Heather couldn't help but feel that, for as long as Mrs Gee continued to buzz around The Elms like a fly in a caravan, she would always have Gwen looking over her shoulder too.

Heather opened the travel brochure she'd hidden behind a cushion on her favourite chair. Despite officially having nothing to do, this was the first real opportunity she'd had to go through the brochure in detail. The cover photo was an iconic image of the whitewashed windmill on Santorini. As she flicked through the pages, taking in the impossibly vivid colours of the photographs, she could feel the excitement building in her fingertips on the glossy pages. Her brain couldn't keep up with the delights her eyes were feeding her. She couldn't find enough shades of blue to describe the colour of the sea, the sky, the hulls of the little fishing boats, the matching doors and shutters of bougainvillea-covered tavernas. The Acropolis shone like gold bullion in the afternoon sun. Churches carved into rocky outcrops conjured up memories of her favourite films. And the food! Her salivary glands tingled beneath her tongue as she imagined sitting down to plates of fresh seafood, crisp salads and honey-drizzled pastries at a waterside taverna as bouzouki music drifted from inside.

Outside the living room window, rain had stopped play. She heard boots on the kitchen tiles and waited for the wrath of Mrs Gee to descend. The long-range forecast predicted a long summer of muddy boots ahead. Heather was desperate for sunshine and with endless rain on the horizon, she remembered a recipe she'd seen in her magazine. She also saw an opportunity. Tomorrow night, she would grill prawns with garlic, and crumble a block of feta into the salad. After dinner they could stream *Mamma Mia!* and the scene would be set to show Alan the holiday brochure. One last-ditch attempt to change his mind.

7

How to bowl a maiden over

THE FOLLOWING NIGHT, AS PREDICTED, ALAN ENJOYED THE prawns and salad, so much so that he offered to load the dishwasher. Unfortunately, Heather's Greek offensive stalled when the internet crashed and they couldn't download *Mamma Mia!* Instead, *Treasures of the Greek Islands* spent the evening behind the sofa cushion while they watched a World War II documentary Kevin had been raving about. It had taken a Herculean effort for Heather not to nod off, and Alan kept checking her every few minutes to make sure her eyes were still open. The urge to sleep was overwhelming, but ironically as soon as she climbed into bed, it disappeared. She was wide awake again.

Alan had been down in the dumps all day since reading about England's disastrous Test series from the previous summer. After this, Heather thought he might abandon his newspaper obsession. If anything, the disappointment had only spurred him on in his quest for good news. Sadly, even the documentary reliving the victory in the Battle of Britain had failed to improve his spirits, and a drop of his favourite red, usually a reliable lifter of Alan's mood, had only made him more irritable. Now she was lying in bed listening to the sound of his reluctant prostate releasing the half bottle of cabernet sauvignon in a series of stop-starts that reminded her of the ill-sequenced traffic lights on the Darlingford ring-road. There was a time when they'd found each other's bodily functions excusable, quaint even. Those days were long gone.

There was a sure way to cheer him up, or rather, to put him in a more receptive mood. If there was one thing her husband enjoyed more than red wine, more than documentaries, or cricket even, it was sex. At least, he used to. Lately, he'd even lost interest in that. At first, she'd put it down to the stress of selling the practice. They'd both been so busy and preoccupied, sex had fallen off the menu. Like Chicken Kiev or Black Forest gateau, at one time a favourite, now consigned to nostalgic history.

Drastic times called for drastic measures. She would be the one to initiate sex for a change. The one to break the drought. Not because Heather particularly craved it but for the sake of their marriage. Not that Alan would recognise it as strategic sex. Sex was sex, and he wasn't a man to look a gift horse in the mouth.

Heather switched off her bedside lamp, leaving only the faint glow from the one on Alan's side. Propped seductively against the pillows, she thought sexy thoughts, imagining she was waiting for Kevin McCloud or Monty Don, then when she couldn't choose between the two, Sam Neill, to emerge from the ensuite. She waited. And waited. The toilet flushed, and she heard water running into the basin. Then nothing.

What was he doing in there? Since when had he performed such a complex bedtime routine?

The sexy thoughts were soon replaced by yawns. By the time Alan finally emerged from the bathroom, Heather was having second thoughts, especially when she was blinded by light beaming through the open door, as if she were an enemy aircraft he'd spotted. Perhaps assuming she was already asleep, he stalked towards his side of the bed, standing on a squeaky toy that Stan had left in the bedroom then bumping into the open wardrobe door with an 'Oof!'

'Sorry, did I wake you?'

'Not exactly,' she replied, resisting the urge to suggest he bring in the entire Notting Hill Carnival with him. 'I can't sleep.'

He lifted the duvet and slipped in beside her. 'I know what you mean. I've hardly been sleeping myself recently.'

Why was it always the people who slept solidly all night who claimed they couldn't sleep? The same people who never believed they snored.

Alan reached for the bedside light.

'Wait,' said Heather, turning onto her side to face him. 'Are you sure you want to go straight to sleep?'

He was a little slow on the uptake, but in the shadows, she watched a smile steal across his face. It was the first smile she'd seen in a while. He turned towards her until they were face to face, her eyes smarting from the arctic draught of Colgate and Listerine fumes. So that's what he'd been up to in the bathroom.

Alan had become rather preoccupied with his teeth lately, spending hours flossing and examining his gums in the mirror as though, having lost most of the hair from his head, he was desperate to hang on to his dental assets. Heather hoped that his dentist gave out frequent flyer points, given the number of visits he'd clocked up this year. Unfortunately, the toothpaste and mouthwash failed to disguise the fact that she'd used too much garlic on the prawns. She should have left the red onion out of the Greek salad too. She found herself wondering if Greek couples found each other's breath off-putting, as Alan searched for her lips everywhere except where they usually resided. After several seconds of exploration, he found her mouth and they kissed.

It was the kind of kiss that might accompany 'Drive safely' or 'Shall I pick up milk or will you?' It was the kind of kiss that wouldn't have felt completely inappropriate coming from an elderly aunt. Heather pressed her mouth more firmly against Alan's until, finally, their startled tongues met. She waited for the tingle in her pelvic floor, tried to will it by squeezing her thighs together. Nothing. Alan, on the other hand, was well under way, his pyjama bottoms tented in an unambiguous sign of his head start.

Heather had never been especially squeamish about the male body. Despite a limited number of sexual partners – the pathetic total of one, including Alan – she'd seen plenty of naked men in the course of her job. She and Alan had even met over a naked man, albeit a dead one. However, there was something about the long grey hairs that corkscrewed through the buttonholes of Alan's pyjama top that was slightly off-putting tonight. They reminded her that the wisteria needed pruning, having once again grown into the timber window frames.

'The window in the back bedroom won't open,' she said. 'Shall I put it on the job list?'

'Mmm?' Alan wasn't listening.

He was stroking slow circles on her back.

Round and round the garden, like a teddy bear.

A jagged nail or possibly a piece of loose cuticle snagged on the thin fabric of her pyjama top, setting her teeth on edge. He inched towards her, trapping her hair beneath his elbow. She gasped out loud. Taking this as a rallying call, Alan picked up the pace and slurped her entire earlobe into his mouth, sparking goose pimples on her arms. She made a conscious effort to relax rather than squirm. Usually keen to get the bedroom proceedings over as quickly as possible, for once Heather wished he'd slow down and take his time. Tease her a little. Meanwhile Alan tore at her pyjamas as if he'd woken up on Christmas morning and found her wrapped under the tree. She supposed she should be grateful he still found her attractive after all these years, and two babies.

'Make love to me, Alan,' she whispered.

Alan stopped abruptly.

Talking during sex had never been part of their usual repertoire. They'd preferred to make their preferences known with a code of non-verbal cues that had been lost in translation over the years. She'd never been good at asking for what she wanted, or needed. Perhaps it was time to spice things up and try something new in the bedroom. It was worth a go.

'Talk dirty to me,' she murmured.

Alan was thrown. 'Like what?'

'I don't know. Use your imagination.' She was sure as hell relying on hers.

'Your lips are so ... plump,' he said breathily as they clashed noses. 'Like two juicy Roma tomatoes.'

He was clearly still thinking about the salad, but it was a start.

'What else?' Heather urged.

Alan nuzzled her neck and breathed in. 'Your skin smells of sweet pea.' He sniffed again. 'No, more rhododendron . . . or possibly a trailing clematis.'

His hand slid to her buttock, giving it a squeeze, as if to check whether it was ripe. 'Do you like that, Heather?'

'Not too hard.' She winced.

'What about this?' he asked. 'Does that turn you on?'

Being asked if something was a turn-on had exactly the opposite effect. They sounded like two low-paid actors in a sleazy porno, the director at the end of the bed giving stage directions, ordering the camera in for a close-up before declaring the scene a wrap. On the other hand, Alan was really getting into the swing of things.

After a while, instead of sending her to new heights of ecstasy, Alan's running commentary, sounding as if he were describing a particularly tedious game of cricket, was starting to put her off.

Now we haven't seen Alan in action for a while. You might remember he's been in the stands following that back injury after trying to lift the dog into the car. It'll be interesting to see if he has any new tricks up his sleeve. I know he'll be relying on tactics given his current lack of flexibility. Here we go. Yes, really shining that ball now. You can see the concentration on his face. Heather is poised at the crease. She'll be looking for clues as to which way he's going to swing.

Alan rushed through the first over. He wrenched Heather's pyjama top over her head and tossed it towards the boundary for an easy four runs. After a little fumbling with the granny knot at the waist, he did the same with the bottoms, which landed across the end of the bed for a disappointing single. Out of compassion, Heather released Alan from the members' enclosure, and by the end of the over they were both naked beneath the duvet. The umpire ordered them to change ends.

Unfortunately, Alan's increasingly heavy breathing reminded Heather that she'd left the prawn heads in the bin. The kitchen would stink to high heaven in the morning.

'Did you put the rubbish out like I asked you, Alan?'

'What?'

'Never mind.'

To give Alan full credit, Heather's ill-timed query failed to derail his enthusiasm. He was a man on a mission. There was a delay when, despite his professional familiarity with the female anatomy, he appeared a little rusty with its real-life layout. His frantic fumbling suggested an amateur safe-cracker anticipating the arrival of the police at any moment. More to get things moving along, she pulled him on top of her.

'Are you sure?' Alan hesitated but his voice was raspy with physical need, and possibly lack of fitness.

'Yes,' she croaked, more the effect of being crushed than from desire.

'Okay then. Here goes.' She could almost imagine Alan rubbing his hands together in anticipation as he did when he was about to syringe out a recalcitrant ear canal.

'Left a bit, Alan.'

'My left or yours?'

She guided him, silently, for fear of sounding like a smutty sat nav.

He took her involuntary groans of discomfort as the sign of a job well done. When it was all over, Alan collapsed like a corpse back onto his side of the bed. They spooned for a while until, mutually overheated, they rolled away to their separate hollows in the mattress. Now would be the perfect time to bring up the subject of the holiday again. Alan would be relaxed and at his most malleable. But it felt too manipulative to ask him now. She wanted him to go away with her because he wanted to, not because he'd agreed in a state of post-coital euphoria.

It was too late anyway. Alan was already asleep in the recovery position, his outline in the glow from the digital alarm clock as familiar and unchanging as a mountain range. Heather thought of all the reasons to love him. He was kind, smart and occasionally hilarious. Sometimes on purpose. He'd been a good husband by all the parameters that mattered, and a good father. Alan Winterbottom was due north on everyone's moral compass. Neither she nor the girls had ever doubted his love for them.

It was unrealistic to expect the infatuation, deep obsession and unquenchable longing of first falling in love to last forever. The limerence was over and they'd temporarily lost their way, that was all. They still loved each other, which was surely all that counted.

Heather imagined many women in the village fantasied about her husband. Any one of the fan club would give their bottom dentures to be in her position, even if it had been only the missionary position. She'd never fantasised about another man, never wondered about how it might feel to kiss anybody other than her husband. Plenty of married people had affairs. A few got away with it, most didn't. It was the reason that half their friends from medical school were divorced, some more than once.

She couldn't be bothered with all that. Even if Alan never found out, Heather doubted she'd have the courage to appear naked in front of anyone else ever again. She couldn't imagine that anyone would find her physically attractive at her age anyway. Maybe now they were both closer to seventy than sixty, they were finally through the danger period in their relationship and safely out the other side. They could both relax. There was nothing left to explore. Nothing left to prove.

Alan was snoring now, stertorous rumblings as the air from his lungs battled the floppy tissues of his soft palate. She'd missed that narrow window of opportunity to fall asleep. How many more nights did they have left together? How long before one of them, heartbroken, spent their first night of grief alone? The thought terrified her. She didn't want to lose Alan, but right now, she didn't know how they could continue like this.

To Heather's surprise a tear ran down her cheek and disappeared into the pillowcase. Unable to sleep, she got out of bed and went down to the kitchen where she bundled the prawn heads into a plastic bag and carried them out in the moonlight to the dustbin.

8

He died with a Ginger Nut in his hand

Netherwood, 1982

'Dr Wilson?' His eyes widened as he approached her in the waiting room. 'Dr *Heather* Wilson?'

'The very same,' said Heather, hoping she sounded confident and professional.

Inside she felt anything but, seeing *him* again after all these years. The penny still hadn't dropped when she'd reported to reception and announced she was here to see Dr Winterbottom. Although an unusual surname, she hadn't made the connection. The invitation to the interview had arrived on the headed notepaper of a Dr Gordon Winterbottom and it had been his name on the brass plaque outside the building. The only other Dr Winterbottom she'd known had had ambitions to be a neurologist and the last she'd heard about him was that he was training up in Edinburgh. Certainly not in a small rural general practice in the south of England.

'I wasn't expecting you,' said the man who offered his hand. The man who wasn't Gordon Winterbottom.

'The letter clearly stated one thirty on Friday the twelfth. Do I have the wrong twelfth?'

'No, you have the right day. It's more that I wasn't expecting *you*.'

'You didn't read my curriculum vitae, Dr Winterbottom?' Should she call him Alan?

He shook his head sheepishly, loosened the shirt collar that looked as if it was strangling him and mumbled something about being completely snowed under. Later, he admitted that there had only been one application for the position, and he'd seen no reason to scrutinise the candidate.

'Netherwood is a long way off the beaten track. It's ten miles to the nearest supermarket. That doesn't trouble you . . . Dr Wilson?'

'Not in the slightest.'

Was he trying to put her off or let her down gently? To save them both the inevitable embarrassment. The remoteness was the reason Heather had chosen this above all the other advertised jobs. She wanted to find a place where she could get to know her patients personally and experience the real essence of general practice. After all those years of training in large district hospitals, a small semi-rural practice in the New Forest had the whiff of adventure she craved. It wasn't famine-ravaged Ethiopia or Somalia, but she'd almost collided with a free-roaming pony on the drive down. The moment her tyres crossed the first cattle grid, she knew this was where she was meant to be.

Alan led her to a consulting room dominated by a heavy wooden desk. The austere room looked as though it should host a bank manager or solicitor rather than a family doctor, but it was reassuring to see shelves piled high with dusty textbooks and other ancient-looking medical paraphernalia. He sat on one side of the desk in a leather captain's chair and gestured to an uncomfortable-looking wooden chair on the other side, no doubt designed to dissuade lengthy consultations. Already Heather could see through him – the languid movements and phlegmatic manner as much an act as her own feigned nonchalance. When he stretched out his long legs under the desk, accidentally brushing her foot, she flinched. And he flinched as if she'd stung him.

'What would you like to know about me?' Heather asked when it seemed he'd run out of words. Really, who was conducting this interview? 'That you don't already know,' she added.

His cheeks flushed scarlet. There was no need for him to study the spare copy of the carefully typed curriculum vitae she pushed across the desk into his hands. He was already well briefed. He'd seen her naked.

To be fair, the interview should have stopped there. There was no way he would – or should – offer her the job. No way they could work together. But Alan went through the motions of examining the typed summary of her qualifications and where she'd worked in the years since they'd last met. She watched him as he read, sandy brows pinched in concentration, eyes obscured by the most luscious eyelashes.

He'd always been fit, with powerful arms and legs, but he'd filled out, as young men do in their twenties. The self-consciousness he'd tried to hide beneath the white lab coat was gone and she was now sitting across the desk from a young man who'd grown into himself. His jaw had squared, and his dark-rimmed spectacles had been replaced with little round John Lennon glasses. He wore his hair fashionably long at the back, curling at his collar. The smooth cleft in his chin that had always reminded Heather of a baby's bottom was all that remained of young Alan Winterbottom.

'That all seems in order,' he said, handing back the CV. 'Any questions?'

Was that it? Was he offering her the job?

'Can I ask about Dr *Gordon* Winterbottom? Will he be joining us?' Heather indicated the framed certificate on the wall behind the desk, hanging at a slight angle.

'I think I'd better explain.' Alan's gaze dropped to the desk and his Adam's apple bobbed. 'Gordon was my father. He died. Recently. Heart attack, we assume. At this desk. In this very chair.' He stroked the armrests. 'The receptionist found him slumped in a pile of repeat prescriptions next to a cold cup of tea. Hadn't even touched his Ginger Nuts.'

'I'm so sorry.' Her hand went to her chest, mirroring without realising what must have been his father's last gesture. 'That must have been such a shock.'

'It was. Ginger Nuts were his favourite.'

Alan smiled ruefully. He'd always had a dry sense of humour, one of the things that had attracted her to him in the first place, but Heather could see the glassy film across his eyes. She wanted to hug him. Should she or would that be inappropriate under the circumstances? Indecision kept her sitting primly across the desk.

'My father was an old-school family doctor,' he continued. 'The only doctor in Netherwood. He was decorated for his service in the Royal Army Medical Corps during the war, and he was one of those GPs who did everything and anything. Things we wouldn't dream of doing nowadays. I never knew him to show fear or doubt or a moment's hesitation. I'm sure he must have delivered half the babies in the district. He was so dedicated he never took a day off.' Alan's voice cracked. He pulled a handkerchief out of his trouser pocket and blew his nose. 'I used to go out with him on visits when I was young. He was so kind to his patients, always going above and beyond. Everyone loved him.'

He paused, as if weighing up whether he should say something or not. 'My mother would tell you he wasn't always the easiest person to live with, especially after my brother died.'

Immediately, he looked uncomfortable, as if used to censoring himself, he'd said too much. He'd never mentioned this when they were at medical school. Never mentioned his father, or that he'd had a brother. Admittedly, they hadn't shared everything about themselves when they'd first met, as they stripped away the layers of skin and fascia to reveal Fred's inner workings.

Then that night. Too much Pimm's. Too few clothes. A split-second decision to tiptoe out rather than snuggle into Alan's warm sleeping body had removed any potential complications or barriers to building her career. It had been better that way, for them both. Having sacrificed her teens to caring for her mother, Heather was keen to make up for lost time. She didn't need any more distractions. She didn't need the complication of a relationship at that stage in her life. The fact that they were unlikely to ever see each other again had eased the guilt a little. It was the one reckless thing she'd done in her entire life, the one thing she'd done for personal pleasure rather than duty. She had done them both a favour by leaving. And yet here they were. It was all very embarrassing. Confusing and embarrassing.

Maintaining a professional persona was something Heather Wilson had always excelled at, and yet as that night returned to her, kiss by kiss, touch by touch, it was proving difficult to keep the heat from her cheeks.

'The job was advertised as an assistant, with a view to partnership. Just to be clear, I take it you're looking for someone to replace your father.'

'Not replace. He was irreplaceable.' His eyes dropped to his lap. 'The worst of it was that my mother had been pleading with him to take on a partner. She kept urging him to consider retirement and that meant planning his succession.'

'You'd never considered taking over?'

'Not me. Not at first anyway. I was destined for greater things, remember that?' Alan shook his head, then looked up again, searching her face for something. She remembered he'd wanted to specialise in epilepsy. He'd never told her why although she'd formed the impression that it was deeply personal. 'My father had always assumed I'd follow in his footsteps. I still remember the look on his face when I told him I thought general practice was boring. It broke his heart. Literally.'

'Now, now, Dr Winterbottom. Even a neurologist knows that myocardial infarction is caused by atherosclerosis not disappointment.' She'd slipped into what she hoped was a passable impression of their old professor of medicine. Luckily, Alan recognised it and his smile returned.

'I came down from Edinburgh to keep the practice running. Call it what you like: duty, loyalty or penance.' Alan threw up his hands. 'What can I say, this place has grown on me. It looks as though I'm here to stay.' Then he added, 'And I hope it will grow on you too. Come on, I'll show you round.'

He stood so purposefully that Heather dropped her handbag. It burst open, spewing its contents – make-up compact, notebook and pencil, folded handkerchief, keys. She dived under the desk to retrieve the items and met Alan face to face, on all fours, surrounded by carpet fluff and dust bunnies.

'This is awkward,' she said.

'It doesn't have to be,' whispered Alan.

He was looking straight into her eyes. *Those eyelashes.* She'd kept her eyes open a fraction longer than he had when they'd first kissed simply to watch his lashes spread like petals as he closed his.

'It was a long time ago. I panicked. I shouldn't have disappeared like that without an explanation or saying goodbye.' What could she say to the man who'd taken her virginity, relieving her of one burden when at that time in her life she'd shouldered so many? Thank you? 'For what it's worth, I'm sorry,' she said.

'We can pretend it didn't happen, Heather. Start all over again.'

'All right then. It never happened.'

'What never happened?'

They smiled.

'So, Dr Winterbottom,' said Heather. 'Are you offering me the job?'

'That depends, Dr Wilson. Do you still want it?'

9

Return of the prodigal daughter

MRS GEE REACHED THE RINGING PHONE FIRST. HER
Hyacinth Bucket telephone voice as she announced that the
caller had reached 'the Winterbottom residence' always made
Heather smile. She was a good sort, and if Alan ever did
get around to that awkward and long-overdue conversation,
Heather was going to miss her.

Heather didn't even need to ask who'd phoned. Mrs Gee
came bustling into the kitchen with an old toothbrush in
one hand and a scrap of paper in the other. She could barely
conceal her excitement.

'It's Tilly. She's on her way.'

Heather was confused. About her daughter, and the
toothbrush. 'On her way where?'

'Home! She's in Singapore waiting to board her connecting
flight.' Mrs Gee handed her a scribbled note. 'This is
her flight number and arrival time, but she says not to worry

about coming to the airport to meet her, she'll get a taxi to Netherwood.'

'Did she say anything else?' Like why she was coming home when they'd already booked flights to spend Christmas with her? Or why she'd only informed them when she was two thirds of the way here?

Mrs Gee shook her head. 'Not really. It was difficult to make out what she was saying with all those announcements in the background.' She smiled at Heather who realised she was wringing her hands. 'You never stop worrying about them, do you?'

'I suppose not,' said Heather. She'd worried about her daughters in the usual ways a mother would. She worried when they were unwell or didn't eat. She worried on their behalf before a presentation at school, and she worried when they forgot their musical instrument on band rehearsal day. But she'd often worried more about her patients, put the needs of virtual strangers and their children ahead of her own flesh and blood. A wave of regret broke over her and she realised that, when it came to her attention, she'd short-changed Sarah and Tilly. Sarah appeared to have escaped relatively unscathed, but Tilly was a different matter.

She found Alan with Kevin in the greenhouse which, over the past few days, had acquired two deckchairs, a mini fridge and an old transistor radio, turning it into a horticultural man cave. Alan was none the wiser about Tilly, unable to shed any light on the surprise phone call. 'It's as much a shock to me as it is to you, Heather.'

'Do you think she's all right?' Heather pondered. Tilly had always been unpredictable, but a surprise visit from the other side of the world was unprecedented, even for her.

'This is probably why she didn't tell us sooner,' said Alan. 'Because she knew you'd worry, try to read all sorts into it.'

'There's nothing wrong with worrying about your youngest child.'

'She's thirty-five,' Alan reminded her.

Heather didn't need reminding. How was she old enough to have a youngest child that age?

As she turned to go, the greenhouse already uncomfortably warm and humid, she asked Alan if he knew what Mrs Gee was doing with his old toothbrush.

'She's scrubbing the grout in the family bathroom,' he said without missing a beat.

'She's doing what?'

'The grout, between the tiles.'

'I know what grout is, Alan. My concern is whether an eighty-year-old woman with osteoarthritis should be on her hands and knees scrubbing it with an old toothbrush. Can't you do something?'

'I could offer her that kneeling pad the Cliftons gave you.' Alan winked at Kevin who was standing awkwardly in the corner with a dibber in one hand and a packet of carrot seeds in the other.

'I'm serious, Alan.'

'So am I. Mrs Gee isn't a woman to be trifled with. Especially when she's only cleaned half the grout.'

'Coward.' Once again, he'd wriggled out of a hard conversation and covered his discomfort with arid humour. If he wouldn't do it, then she would. One of them had to say what needed to be said.

Heather knocked, then poked her head gingerly around the bathroom door. All she could see of Mrs Gee was the back of the daisy-print housecoat she'd worn to work ever since Heather could remember.

'Would you like a cup of tea, Mrs Gee?'

Mrs Gee sat back on her haunches and wiped her forehead with the back of her marigold glove. 'No thank you, Dr Winterbottom.'

'Are you sure? I thought we could have a talk.'

'What about?'

'Oh, things.'

'What kind of things?' Her eyes narrowed suspiciously.

'I was thinking that the house might be getting a bit much for you to manage now. At your –'

Mrs Gee stopped mid-scrub. 'Are you saying you're not happy with my work, Dr Winterbottom? The last Mrs Winterbottom never had any complaints.'

Half the bathroom floor was gleaming white, the other half still grey and grubby. Alan was right. Maybe this wasn't the ideal time to have this conversation.

'No, no. Not at all. Far from it. I don't know what we'd do without you. It's more that I wouldn't blame you if you decided you'd had enough. I mean, Alan and I would completely understand if you announced it was time for you and Mr Gee to retire down to a lovely cottage in Devon, or if you wanted to spend more time with your grandchildren. How many is it now, seven?'

Mrs Gee laughed. 'Eight now. And four great-grandchildren. Truth be told, I come here for a break. Mr Gee too. It keeps us young. No, I'm a firm believer in good honest hard work. At our age it's important to have a sense of purpose. Don't you think?'

'So important,' Heather agreed. *So important.* Her shoulders dropped.

'Well, I'd best crack on, Dr Winterbottom.' Her knees clicked like cocked triggers as she shuffled across to the next row of tiles. 'There's so much to do before Tilly arrives.'

~

After two years apart, Heather's first impression of her daughter was that, despite the baggy sweatshirt and jeans she wore, she'd lost weight. She stopped herself from passing comment. Mothers were invariably obsessed with their daughters' weight, either gain or loss, as if the scales held some secret code for happiness or heartbreak. Tilly's travel-weary face was implacable as the taxi pulled out of the drive with a final crunch of tyres.

Mrs Gee, who'd arrived especially early that morning, and had spent an hour and a half polishing the brass door knocker, was first in the meet and greet line-up. She pinned Tilly's arms to her sides in an eager embrace and promptly burst into tears.

Heather found the relaxed, welcoming smile she'd rehearsed in the mirror that morning. She opened her arms but, instead of falling into them, Tilly handed her a small backpack.

'Thanks, Mum,' she said, brushing Heather's cheek with her own, before side-stepping to meet Stan's enthusiastic welcome.

'I've missed you soooo much,' she told the dog.

'Did you have a good flight?' Heather asked.

It hadn't been a good flight – long, cramped, the food terrible. Good to know Tilly hadn't lost her ability to find the cloud in the silver lining.

'I'll put the kettle on,' said Mrs Gee.

'Thank you, I could murder a cup of tea.' Tilly slumped into one of the chairs at the kitchen table.

'How about I make you your favourite, toast and Marmite?' Heather offered brightly, not wanting to be outdone.

'Do you have any Vegemite?'

'Er no, sorry.'

'Don't worry. I'm not very hungry,' Tilly replied blandly. 'Quite honestly, my body doesn't know whether it's breakfast or dinnertime.' She cracked her neck, something she knew her mother hated.

'Okay. Make yourself at home.' How silly, thought Heather. Tilly had moved in and out like the hokey-cokey, but this was still her home.

Not wanting to dive straight into an interrogation, but struggling for safer topics of conversation, Heather dithered, fussing with the mugs, and colliding with Mrs Gee who was already fetching the milk from the fridge.

Alan walked in. 'Your suitcases are upstairs, Tilly. In your old room.'

'Oh, Dad, you shouldn't have,' Tilly called after him as he shuffled back out into the garden. 'Not at your age.'

Heather stifled a snigger. There was no getting away from the fact that Alan looked tired and drained. Old, she supposed. Heather rarely bothered looking in a mirror herself. Since she and Alan were only a year apart in age, it was a fair assumption that she looked old too. What was more of a shock was to see that Tilly had the first crow's feet around her eyes and the first white hairs at her temples, like dried paint clinging to the bristles of a paintbrush. She was entering middle age and yet, in Heather's eyes, she still looked too young to be out in the big wide world on her own.

Mrs Gee insisted on carrying the heavy teapot to the table but refused a cup herself, saying that she had to make the most of the weather and peg out another load of washing on the line.

'I see we have a greenhouse,' Tilly remarked, looking out of the kitchen window. 'Nice.'

'Your father has decided to save the planet,' said Heather, trying not to smirk.

'I think that's amazing. It's about time you both reduced your carbon footprint.' She glanced across at the gas-powered Aga, the primary purpose of which seemed to be to keep Stan's bed nice and cosy in winter. Heather decided not to point out that Tilly had just flown halfway across the world, apparently on a whim. 'Who's that with Dad?'

Heather joined her at the window. 'That's Kevin.' He must have arrived early and snuck in around the back. 'He's your father's new *friend*.'

She hadn't meant to italicise the word friend. It had just come out like that. Tilly gave her the side eye.

'You mean a *Brokeback Mountain* kind of friend?'

They watched Alan take Kevin's hand and bring it to his lips.

'I'm not sure, but they've become quite the item.'

'I wouldn't have thought he was Dad's type.'

'I'm not sure your father has a type anymore.' It came out sounding sadder than she'd intended.

Tilly said, 'It's not unusual for men of Dad's age to finally come out.'

Heather knew. Of their admittedly limited circle of friends, two of the husbands had ended up together, which made for interesting dinner parties. And tricky Christmas cards.

'That's odd,' Tilly said. 'Dad usually goes out of his way to avoid the garden.'

'Kevin has initiated your father into the sacred order of organic growers of Netherwood.'

Tilly nodded, as if she understood. 'Is that like the Knights Templar?'

'Similar.'

They smiled at each other. If making fun of Alan was the bridge she had to cross to her daughter, then so be it. And Alan made himself such an easy target. Especially when he appeared at the back door moments later, holding Kevin's hand. He led him to the kitchen drawer where he rummaged around for a pair of eyebrow tweezers.

'Splinter,' Kevin said, holding up his finger while Alan probed the pulpy flesh at close quarters.

Heather and Tilly exchanged looks.

'I thought I'd bake some salmon for dinner,' said Heather, while Alan poked about. 'How does that sound?'

Tilly screwed up her face. 'Is it farmed?'

'The salmon? I don't know. It's Scottish.'

'Have you any idea the kind of conditions these poor creatures live in?' Kevin chimed in. 'Crammed into cages being eaten alive by sea-lice? Salmon are sentient beings.'

Tilly stared at him as if he'd told her he could speak fluent salmon.

'Got it!' Alan inspected the sliver of wood at the end of the tweezers.

He had several attempts at applying a band-aid to Kevin's bleeding finger. Eventually, after he'd stuck half-a-dozen to themselves, Heather came to his rescue. To think that only weeks ago this man had been allowed near real patients.

Kevin and Tilly sized each other up until Alan finally performed the introductions.

'Kevin is helping me with my sustainability goals,' he said.

'This planet simply cannot feed the people it already has, let alone the growing population,' Kevin said. 'Intensive modern farming practices and the use of pesticides have destroyed the natural world and if countries can't even agree on a target for how quickly the planet dies, then what hope is there?'

Tilly's mouth had fallen open. She was a contrarian by nature and Heather couldn't wait to see how she planned to counter this statement.

'The henhouse is arriving tomorrow,' Alan announced, before she could speak. 'We'll be self-sufficient in eggs in a few weeks.'

'You don't even like eggs,' Heather pointed out. Alan pretended not to hear.

'You should get a goat!' Tilly said.

Everyone turned to look at her in amazement.

'Great idea,' said Alan.

'Why stop there? How about a cow and a few pigs?' Heather muttered as she cleared the mugs from the table.

'I might go upstairs and unpack.' Tilly stretched her arms above her head and yawned.

'Well, those butterheads won't plant themselves,' said Kevin with a little laugh and headed outside.

That left Alan and Heather alone in the kitchen. Mrs Gee, who'd been given a pair of headphones for her birthday, was singing along tunelessly to what was possibly Elton John's 'Rocket Man'.

'How long do you think Tilly's planning to stay?' Heather asked Alan.

'Didn't she say anything to you? You are her mother.'

'I didn't like to ask. You know how she can be. A simple enough question but it would be bound to come out the wrong way.'

'She's tired,' said Alan. 'It was a long flight. I'm sure we'll find out more when she's had a good rest. Though, judging by the weight of her suitcase, it looks as if she's back for a while.'

10

Beware the Sirens

STAN STRAINED AT HIS LEAD AS HIS CLAWS SCRATCHED AND skittered across the stone-floored entrance hall to get to the courtyard where Esme was waiting on her bench.

'Good morning, Dr Winterbottom.'

'Morning, Miss Clark.' Heather sat down beside her friend. 'It feels strange to hear the doctor bit now. People have started to call me Mrs Winterbottom, which makes me sound like my mother-in-law.'

'Once a doctor, always a doctor, surely?'

Until she cancelled her direct debit to the General Medical Council. One email and her career would be over, all those years of experience redundant. Heather stared wistfully into the distance.

'Are you having second thoughts?' Esme asked.

'What makes you say that?'

'I know what the job meant to you.'

'Nah,' said Heather. 'I was ready to give up the daily grind. I won't miss the stress and long hours.'

'Why don't I believe you?'

Heather smiled at her friend. 'Because you know me too well?' She took a breath. 'I'll be fine once I've adjusted to civilian life again.'

'And Alan?'

'Oh, he's hit the ground running. He's found a new hobby and a new friend. To think I was worried he'd be under my feet all day! I hardly see him.'

High above Esme's bench, two solitary wisps of cloud floated across the sky on the jet stream, both heading in the same direction, destined never to meet. Heather watched them, mesmerised.

'So, you're lonely?'

Was she? Was it possible to live with someone, sleep with someone, and still be lonely?

'I miss our working relationship. I realise now how much I miss talking about medicine, discussing patients, brainstorming ideas for the practice or sharing those little clinical pearls of wisdom. Now, we hardly talk at all unless it's to ask if the dog's been fed or what's for dinner.' Had she seen his socks? Had he seen her phone charger? Aside from the disagreement on the first morning, their conversation had shrunk to domestic matters. They'd become co-administrators of their marriage rather than enthusiastic participants; housemates who shared the same bed.

'You were a good team.'

'We were. We've always worked well together, respected each other's clinical strengths and interests. Sometimes I admit it felt as though, as the "lady doctor", I dealt with all the gynae stuff and mental health problems. But that's what I was good at. I was more than happy to leave all the prostates to Alan. We complemented each other.'

'Symbiosis.' *Typically, but not always, to the advantage of both.*

There had been times when Heather had been resentful. Once, after a particularly heavy morning during which she'd broken the news to a woman of fifty that she had breast cancer, arranged a hospital bed for a withdrawing alcoholic, and supported a mother of five who was about to leave her abusive husband, she'd found Alan talking cricket to a sixty-year-old man while removing a perfectly harmless fatty lump from his back.

'I wouldn't mind doing a bit of minor surgery once in a while,' she'd snarked.

'By all means,' he'd replied benevolently, examining the pale lump of tissue floating in the specimen jar in one hand while in the other, he held a mug of steaming hot tea. 'And I'll do the family planning clinic.'

A month later, they'd both drifted back to their own lanes and the subject was never raised again.

Heather produced a cardboard tray of glistening pastries. Esme's eyes lit up. If Stan had been awake, so would his. Lying across Esme's feet, he was reliving some highlight of his puppyhood, back legs twitching as he gambolled across the Elysian Fields of his dreams.

'You'd be surprised what exotic wares the village store is stocking these days. They're going all Continental.'

'Tell me, doctor, do baklava count as part of the Mediterranean diet you're always telling me to follow?'

'Most definitely.'

They bit into their baklava at the same time, and Heather watched Esme's eyes widen at the sweet, nutty taste. The older woman wiped crumbs away from her lips with a napkin.

When she'd finished, Esme picked up her knitting from the bench. The baby blanket had grown several inches since Heather's last visit. Or had Esme's hands shrunk?

'Would you like to try?' Esme offered Heather the giant needles that made her hands look so tiny and fragile.

Heather shook her head. 'I don't know how.'

'It's not too late to learn. Someone needs to carry on with this blanket if I pop my clogs before it's finished.'

'Don't talk nonsense, Esme! In fact, as your doctor, I forbid you to ever pop your clogs.'

They laughed, the mood lightened again as Heather took the needles and, dropping four stitches in her first row, proved that perhaps it was too late for her to take up knitting.

'I do have some exciting news to share,' said Heather.

'Sarah's pregnant?'

Heather shook her head. 'Almost as miraculous. Tilly's home.'

'Tell me all about Tilly,' said Esme, rubbing her hands together. 'How is she?'

Her daughter looked pretty much the same, even sounded the same. Conversations with Tilly had always been unpredictable, like dancers dancing to slightly different versions of the same piece of music. Whether she was involving you in a hypothetical discussion about the pros and cons of colonising other planets, or asking, if given an envelope with the time and date of your own death inside, whether you would open it or not. She'd once spent an entire summer holiday trying to fold a piece of paper in half more than seven times, having read that it was impossible.

'Tilly is still Tilly,' said Heather. An enigma, even to herself.

Just then, singing floated across the courtyard garden, a cacophony of female voices that set Heather's teeth on edge, almost as much as the sweetness of the honey-filled baklava she'd just finished eating.

'What is that noise?' Heather couldn't quite make out what they were singing but, as was usually the case, a single soprano drowned out all the others.

'That's the new ladies' choir,' said Esme. 'Brenda Bishop thinks she's Netherwood's answer to Sarah Brightman. She has designs on Handel's *Messiah* for the end of year concert. They tried to get me to join but I told them not until I'd finished knitting Laertes his funeral shroud. They already think I'm a crazy old duck, so nobody questioned it.'

'If you don't mind me asking, who is Laertes?'

'Penelope's father-in-law,' Esme clarified.

'I haven't heard you mention a Penelope before. Is she a new resident?'

Esme laughed as if this was the funniest thing she'd ever heard. She picked up a small brown paperback that Heather hadn't noticed sitting on the bench beside her friend. The spine of the old paperback was cracked, and the lettering faded and aged by exposure to sunlight. The words on the cover were still readable despite the dappling of the paper.

'Penelope is the long-suffering wife of the Greek hero, Odysseus. I finished with Mary Oliver. Next on my bookshelf was Homer's *Odyssey*. Since you'd mentioned your desire to visit Greece, I thought I'd do the same.' When she saw

Heather's confusion, she said, 'Tell me you studied Homer at school.'

Heather shook her head. 'Can't say I did. Blame the ignorance of a modern secondary education. Not much call for epic poets where I grew up.'

Esme examined the book, squinting as she flicked through the yellowed pages.

'I happen to think it's one of the better translations. Amazing that something written in the eighth century BC, about something that happened three thousand years ago, can still be relevant today. I suppose it goes to show there's nothing new under the sun. Take it from me, you don't need to have studied Classics to appreciate Homer. There's nothing the ancient Greeks had to say about human nature that as a doctor you don't already know. They simply added the monsters and fantastical beasts, the obligatory heroes and villains, and threw in a few sex-craved gods and goddesses to wreak havoc over the hapless mortals.'

'You're right. That sounds suspiciously like Netherwood to me.'

Voices rose again from nearby. It really was hard to ignore Brenda's dominance in the chorus.

Hallelujah! Hallelujah! Hal-le-lu-jah!

A smile twitched at Esme's lips. As soon as she caught Heather's eye, they burst out laughing.

'Ironically, I've reached nearly ninety and there is nothing wrong with my hearing.'

'How do you put up with it?'

Esme waved her book. 'I told you; Homer has the answer.'

'So, what does Homer have to say about Brenda Bishop?'

Flicking through her copy of *The Odyssey*, Esme stopped at a page, one of many with the corner folded down. 'This is one of my favourite parts,' she said, scanning the line with her finger. '"Stuff your ears with softened beeswax and tie me to the mast with chafing ropes lest I surrender to those honeyed voices!"'

Seeing Heather's blank expression she added, 'He's warning his crew about the Sirens.' She closed the book and turned towards Heather. As patiently as if she were teaching a class of five-year-olds to use scissors, she explained the plot.

'Odysseus, King of Ithaca, is sailing back home to his island after ten years fighting in the Trojan War. His wife, Penelope, is waiting there for him, not knowing if he's alive or dead. Unfortunately, the royal house has been taken over by hordes of young men, or suitors, who are hoping to marry her.'

Heather sat in stunned silence as Esme continued to retell the story of Odysseus's encounter with the half-bird, half-maiden enchantresses called the Sirens who tried to lure sailors to their death with their irresistible voices.

'And to think that in forty years as a GP I thought I'd heard everything.'

'That's just for starters.' Esme went on to regale Heather with how Calypso the libidinous nymph kept Odysseus as a sex slave for seven years; how the sailors escaped Polyphemus the one-eyed giant; as well as a sexy sorceress who turned men into pigs. After that she lost track, gathering that the story was basically a series of implausible excuses for why Odysseus was late home to his wife.

'I'll bear the earplugs in mind for next time.'

Esme grasped Heather's arm with her cool hand. 'Thank you,' she said, earnestly, searching until she had Heather's full gaze. 'I mean it.'

'Thank you for what?'

'For this.' She indicated the bench, Stan, the empty cardboard tray. 'For not forgetting me.'

'Don't be silly. I love our chats. I always look forward to coming here.' It was the truth.

Esme's sunken face lifted as if to say, 'You do?'

'My life is so small these days,' she said. 'I feel as if I've been shrink-wrapped into this place. It's nice to enjoy the outside world, even if it is vicariously. Talking of which, how are your holiday plans coming along?'

'What holiday plans?'

'The trip to Greece.'

'On hold, I'm afraid. The subject is moot in our house. It's as if he's stuffed his ears with beeswax and lashed himself to the treated wooden sleepers of his new vegetable garden to avoid hearing what I have to say. He claims he's too tired to go on holiday. Honestly, who's too tired to take a break? Or he will go away but not until his seeds have germinated, then it's not until he's propagated his seedlings, then not until they're established. Just when I thought he might be coming round to the idea, he bought a henhouse. The hens arrived yesterday and he's already named them.'

'How many are there?'

'Four so far. Alice, Belinda, Chantal and Dee. I suspect he's calling them after all his ex-girlfriends. Who knows how far down the alphabet we're likely to go.'

'What about Tilly? Would she go with you?'

'Did I ever tell you about the incident on Bournemouth Beach when she was six?'

Esme chuckled. 'No, but I read about it in the paper.' Her face grew serious again. 'Give Alan time. He'll come round to the idea eventually.'

Heather doubted that. She now had an inkling of how it felt to lose a loved one to a cult. Alan had been brainwashed by the Netherwood Organic Gardening Group and its charismatic leader, Kevin.

They watched an elderly couple shuffle slowly past, arm in tightly wrapped arm, giving the impression that if one of them let go, they would both crumble.

'Can I ask you something, Esme? When you look back at your life, do you have any regrets?'

Esme thought for a moment. 'Of course. Only I regret the things I didn't do, not the things I did.'

'Such as?'

'Smoking pot.'

'Miss Clark! I never thought I'd hear those words coming from you.'

Esme smiled mischievously. 'I'd like to have tried it once in my life. See what all the fuss is about.'

'Anything else on your bucket list of regrets?' Heather asked, still reeling at what she'd just heard.

'I wish I'd travelled more, watched more sunrises, learned another language.'

'Those are on my bucket list too.'

Esme added, 'And I wish I'd had more lovers.'

Heather snorted.

'Was Aubrey your first?'

'And last, yes.'

'I'm so sorry,' Heather said. 'There's me going on about my husband . . .' The sentence ended in an apologetic shrug.

How could I have been so insensitive, thought Heather, remembering only too well the day Aubrey's aneurysm had ruptured. Alan had sprinted across the village green and attempted to resuscitate Aubrey where he'd fallen, in his beloved front garden, secateurs and scattered rose heads still within his reach. There was little anyone could have done to save him, according to the coroner, and yet, as his GP for many years, Alan had taken it very hard.

Heather and Esme joined hands, holding onto one another as the memories and regrets jostled the peaceful morning like a sudden bout of turbulence. The back of Esme's hand reminded Heather of a speckled egg.

Eventually, Heather spoke. 'I suppose it's only natural to wonder how green the grass is on the other side of the fence.'

'The grass may look greener over the fence, but if you water your own grass, it can grow just as green. Unfortunately, I've left it too late to water anybody's grass.'

Whichever way Heather looked at it, she was back to lawns. Already deflated, there wasn't enough air left in her chest to sigh.

'Why don't you go on your own?' Esme dropped her hand and sat to attention. 'If Alan doesn't want to go with you, then go alone.'

'Do a Shirley Valentine, you mean?' And be another embarrassing older woman making a fool of herself with a young Spanish waiter, like Jim Fielder's wife. 'It's too late for that. I should have done it when I was younger. When I should have been backpacking around the Greek islands, drinking retsina and sleeping with waiters, I was sailing with my parents on the Norfolk Broads. Five years in a row we thought it would be Mum's last holiday. I'm afraid I misspent my misspent youth.'

'I'm not saying you should strip off and bare your breasts to a local Lothario like Pauline Collins did but go and have some fun. Don't leave it too late like I did.'

11

Hors d'oeuvres

THE DOWNPOUR STARTED AS SOON AS SHE LEFT THE Willows. Thick grey choked the sky, swallowing the wispy pair of clouds she'd watched from Esme's bench. They must still be up there, high in the stratosphere, invisible now behind a sudden storm.

She longed to go back, return to the perpetually sunny courtyard and Esme's bench where she'd felt seen and heard. If only she and Alan could converse like that, listen to each other's hearts. But they were both equally pig-headed. They couldn't go on like this, tiptoeing around each other pretending everything was fine. One of them needed to bring this situation to a head.

Heather leaned into the gusts that drove the rain like needles into her face, dragging Stan behind her, his sodden fur weighing him down like a lead X-ray apron. Water was already pooling in the potholes along the lane. Should she run or walk? Her mathematical brain wrestled with the calculation and decided it made no difference. If she walked, she'd get hit by a certain number of droplets over a certain period of time. If she ran, she'd hit more droplets over a shorter time. It was the kind of equation Tilly would stay up all night trying to solve.

Before she'd decided whether to make a run for it, she reached the notorious Bridgestone Lane blind bend. The narrow, winding lane was a popular shortcut to the school, and twice a day laden people-carriers duelled head to head. Occasionally, a New Forest pony would decide to stand in the middle of the road, and not even Darlingford Dings and Dents could repair the damage a pony could do. Nor the vet hospital mend the damage a large vehicle could do to an animal like that.

Stan, who hated getting his paws wet, pranced like a frisky show pony in protest at the deepening puddles. Heather walked on the soggy grass verge, where the lane was too narrow for a footpath. The moist earth sucked at her canvas shoes. Her linen trousers and Breton t-shirt were equally saturated, and her hair fell in Medusa tendrils around her face. She was so focused on her physical discomfort that she almost walked into the back of a vehicle that had stopped in the middle of the road, hazard lights flashing. Immediately, her body launched into rescuer mode. It wouldn't be the only time she'd been the first responder on the scene of an accident and her body knew exactly how to prepare. Racing heart: tick. Dry mouth: tick. Sweaty palms: difficult to say in the rain. Instinct to run away: tick.

It took a moment for her to realise that it was Alan's silver Honda. Fearing the worst, she broke into a run. She squeezed past the car, snagging her arm on a bramble and came across a hunched figure, hands on knees and breathing heavily.

Alan.

She called out. He didn't react as she approached. Was this it – the heart attack they'd both secretly dreaded? There'd been times in the past few weeks when she'd imagined murdering him in his sleep. It would be simple enough to give the appearance of death from natural causes – insulin overdose, a high-dose opiate patch stuck onto his back as he slept, a dozen glyceryl tri-nitrate tablets crushed into his tea. Now, the thought of losing him was unbearable. He was an old fool, but he was her old fool. And she loved him.

'Alan, are you all right?'

This time he turned to the sound of her voice.

'Of course, I'm all right.'

'Oh Alan, those are your best trousers.' He was wearing his father's Aquascutum raincoat and the trousers she'd recently collected from the dry cleaners, tucked into a pair of Wellington boots. 'What on earth are you doing?'

'What does it look like?' He was leaning on the handle of a shovel. Beside him a hessian sack was half-filled with horse droppings.

'Why?' So many whys. Why horse shit? Why on a blind bend? Why in the pouring rain?

'It's for the rhubarb,' he explained as if to someone of limited intelligence.

The screech of tyres cut the conversation short. A blue van skidded to a halt a hair's breadth from the back of Alan's car. The driver released a torrent of abuse and the full force of his van's horn.

'Quickly, Alan, move this thing before you cause an accident.'

'You'd better get in before you get soaked,' he said, glancing at her sodden clothes.

Alan dragged the sack of manure to the back where it joined several others and was eagerly accompanied by Stan who leapt into the boot like a gazelle. The smell inside the car was overpowering. Heather wound down the window, then shut it again when a gust of wind blew rain inside.

'What were you thinking?'

Alan launched into a well thought out defence. 'You wouldn't believe the price of rotted manure. I popped into the garden centre for a few bits and pieces while you were gone, and I was shocked. Kevin calls it daylight robbery. Thanks to all the free-roaming shit-machine ponies, he pointed out there's a plentiful supply, free for the taking.'

Kevin again.

Behind them, the driver of the blue van was growing impatient. Alan found first gear, seconds before he became Netherwood's first road rage victim.

'I was thinking that we really need a four-wheel drive out here in the sticks.'

'We've managed perfectly well for forty years without a four-wheel drive, not to mention that we live half a mile from the ring-road and then it's dual carriageway all the way to Darlingford.'

Alan raised his hear-me-out finger, his tone suggesting that, after Pericles, she owed him not to interrupt.

'I'm worried about global warming. Flooding, in particular.'

'Hold your horses, Noah. This is a passing shower. We don't need to panic just yet.'

They drove in silence, Alan apparently steering through every flooded pothole to make a point.

'You didn't answer your phone. I was worried about you,' he said finally. 'I thought you might have been kidnapped.'

She glanced at her phone. Two missed calls. She always kept her phone on silent, as a matter of habit, so as not to interrupt her consultations at work. And also because she'd forgotten how to turn the ring tone back on again. Her skin prickled with irritation. It wasn't unreasonable of her husband to wonder where she was. He wasn't stalking her. At the same time, Heather didn't like having to account for her every movement.

'Alan, I'm sixty-six, with cellulite. I'm hardly likely to appeal to sex-traffickers. Besides, this is Netherwood. Nothing ever happens in Netherwood.'

Wasn't that the truth?

'Seriously though, where have you been all morning?' Alan glanced across to where Heather sat in a pool of water on the passenger seat.

'I went to visit a friend. We got talking and I forgot the time.'

He eyed her suspiciously. Did he think she was having an affair?

'Anyone I know?'

'As a matter of fact, yes. Esme Clark at The Willows.'

'Miss Clark is still alive?'

'Very much so.'

He seemed to weigh up his next words, tapping them out on the steering wheel before trusting his mouth to say them.

'What's going on with you, Heather?'

'What's going on with *me*?'

Alan's knuckles blanched on the worn steering wheel. 'See? This is what I'm talking about. I can't do anything right. I thought this was going to be our special time, a chance to relax and reconnect, to enjoy growing old together.'

'I don't want to grow old!' Her shout echoed in the ensuing silence. Stan tried to hide his head between his paws. 'Not yet. Not until I've had my chance to be young.'

'I don't understand. Explain it to me.'

They were back home. Alan parked and turned off the engine. Stan reappeared over the back seat, his eyes flitting nervously from one to the other. It may as well be now, thought Heather. Upstairs, the curtains were drawn at Tilly's window. She must be having a jet-lagged nap. It was Mrs Gee's half day. Heather took a deep breath and, concentrating on maintaining a calm, non-confrontational, non-judgemental tone, set out her grievances.

'I have dedicated my whole adult life to attending to other people's needs. And I don't regret any of it, not one brow mopped, hand held, or nappy changed. It was satisfying, fulfilling. It's who I was, and am. Yes, there were times when I was exhausted, resentful and, I admit, self-pitying, but I fought so hard not to let that show.'

Alan regarded her intently. To his credit he didn't try to tell her what she should think or feel. He simply listened.

'I have become the sum of my obligations to other people. For once, I want to do something for myself. I want to make it up to the young woman who missed out.'

'Is this about the Greece thing?' Alan asked, turning the windscreen wipers off. It had stopped raining. 'I don't understand why it can't wait until next year. Or the year after –'

See? Heather wanted to say. The goalposts were shifting already. She thought about Esme and Aubrey. She didn't want to reach ninety with a bucket list of broken dreams.

'I can't wait that long.' *Risk* waiting that long, she nearly said. 'The whole idea of retirement is that we can take off when we like rather than plan months ahead. I mean, it's one thing to work around the junior partners, but quite another to schedule trips around bloody rhubarb.' *Or hens named after ex-girlfriends.* 'I don't want safe, boring and predictable any longer. I want spontaneous, fun, adventure.'

He looked at her as if she was speaking in tongues. What was the point? They were going round and round in circles, as usual. She tried to open the door, to jump off this carousel. The door was jammed. Stuck like the bedroom window, the kitchen cupboard that still hadn't been fixed, the mirror still resting against the wall. Stuck like their marriage.

Heather threw her weight into her shoulder and the door gave way, spilling her out onto the wet gravel. In the porch, she threw her muddy shoes into the pile of assorted footwear. So as not to drip on Mrs Gee's freshly waxed floor, she wrapped herself in the brown towel she always left at the door to wipe Stan's paws. Dog towels now outnumbered the human towels two to one. She'd smell like Stan, but that was a small price to pay not to upset Mrs Gee.

Heather scrubbed at her dripping hair and patted her cheeks that were damp from not only the rain but tears too. She buried her face in the threadbare fabric. Then she remembered the reason she'd kept this tatty old towel all these years.

12

Hatching and matching

Netherwood, 1983

WHEN THE PHONE RANG, HEATHER WAS STILL IN HER LAST appointment of the day, one of Alan's regulars the receptionist had fitted in as an extra, assuring her that the man only wanted a quick prescription. An hour later, having unburdened himself of a secret he had never told another living soul – including Alan – the patient left again, leaving a shell-shocked Heather trying to stuff the thick wad of handwritten notecards back into their Lloyd George envelope. She didn't know why Alan bothered writing any notes, since even he admitted he couldn't read his own handwriting. In his defence, he claimed that if he couldn't read his notes, then neither could a judge in court.

The evening receptionist already had her coat on when Heather walked in with her teetering pile of the day's completed patient notes.

'Don't worry about filing these now,' she told the receptionist. 'You get home before the snow settles.' Outside, the light had changed from the gloom of a mid-winter evening to the silvery glow of falling snow. 'Did I hear the phone?'

The receptionist looked worried. 'It was Mr Lawson. Rosemary's waters have broken. The midwife is stuck in Darlingford with twins.'

'I'll call in on my way home,' said Heather.

'No need. Dr Winterbottom said he'd go. He left not five minutes ago.'

'But it's my night on call.'

'He told me to tell you to go straight home. He was worried about you driving back to Bournemouth if the roads get blocked.'

It rarely snowed as far south as Netherwood, but tonight of all nights, the heavily pregnant clouds that had blanketed the village all day had finally delivered. The first fat snowflakes melted against the glass of the tall sash windows. Minutes later the snow was an inch thick on the sill. Outside, the village green, home to summer fetes and cricket matches, was hidden beneath a thick carpet of white. Snow had already settled on the thatched roofs, the box hedges, and the bare branches of every winter tree. With the lights shining through the stained-glass windows at St Luke's church, the village resembled a Christmas card.

The heater had never worked properly in Heather's Triumph, and her feet were already numb on the pedals. She crawled along the familiar road in the rapidly disappearing tracks of another vehicle. It was good of Alan to suggest she go home early. He lived barely two hundred yards from the surgery, and while she had been officially promoted from assistant to associate, it was his practice, after all.

At the edge of the village, the road forked. Usually, Heather turned left and headed towards the main road to Bournemouth. Several cars before her had kept this route relatively clear of snow. A single set of tracks headed right, towards the Lawsons' farm.

'Call it a sixth sense,' she said later, explaining why she chose to turn right and follow those tracks rather than head home. She'd felt the sensation in the same part of her body that told her which patients to phone to check up on late at night, when to order that extra X-ray or blood test, and when to probe a little deeper, to ask, 'Are you *really* all right?'

Gestalt. It was a German word, meaning pattern or shape, that was used to describe when something was greater than the sum of its individual parts. It would be easy to call it a gut feeling since that's where it resided. But that kind of intuition was so much more, coming only after years of training and experience. It was the ability to recognise when something didn't fit the usual pattern. A symptom, a sign, or body language that wasn't quite right. Something the patient said. Or didn't say. Or why the tyre tracks at this junction, after turning right, appeared to vanish into thin air. And thereafter, lit up by the Triumph's headlights, Heather saw the rear end of Alan's car half buried in the hedge.

Leaving her engine running, Heather slid and slipped her way over the verge to the mangled wreckage. Having seen plenty of car crash victims in casualty, faces sliced and pebble-dashed with broken glass, she prepared herself for the worst. But the car was empty. Footprints led away from the crumpled vehicle, heading up the road, towards the Lawson place. She jumped back into her car and followed them. A hundred yards further on, she came across Alan, coat collar turned up against the driving wind and snow, his father's Gladstone bag in his hand.

'Get in!' Heather shouted, leaning across to open the passenger door.

Seemingly more concerned about Rosemary Lawson than his brush with death, he climbed into the Triumph and urged Heather to hurry. His woollen coat was heavy with snow and already smelling like a sheep. Heather was relieved to find Alan unhurt, surprised by quite how relieved she was.

Mr Lawson greeted them at the front door of the old farmhouse, his features alternating between relief and concern.

'This one isn't like the others,' he said. 'Usually, she coughs, and they fall out.'

No wonder. Six strapping lads, all showing early promise on the rugby pitch, had neatly evicted themselves from Rosemary Lawson's womb. Number seven – somehow, they all knew it would be another boy – should have followed suit. The snow from their shoes melted on the wooden stairs, as they followed Mr Lawson to an overheated bedroom where a small fire was burning in the grate. Alan dispatched Mr Lawson to fetch towels and boil water while he assessed Rosemary. Steam was already rising from Alan's thick winter coat when he rested it over the back of a chair in the corner.

Watching Alan wash his hands in the bowl, Heather found herself hypnotised as he massaged the bar of carbolic soap between his palms, stroking the creamy lather over the backs of his hands and down into the clefts between his elegant fingers. Slow and sensual. The writhing of slippery skin on skin. When Alan dried his hands on a brown towel, all the saliva had vanished from Heather's mouth.

'Let me have a look,' said Alan, folding back the nightdress to reveal the pale skin of Rosemary Lawson's abdomen, stretched skin laced with purple ribbons that radiated like spokes around a bicycle wheel. Heather averted her eyes when he performed an internal examination.

Alan's eyes found hers. 'Breech,' he said quietly.

'Are you sure?' Heather whispered.

'Quite sure. I've just put a finger up his arse.'

Rosemary knew enough to look scared. The wind rattled the window in its loose frame. There was no way they could get her to hospital in this weather.

'You've delivered a breech before,' Heather whispered as Alan searched through his bag for his pinard stethoscope, trying not to make it sound like a question in front of the Lawsons.

'I watched my father do it once.'

'That's something,' said Heather, encouragingly.

'I was eight,' he added.

'Listen, I've done obstetrics, I can talk you through it,' said Heather. 'Or . . .'

The relief was written all over his face. If you had a tremor in your right hand or tingling in your face, then Alan Winterbottom was your man. If his father hadn't died, Alan would have been a fully fledged neurologist by now. He was never supposed to end up here, delivering babies in the middle of nowhere. For Heather, on the other hand, this was the reason she'd dreamed of being a rural GP.

Alan handed her the pinard and through the miniature silver trumpet she heard the baby's heartbeat, reassuringly fast in her ear.

'Try to relax, Mrs Lawson,' said Alan from the foot of the bed. 'You're in excellent hands here.'

A contraction racked Rosemary Lawson's body, an awful guttural sound exploding from her pursed lips as she tried to push her son from his tight cocoon of muscle. A foot appeared.

'He's in a hurry to kick that ball,' Alan joked while Heather released both the baby's slippery legs.

Slowly, slowly. Heather felt a trickle of sweat down her spine. *Let Nature do the hard work.* One shoulder, then an arm. Another arm. An enormous head followed, and in seconds the room was filled with Billy Lawson's ten-pound-two-ounce cry, just as in years to come, the bar at The Four Candles would resonate with his bawdy rugby songs on a Saturday night.

As a token of his appreciation, Mr Lawson insisted they keep the brown towel. They passed it between them, wiping sweat from their brows. Alan's shoes were soaked and while the Triumph's pathetic heater merely recirculated the sub-zero air, Heather insisted he dry his feet on the towel to prevent chilblains. Her own body was still flushed and warm from the adrenaline.

Later, over mugs of steaming Horlicks in the kitchen at The Elms, Alan said, 'You were very impressive back there, Dr Wilson.'

'I couldn't have done it without you. We make a good team, Dr Winterbottom.' She clinked his mug with hers, bringing a smile back to his face.

'You're right. We are good together. In fact, there's something I've been meaning to ask you.' He was looking straight at her now. 'Now seems as good a time as any.'

Here it was, she thought. The offer of a partnership. At last. Her future secured in the community she'd come to love, and hopefully, with a pay rise, a chance to move out of that draughty old flat in Bournemouth.

'Go on then,' said Heather, beaming. 'Ask me.'

To her surprise he took the mug from her and placed it on the kitchen table. Then he dropped down onto one knee on the flagstone floor close to where the brown towel and their damp coats were drying on the Aga.

He looked up from beneath those long, lustrous eyelashes, blinked away what looked like tears and said, 'Heather Wilson, will you marry me?'

13

Where the wild thing is

'HOW IS ATILLA?'

'Sarah, don't keep calling her that,' said Heather, secretly pleased that there was a telephone between them to hide her smile. She had to admit she still found Sarah's childhood mispronunciation of Matilda hilariously apt, now an ironic term of endearment by an adoring older sibling. 'She's fine. Or she will be once she's over the jet lag.'

Alan appeared at the front door, beckoning to Heather to come outside.

I'm ... on ... the ... phone, she mouthed, pointing to the handset. He would know it was Sarah, since only family and scammers knew the number for the landline and the age-yellowed curly cord telephone the girls considered so old-fashioned to be 'retro' and forbade their parents to ever upgrade.

'Is that Dad?' Sarah asked.

'Yesss,' Heather hissed.

'Uh-oh, is there trouble at The Elms?'

'Don't say anything to Ravi, but he's driving me mad. He's approaching retirement as if it's the start of a zombie apocalypse. He wants us to become self-sufficient, of all things. Grow all our own food. I wouldn't mind except he's spent more time working on the greenhouse and henhouse than the house we live in, which is crumbling around us.'

On the other end of the line, Sarah laughed. 'You two are so funny.'

'Not so funny from where I'm standing.'

Sarah's tone changed. 'Mum, have you thought this sudden obsession might have anything to do with what happened to Uncle Ambrose? Dad told me once that he and Ambrose used to help Grandad in his garden, that they each had their own plot they were responsible for. He said it was the only time he felt they had their father's full attention because he was always so busy working.'

'I don't know. He won't talk about Ambrose, or the accident. I know your grandfather used to give away fresh vegetables to his patients during post-war rationing. People used to come and help themselves if they needed anything.'

'Like a foodbank?'

'Yes. I gather he believed that good nutrition was the key to health. When I first joined the practice, I remember there was a framed quote by Hippocrates hanging on the wall in the waiting room. *Let food be thy medicine.*'

'Do you think that by resurrecting the garden, he might be trying to resurrect the past?'

It made sense. Sarah had always been astute. So good at reading between other people's lines. The problem was that she absorbed their feelings too. Now Heather regretted unburdening on Sarah. Especially when she was trying to get pregnant. The stress response wasn't good for fertility. In fact, Heather was so keen not to stress Sarah that she deliberately avoided asking about her last embryo transfer. As always, Alan had marked it on the calendar. Five calendars' worth now.

They both wanted grandchildren, of course they did, but for Alan the need to be a grandparent was like a thirst he couldn't quench. Though he tried to disguise his disappointment, he was becoming more morose with each failed cycle. Heather had begged him to stop asking, and it was a relief when Sarah, brave Sarah, had stopped telling.

Alan marched in and out of the front door, waving and gesturing like an impatient bouncer for her to come outside.

'I've got to go,' said Heather irritably. 'Your father wants to show me something. Why don't you and Ravi come for Sunday lunch? It will be a good opportunity for you and Tilly to catch up.'

'Great,' said Sarah. 'I can't wait to hear all about her gap year.'

'Her what?'

Before she could process what she'd been told, Alan walked in and, grinning, took the receiver from Heather's hand.

'Sarah, it's Dad. Mum will phone you back, okay, love?'

He covered Heather's eyes with his hands and marched her outside.

'Where are we going?'

'Wait until you see what I found,' Alan said.

It took a moment for her vision to adjust.

'What do you think?' Alan beamed a lighthouse smile and indicated his 'find' with triumphantly outstretched arms.

'I'm speechless.'

It was the truth. Heather could not think of a single thing to say as she took in the boxy, green Land Rover in front of her. It had four thick wheels and a canvas roof. It looked as if it had driven around the world several times.

'I knew you'd love her.'

'Who does it belong to?'

'Me. Us.'

'Hang on,' said Heather, head whipping round. 'Where's your Honda?'

'I part-exchanged it.'

Part-exchanged? Unless she was mistaken, this meant this ancient relic had cost more than Alan's old car. 'For this?'

'I was lucky to find one in such good condition. She's a beauty, isn't she?'

She. The old rust bucket already had a gender. Next it would have a name and an identity.

Then it dawned on her. 'Isn't this like the one your dad used to drive?'

'The very same model. Same year even.'

She softened at his boyish grin. Heather had never met Gordon, but she'd seen the photos and heard the stories. Back then, many of the roads in the area were unsealed and the only way to reach the patients on some of the more remote or inaccessible properties was by four-wheel drive. *Sentimental old fool.*

'Aren't you meant to be dyeing your hair and chasing younger women in a yellow sports car?'

'It's a bit late for a mid-life crisis, unless I make it to a hundred and thirty-six. With my genes, I'm lucky to have made it this far.'

She understood then, was almost relieved, that he planned to have a little fun. 'Go on, you enjoy her.'

'I knew you'd understand. You're going to love driving her.'

'Me? Oh no, this is *your* baby, Alan. I can assure you I will be just fine in my watertight, air-conditioned Golf, thank you very much.' Alan's face dropped. She looked around. 'Speaking of which, where is my car?'

'As I said,' Alan continued, 'I was lucky to find this model in this condition. They're appreciating in value all the time. She's a collector's item. Think of her as an investment.'

'What have you done with my Volkswagen, Alan?' Heather was fond of the nervous little car that always seemed to take her safety so seriously and could park itself.

'Think of how much we'll reduce our carbon footprint by becoming a one-car household.'

'Explain how replacing two low-emission, energy-efficient modern vehicles with a single gas-guzzling, fume-spewing miniature tractor is going to save the glaciers.'

Heather stormed back inside the house, pausing on the front step to shout, 'You should have asked me before you sold my car, Alan!'

He looked confused. 'I wanted to surprise you. You were the one who was fed up with boring and predictable. The one going on about fun and spontaneity.'

Her response was an incoherent mishmash of hard consonants.

'Where's your sense of adventure, Heather?' Alan called after her.

Tears of fury pricked her eyes. Where was *her* sense of adventure? He was the one who'd turned his nose up at all her suggestions for adventure. He was the one who wanted to stay at home and grow potatoes rather than explore Greece with her. They were so far from being on the same page, she doubted they were even reading from the same book.

Heather shut herself away in the bedroom with *Treasures of the Greek Islands*. She thought about what Esme had said, about going away on her own. It was the obvious solution. Plenty of women travelled solo. The appeal was undeniable: the freedom of having no one to answer to but herself, to meet new and exciting people, to do exactly what she wanted, when she wanted, without compromising.

There were downsides too, apart from the obvious worry of personal safety. No one to share experiences with. Eating dinner alone. Embarking on a trip like this at her age was a big deal. The stakes were so much higher than if she'd done it at nineteen when she was young, free and single. She was married, even if it was obvious now that her marriage was in trouble. Jetting off to a foreign country without resolving things with Alan might signal the end. The message would be clear. She would be walking away from so much more than a rough patch. She would be walking away from Alan.

Through the bedroom window she watched her husband pat and stroke the Land Rover, lavishing it with the care and attention he might a new lover. A dark moth of suspicion flitted into her mind, landing long enough for her to examine it in all its ugliness. Was Alan having an affair? Was he double bluffing by refusing to lose weight and get fit, by wearing his oldest, tattiest clothes and buying the least sexy vehicle he could find? Had one of the fan club finally tempted him with more than a slice of fruitcake?

The moth flapped its wings and was gone. Alan having an affair? Heather's gestalt was in stitches.

~

Now they were down to a single vehicle, if Heather wanted to go anywhere, ever again, she was going to have to put her petulance aside, don her big girl pants, and drive the damn thing. She was overdue a visit to Mandy, her melancholic hairdresser, and the receptionist had managed to squeeze her in after a cancellation. There was another reason Heather needed to see Mandy. If she could pluck up the courage to ask her.

She found Alan in the kitchen, dissecting a baby beetroot. 'Fancy a sandwich?'

'No thanks,' Heather replied, trying to ignore the blooming purple stain on the benchtop. 'I'm heading into Darlingford for the afternoon.'

'Look at this, would you.' Alan held out the empty baby beetroot jar for her inspection. 'Ninety-nine p! It's extortion. Daylight robbery.'

'It's not that expensive in the grand scheme of things, Alan.' Compared to a new stone benchtop, for instance. She handed Alan a chopping board.

'But we can grow our own for nothing.'

She looked up to see Alan, still standing at the kitchen bench, take a bite of his sandwich. It disintegrated in his hands, sending beetroot slices tumbling down his clean shirt before landing on the tiles at his feet. The tiles he'd been promising to reseal for months. Heather bit her lip so hard she tasted blood.

'I need the keys. To the . . . car.'

He straightened up. 'Shall I show you how –'

'No need,' she replied. 'Just the keys, thank you.'

Heather soon discovered that the old girl did not like to be rushed. Her bronchitic engine hacked several times before spluttering to life. After a nine-point turn in the driveway to avoid the sacks of rotting horse manure that still hadn't trotted their way into Alan's vegetable garden, and with her arms aching from hauling the ancient steering wheel repeatedly clockwise then anticlockwise, Heather called a truce.

'Now listen to me,' she said. 'I will admit I wasn't as welcoming as I could have been, but since you and I are both ladies of a certain vintage, we need to pull together. Understood?'

The engine hiccupped but didn't stall and by the time they hit the bypass, they were doing a steady sixty, the engine sounding less like the purring of a cat and more like one trying to cough up a hairball at every gear change. Heather turned on the radio, tuning it to her favourite classic hits music station. Lolly, because for some reason the name suited the Land Rover perfectly, responded with an unexpected message of encouragement.

Wild thing!

'Very funny,' Heather said. She turned up the volume, letting her heart sing. Everything was groovy. The wind through the open window wound her hair into a knot. Heather tried to keep the wisps out of her eyes. *Damn hair.* It was way too long and her almost white roots were in desperate need of attention. Mandy was going to have her work cut out for her today.

Heather checked her reflection in the rear-view mirror. She was the very opposite of wild. Tame. Dowdy. Careful. Small-c conservative. *Sensible.*

The style she'd cultivated throughout her adult life could best be described as semi-rural professional, with a side helping of dog owner. She'd always favoured practicality with tailored separates for work, and forgiving dresses, or cotton trousers and tops at weekends. What had never been in fashion would never go out of fashion, she reasoned. Even her job had been sensible. There were few professions more respectable, sober and responsible than general practice. It was hardly the wild child of specialties. GPs were the labradors of the medical profession: friendly and loyal, capable of short bursts of excitement and activity, but mostly content to sit and wait for the crumbs under the table.

Heather had been thinking about Mary Oliver's poem since that day on the bench with Esme, namely, what *was* she going to do with her one wild and precious life? It was time to work on the wild part.

Mandy, who had been doing Heather's hair for donkey's years, wasn't known for edgy transformations. Heather fell squarely into the colour, trim, blow-dry category. Facing her reflection while Mandy tortured her scalp was the one time she really saw herself as others did. Today, Heather studied the woman in the mirror. Her face revealed her age but her dyed hair lied about it. It was becoming harder to ignore the incongruity of the two. Ironically, the more she tried to disguise the passing years, the older she looked. And at what cost? Forget the dent in her credit card, it was the wasted time she resented most. Two and a half hours, every five or so weeks. That was twenty-five hours a year, or two whole days a year sitting in this sweaty vinyl chair reading gossip magazines, drinking disgusting coffee and hearing about Mandy's latest romantic misfortune. Heather calculated that if she lived another twenty years, the time spent pretending to listen to Mandy would equate to three entire weeks of her one wild and precious life. Three weeks when she could be sitting at a whitewashed taverna under a brilliant pink bougainvillea, sipping retsina.

Bloody hair.

They'd been fighting one another for years. With widow's peak and cowlick to contend with, Mandy had always made Heather's hair sound like something out of a Thomas Hardy novel. Having spent a small fortune on chemicals to alter the colour, texture and style of the hair that always reverted to the genetic code that programmed her follicles, it was time to let nature take its course. Five minutes later, when Mandy had finished with her previous client, she stood behind Heather and, as she always did, frowned into the mirror at her white roots and tangled ends.

'The usual?'

'No,' said Heather. 'Cut it off.'

Heather's sensible side tried to warn her, demanding doubts and second thoughts instead. What would people think? What would Alan think?

'Stand down,' she told the sensible thing. 'The wild thing is taking over.'

Mandy clutched a couple of centimetres between her scissor fingers. 'How much do you want me to take off?'

'All of it.'

'Are you sure?'

'I've never been more certain of anything.'

14

Breaking bad

HEATHER'S CERTAINTY WANED THE MOMENT SHE DROVE away in Lolly. It had all been too easy. Mandy had been shocked and somewhat reluctant to crop Heather's hair so drastically but had barely batted an eye at her client's casual enquiry as to where she could buy cannabis. Thanks to a series of unsuitable mates, seemingly a new one at each six-weekly appointment, Mandy had collated a list of contacts so that, like a one-woman search engine, all Heather had to do was give her postcode, and just like that, she had not one, but half-a-dozen local dealers, each with Mandy's personal rating and review.

'Netherwood, you say?' Mandy had tapped her chin, made a call and written down a name and time on the back of an appointment card.

Dan. 5.30 pm. St Luke's church carpark.

Heather's feigned nonchalance did not extend to asking how she would recognise 'Dan', nor what it was she needed to ask for, the correct jargon for buying illegal drugs. Would there be options, different types and doses, or more of a one-size-fits-all arrangement? But that was the least of her worries because it was virtually impossible to arrive anywhere by stealth in a 1959 Land Rover, let alone to visit a drug dealer in the carpark of the very church where she was married, where Sarah and Tilly were both baptised, and where hers was one of the most recognised faces in the tightknit community. Why on earth hadn't she chosen one of the less salubrious suburbs in Darlingford, where no one would give her a second glance? Or since she still hadn't got around to cancelling her licence to practise, simply prescribed some medicinal cannabis instead? Neither of those was now an option.

At half past five exactly, Heather pulled into the empty carpark. Thankfully there was no one about. Hardly surprising since, sadly, Netherwood's pretty Norman church attracted more tourists than congregation these days.

She tried to remember which night was bell-ringing practice and which was when the flower-arrangers gathered. It was all there on the parish noticeboard, along with a request to report any suspicious behaviour in the church grounds to the police. She skulked behind a pair of dark sunglasses, convinced she could see people hiding behind each gravestone with binoculars and telephoto lenses trained on her. She could almost see the headlines: *Local doctor in drugs bust. Husband says wife acting out of character recently.* This was the most outlandish thing she'd ever done. And yet, as the blood surged around her body, the sheer danger of it was intoxicating.

At five thirty-seven, Heather heard a car. She watched the unassuming blue saloon park a few spots away from her. It certainly didn't look like the kind of car a drug dealer would drive. She held her breath, waiting. Perhaps she'd misread the sign and tonight was Bible study, or an extraordinary parish council meeting. But the driver, whom she couldn't see clearly, remained in the car. Eventually, the driver's window opened and a young man poked his head out.

'Are you Heather?' he called to her.

She wound down her window. 'Dan?'

The young man's face lit up with recognition. 'Dr Winterbottom! I almost didn't recognise you. I like the hair.'

Heather tilted her sunglasses and peered over them. *Dan Dixon.* She'd known him all his life. His parents and grandparents had been patients at the practice. He'd had a few problems in school, acted out as a young teen, had an early brush with the law, but had seemingly sorted himself out.

'Lovely evening, isn't it?' Heather remarked. How did she know this was the right Dan? If it was, how on earth did she begin the conversation?

'Heard it might rain later though,' Dan said, looking up at the rosy sky.

Exactly how much had Dan Dixon sorted his life out? Enough to attend Bible study or arrange flowers? Or was he toying with her?

'Mandy sent me,' said Heather, trying to keep her voice steady.

'Okay,' said Dan, nodding his head and smirking.

'It's for a friend,' Heather assured him.

'Always is.'

A blackbird landed on the fence nearby. Heather startled at the movement. Suddenly her lungs were full of helium, and she could barely form the words.

'She's not sleeping well,' she said.

'Hasn't your friend heard of sleep hygiene?' Dan asked. 'No screens before bed, avoid caffeine in the afternoons, get up if she hasn't fallen asleep after fifteen minutes?'

Heather remembered now. A few years ago, Dan's mother had found his stash and dragged him in to see Heather, begging her to talk to him. He'd claimed he was only smoking pot to help him sleep, and Heather had used the consultation to educate him about sleep hygiene.

'Look, Dan, can we cut to the chase here? I'm in a hurry.' In a hurry to get away before the police drug squad arrived, or worse, Reverend Samuels. He was getting on in years but continued to minister resolutely, despite a dwindling congregation and inconvenient bouts of diverticulitis that could strike without warning. He was a man of God, through and through, but his wife was a renowned gossip.

'Righto, Dr Winterbottom.'

'Could you please not call me that.'

'All right, *Mrs* Winterbottom. What are you in the market for?'

Pot, weed, grass, cannabis? What was she supposed to ask for? What was the generic term?

Heather squirmed, as if she was in her final pharmacology exam and her mind had gone blank. 'Marijuana.'

Dan cupped his ear. 'Sorry, what was that?'

'Marijuana,' she shouted through the open window.

Dan was having trouble keeping a straight face. 'What kind?'

There was more than one kind? This was worse than her pharmacology finals. 'What would you suggest? For a beginner.'

To her relief, he held up a tiny ziplock bag. 'This is top quality. Would you like to try some before you buy?'

'No thank you,' Heather answered primly.

'Okay. How much do you want?'

It was like being at the deli counter with a long queue behind her as she tried to picture how many slices of leg ham she'd get for two hundred grams. Or were illicit drugs sold in imperial measures, by the ounce? She had a vague feeling they were. She now wished she'd paid more attention to the TV shows Alan liked to watch.

'About that,' she said, pointing to the small bag. 'How much is it?'

'Seeing as you were my doctor, I'll give you a discount.' He told her the price and Heather rummaged through her purse.

'Do you take Visa?' she asked, realising she hadn't enough cash.

He roared with laughter. 'Give me what you've got. Let's call it a special introductory offer. Full price next time, mind.'

'I can assure you there won't be a next time, Dan. This is purely a one-off. It's my friend's birthday you see.'

It struck her now how much easier it would have been to buy Esme flowers or bake her a cake for her ninetieth birthday. Or pop into the department store to buy her one of the velvet turbans she favoured, or a silk headscarf.

'Has she smoked pot before?' Dan asked.

'No. She's a complete novice.'

'In that case I'd warn your friend to go easy at first.'

'Start at a low dose and gradually increase, titrating to clinical effect?' Heather asked, realising now that she might know more than she thought.

'Exactly. I take it your *friend* knows about the potential dangers of smoking cannabis? Lung disease, anxiety, paranoia, schizophrenia, addiction?'

She didn't want a lecture. Not like the kind of lecture she'd doled out to dozens of patients she'd counselled over the years.

'It's no big deal,' she said defensively. 'Cannabis is quite safe, you know.'

Dan raised his eyebrows, then cupped his ear. 'What was that you said?'

She'd stepped into that one. 'Never mind. Can we please hurry up?'

They exchanged the goods and the cash, Heather making up the shortfall with loose change from the bottom of her handbag. She only hoped that when it came to confidentiality towards their clients, drug dealers pledged something similar to the Hippocratic Oath, and word of her dalliance with Netherwood's dark underbelly would never get out. With a brief nod of acknowledgement, she turned the key in Lolly's ignition.

The engine stalled. Heather tried again. Nothing.

Dan was watching, one elbow leaning through his open window, a faint look of amusement on his young face.

Heather tried to start the engine again. *Shit.*

'Everything all right?' Dan asked.

'Perfectly.'

'I have a set of jump leads in the back of my car. I can get you started if you like.'

'Thank you, but that won't be necessary, Daniel.'

After half-a-dozen more attempts, Heather was faced with two options, three if she counted phoning Alan and confessing all. She could either phone the AA and wait who knew how long for Roadside Assist, or accept Dan's offer to help start the engine.

Just then, another car turned into the carpark, followed by another and another. Soon, she was surrounded by people getting out of their cars and congregating nearby on the path that led to the church door. The bell ringers. It was ten to six already. Someone caught her eye and waved.

'Come to join us, Dr Winterbottom?'

How else to explain what she was doing at the church at this time of day?

Dan took this as his cue and reversed out, rap music blaring from his disarmingly normal-looking car, before skidding away on the loose stones. Heather hid the plastic bag of pot in the very bottom of her handbag and climbed out.

'Yes, I thought I'd give it a go,' she called across to the assembled group. 'Assuming you're taking new members.'

~

It was dark when she finally arrived home. Between them, the bell ringers had managed to successfully push-start Lolly after the practice. They were a lively bunch, and though Heather was happy to spectate while they demonstrated the surprisingly complex art of campanology, they insisted she help herself to the sherry and biscuits they kept up in the bell tower. Who knew there was so much to it? It was early days and she still didn't know a Plain Bob from a Bob doubles, but this was the most fun she'd had in a long time. From now on she would definitely keep her mind open to new experiences. When Heather pulled up at her front door, ears still ringing, Alan was waiting for her. His reaction wasn't what Heather had expected. He didn't comment on her dramatic change in appearance, nor ask her where she'd been, given it was nearly eight o'clock by now.

'You'd better come inside, Heather,' he said, solemnly.

Heather ran her fingers through her spiky hair. So what if Alan hadn't noticed? She had decided she loved her new look. The bad-assness of it. The wildness of it. Even Dan the drug dealer had commented on it. She loved the weightlessness of her head. It felt as though Mandy, however reluctantly, had excised the last traces of the old Heather, and finally set her free. She could feel the power growing through her scalp.

In the kitchen, Alan pulled a chair out, pressed her gently down into it. He knelt beside her as he had when he'd proposed. She smiled, growing nervous when he didn't say anything. His once-luscious eyelashes were now obscured by eyebrows that resembled cartoon caterpillars. Or seaweed, yes, that was it. Who needed the Shipping Forecast when Alan's eyebrows could predict the weather?

'What's the matter? Do you really hate it?' For all her bravado, it did matter what her husband thought of her hair. She wanted him to like it, to tell her she looked gorgeous. *Hot.* Could he not, just once, call her hot?

He shook his head. 'I don't hate it,' said Alan, tears collecting in the gutters under his eyes.

'Then what is it? You're acting like somebody died.'

He squeezed her hand. She jerked it free and covered her mouth. *Oh god.*

'The manager at The Willows has been trying to get hold of you.'

Heather grabbed her phone, opened the flap cover. Six missed calls. While she'd caught up on secret babies and royal bust-ups, while she feigned interest in Mandy's sister's ex-husband's new girlfriend, while she'd been buying pot from a drug dealer and swigging sherry in the bell tower, she'd missed the chance to say goodbye to her dearest friend.

15

Mind the gap

IN THE DAYS THAT FOLLOWED ESME'S FUNERAL, HEATHER barely left the house. She spent hours at the kitchen window watching Alan's progress on his garden, including the morning when four NOGGINs had arrived to help him erect the rectangular raised beds and fill them with soil and, finally, the horse manure that had proved so irresistible to Stan.

Heather was genuinely pleased for Alan; happy that he'd discovered a passion, and with it a group of new friends. And, if she was honest, also a little jealous. Alan was doing what she'd been advocating all along. He was getting out there, developing a new skill, nurturing a new hobby, and at the same time expanding his social circle. He was growing into himself, and away from her.

'I thought I'd do a nice piece of grass-fed beef for lunch tomorrow,' Heather had said on the Saturday morning as she prepared her shopping list. 'I could buy the meat at that new farm shop in Darlingford.'

'Kevin doesn't eat red meat.'

'Kevin's not coming.'

'Couldn't we invite him?'

'It's a family lunch, Alan.'

'But he's like family to me.'

They'd argued back and forth for several minutes until, keen not to waste any more of her dwindling lifespan, Heather agreed that Alan could invite his friend to join them. If grief came in waves, as people said it did, then this was the seventh wave in the set, the largest and most powerful since Esme had died, as she thought how nice it would have been to invite a special friend to lunch too. Why hadn't she thought to do it while Esme was alive?

'All right, roast chicken it is. Which one of your exes are we going to sacrifice?'

Alan had raised his leave-it-to-me finger.

Three hours before Sarah and Ravi were due to arrive, Heather took the chicken out of the fridge. The plucked bird looked more like roadkill than something Alan claimed was organic and free range. Ignoring the feel of the cold, pimpled flesh, she thrust her hand inside the bird's cavity and manually evacuated the giblets, dropping them into Stan's bowl. The redundant organs hit the metal with a plop.

Out of the corner of her eye, Heather watched Alan drop two slices of stale bread into the toaster. She was sure she'd already thrown out the stiff remains of the week-old supermarket loaf.

'Why aren't you using the fresh bread?'

'No point wasting perfectly good food.'

'It's budget bread, Alan. About twenty p's worth. By the time you've used it up, the nice fresh sourdough I bought will be stale too.'

Sarah and Ravi were on time as usual, the crunch of Audi tyres coinciding with the twelfth chime of the grandfather clock in the hall. Heather answered the door to her son-in-law who was wearing box-white trainers that matched his expensive teeth. He beeped his electronic key fob not once but three times to be sure.

'This is Netherwood, not Cricklewood, Ravi,' said Heather.

'Can't be too careful out here in the sticks,' he said, kissing her on both cheeks before presenting a dozen tightly clenched pink roses. His gaze diverted briefly from her face to her hair and back again, as if he'd been warned not to say anything. He told her she looked well, as he always did. This time he said it with such sincerity, it was as though he was surprised to find her retired *and* still alive.

Sarah was next in the meet-and-greet line-up. Heather examined her for any tell-tale signs. Sarah's last embryo transfer had only been eighteen days ago; it was too early for news. Heather couldn't bring herself to ask yet. She wouldn't get her hopes up again.

Ravi, who worked for a high-end London wine importer, had brought along Alan's favourite red, and Heather noted with interest, a bottle of Champagne. Were they celebrating something? He cradled the bottles like twin babies. The labels meant nothing to Heather but knowing professional wine-ponce Ravi, he would hold court over lunch about the sparkling wine's provenance.

Alan dreamed of being a wine-ponce like his son-in-law, who'd installed a top-of-the-range wine fridge in his kitchen that for the price should have come with its own sommelier. There was only room for one wine-ponce in the family though, which was why whenever Heather saw Alan and Ravi talking wine together, she had an image of two male sea lions barking at each other and banging chests to establish seniority.

Alan appeared halfway down the stairs. 'I thought I heard voices.'

He was wearing his new *You're Never Too Old To Play In The Dirt* t-shirt, a pair of shorts that last fit him in the 1980s, grey socks and his newly resuscitated deck shoes. He looked ridiculous, but she would not say anything. She would not.

Ravi pumped his father-in-law's hand. 'You're looking well, Alan.'

'Loving the new look, Dad,' said Sarah, tugging at the t-shirt.

So far, no one had mentioned Heather's hair.

'Where's Attila?' Sarah asked.

'She's taken the dog for a walk.' Heather frowned at the grandfather clock. 'She should be back by now.'

Perhaps Tilly had run into someone she knew in the village. Or decided to stop off at the pick-your-own berry farm. Or hopped onto a bus and headed into Darlingford, or London, to visit a museum. She would completely forget it was a Sunday, that the sister and brother-in-law she hadn't seen for two years were coming for lunch, and that she had a large dog with her. How much easier it had been for Heather not to worry about her when she was on the other side of the world.

By the time Tilly returned with a heavily panting Stan, Alan and Ravi were at loggerheads over the Médoc. Alan was in favour of decanting while Ravi insisted he would ruin the aromatics. Sarah abandoned the convoluted story Heather had lost track of about a company restructure at work and threw her arms around Tilly.

'Come here, you weirdo,' she said as Tilly tried to struggle free of the embrace.

With five adults in the kitchen, the path to whatever pot, pan or utensil Heather needed now involved a sidestep or a duck. Cooking Sunday lunch had turned into a game of Twister. She tried shooing them away, but they soon returned, like pigeons to a park bench. At the very worst moment for an audience, with saucepans boiling over, the oven timer pinging, and Stan an ever-present trip hazard, Kevin arrived.

'I brought you some apples,' he said handing over a cardboard box of misshapen, bruised and frankly unappetising apples. 'I thought you could whip up a pie.'

She wasn't a 'whip up' kind of cook, but she thanked him anyway. 'How thoughtful of you, Kevin.'

'I scrumped them myself,' he said proudly. 'No point letting perfectly good food go to waste, or paying through the nose when you can pick your own for free.'

Tilly appeared beside them. 'I couldn't agree more. Mum wastes far too much food. Don't you, Mum?'

They continued to hover over her, scrutinising her every move. As she'd feared, when she took the roasting tray out of the oven, the chicken had shrunk to the size of a quail.

'Is that free range?' Tilly frowned.

Heather sighed. 'Ask your father, he's the one who scooped it up off the side of the road.'

'It was about as free range as they come,' Kevin interjected. 'I liberated it myself.'

'You stole it?' Tilly's eyes widened.

'Let's just say I encouraged her and a few of her friends to roam outside the confines of their unnatural enclosure.'

'Battery farming is abhorrent,' said Tilly. The pair moved off together, discussing animal welfare and how food production in a capitalist society contributed to destruction of the environment, exploitation of the workforce and animal cruelty. So far nobody had offered to help Heather with lunch.

Alan and Ravi's conversation had moved on to crypto-currency. Heather helped herself to a drop of Ravi's red, the bottle having been conveniently left to breathe before lunch. With all the wine glasses now on the table, Heather poured the wine into her retirement mug. *Living the Dream*, indeed.

It wasn't a bad drop. Heather refreshed her mug and added a good slug to the gravy she was stirring. For once she was glad Stan was on hand to lap up the spillage from the tiles as she sloshed the gravy into the china gravy boat.

After a round of musical chairs, everyone was seated at the kitchen table.

'It looks delicious, Alan,' said Ravi as Alan carved the chicken. Heather recalled the care and precision with which he'd dissected Fred's brachial plexus in first year anatomy. Such steady hands. Such beautiful, soft, clean hands. Now they were polka-dotted with age, the nails thickened and rimmed with dirt from the garden.

Alan arranged the sliced breast and thigh meat on a vast white serving platter that merely emphasised the paltriness of the poultry.

Heather reached for the wine.

'It's still breathing,' said Ravi, swooping protectively on the bottle.

Still breathing. Heather thought about Esme, and how she'd been alone when she took her last breath, slumped over on her bench as if asleep, her knitting still in her hands when a gardener found her. This time, as the wave rolled in towards her, Heather was buoyed from its undertow by two mugs of wine. She had reached that lovely stage of early intoxication when the mind is light and easy, the body warm and supple. It made her question why she didn't drink more often. There was no work tomorrow. No Esme to visit. If she had a hangover, she could stay in bed all day. Ta-da! She'd accidentally uncovered the secret to a happy retirement, and a brand-new drinking game. Why hadn't she thought of it before? Every time anyone mentioned the 'R' word, she would have a drink. A bloody big one.

'I think that red has taken quite enough breaths, don't you, Ravi? It must be hyperventilating by now.'

She stood up from the table to fetch the bottle. It weighed less than she remembered and while conversation continued at the table, she held the bottle up to the light. Half full. That mug must have been bigger than she realised.

Sarah asked, 'So, how are you both adapting to retirement?'

Retirement! Heather helped herself to another mug of red and gulped.

'Your father is re-enacting *The Good Life*.' Her words sounded slurred, even to herself. *Must try harder to speak normally.*

'The what?' Sarah asked.

'It's a sheventies shitcom about a couple, Tom and Barbara Good, who drop out of the rat race to become shelf-shufficient by turning their home in Shurbiton into a schmallholding. Your father ish rather taken with Felicity Kendal's bottom.'

Much better.

A beat of silence at the table.

Ravi cleared his throat. 'That's interesting. My company are looking into sustainability. I'd love to hear more about your plans, Alan.'

While Sarah helped Heather to clear away the plates, Alan spread his drawings for the garden over the kitchen table. Ravi couldn't have been more interested if Baron Rothschild had been showing him a map of a secret underground cellar.

'Anyone for apple pie?' Heather held the hot pie dish over the table between two tartan oven gloves. Kevin's eyes widened, but Heather wasn't about to confess that this was a pie Sainsbury's had already prepared.

'Talking of apples,' said Tilly, 'how about planting an orchard over here?' She pointed to a redundant patch of lawn.

'I was saving that part of the garden.'

'What for?'

'For . . . never mind.'

A child's swing and climbing frame, Heather guessed from the pain in his expression. He forced a smile and wrote ORCHARD in pencil instead.

The pie dish was growing heavy in Heather's hands. 'Excuse me,' she said to the backs of five heads. When no one responded she placed the steaming dish in the middle of the orchard, followed by a jug of custard directly on top of the area marked GOAT PEN.

Alan took the hint and rolled up the drawings while Sarah fetched dishes and spoons.

'What about a vineyard too? We could grow our own *Champagne*,' Heather asked, remembering the untouched bottle she'd spied in the fridge.

'You know, Heather, that's not such a bad idea,' said Ravi, the hint missing the stumps by a mile.

'What, plant a few vines?' Alan was all ears.

Ravi continued, 'Why not? It's south-facing and far enough from the coast to benefit from a chalky soil. I reckon we have the perfect terroir to grow a cool-climate grape. The Champagne houses are already jumping on the English sparkling wine boom.'

'Talking of Champagne,' she said, 'shall I open the bottle in the fridge?'

Ravi jumped up as if he'd been electrocuted. He clearly wasn't about to entrust the opening of his Chateau Fancy-pants to an amateur.

'It's hand-harvested, Alan,' Ravi said as he removed the cage and foil from the neck of the bottle. He popped the cork and poured it into perfectly tilted flutes with a practised hand.

'This is a 2013 *Lelarge-Pugeot les Meuniers de Clémence*, unless I'm very much mistaken,' said Alan, remarking on the tightness of the bubbles rising in his glass. Heather had seen him read the label as Ravi poured and raised her eyebrows to let him know he'd been sprung.

'Yes, well done Alan. I believe it's currently in the hands of the seventh generation of Lelarges,' Ravi said.

Tilly rolled her eyes at Kevin who stifled a snigger.

'What are we celebrating?' Heather asked, noticing that Ravi had handed everyone a glass except Sarah. Under the table she crossed her fingers. Were she and Alan going to learn that they were about to become grandparents after all?

Ravi handed her the first glass. 'To start with, I am delighted to welcome home my favourite sister-in-law on her gap year.'

'Only sister-in-law,' Tilly corrected.

Sarah punched her in the arm. 'Yeah, welcome home, Attila.'

'Isn't the idea of a gap year that you leave home and travel overseas, not the other way round?' That's what Heather was thinking to herself, but, judging by their looks, she'd said it out loud.

'A gap year can be anything you want it to be,' Tilly said defensively. 'I need a break from academia. I want to decide if it's what I still want to be doing in twenty years' time.'

'I thought it was meant to be a rite of passage into the adult world, not wriggling out of it.'

To Heather's surprise, Alan leapt to Tilly's defence. 'It's better than rushing into a decision she might later regret. She's moving into a whole new phase of her life. Far too many people live their lives based on arbitrary decisions they hardly give a moment's thought to.'

Like saying yes to a marriage proposal?

Ravi cleared his throat, looked to Sarah for guidance.

'Sorry, Ravi,' said Heather. 'Cheers to Tilly's gap year. May she find what she is looking for.' *Having travelled to the far side of the world and back looking for it.*

'Thank you, Heather. Now, as I was saying, secondly, I'd like to congratulate you and Alan on your retirement.'

The R word! Everyone took a sip. Heather drained her glass.

Heather waited for a thirdly. Ravi sat down again. There wasn't a thirdly. No baby announcement. If Alan had deduced the same and shared her disappointment, he wasn't showing it.

'It's good to see you so busy and engaged, Alan,' said Ravi. 'I think it's great you're resurrecting your father's garden.'

'I agree,' Tilly said. 'I'm so proud of you, Dad.' She leaned over and patted his arm. 'It's so important to leave a legacy, something people will remember you by.'

'If his marrows live up to their potential,' said Kevin, 'you could be seeing his name in the paper.'

Alan blushed.

'Have you taken up any new hobbies, Mum?' Sarah asked. 'Joined any groups?'

Esme had tried to teach her to knit, but the co-ordination required to loop wool round two long needles in a specified sequence had eluded her. And to think she used to be able to tie surgical knots one-handed. What about bell-ringing? Should she tell them she'd taken up campanology? But that would require too much explanation.

'My mother is busier than ever since she retired,' said Ravi to fill the awkwardness when Heather didn't reply. 'She does conversational French on a Monday, genealogy on Tuesdays, and choir on Thursdays.'

Of course she did. Bloody Ravi's mother. She was well read, well travelled and an excellent cook. And a retired high court judge. She'd raised three perfect boys in a pristine home, and already had four perfect grandchildren. 'I do everything myself,' she'd once said in a not-so-subtle dig at Heather's reliance on Mrs Gee.

'She claims U3A saved her life after my father retired,' Ravi said.

'Oh, really, are they doing resuscitation courses now?'

Heather excused herself from the table, leaving the others tucking into their hot pudding and planning her future for her. She heard them, talking about her in hushed voices.

She should join the Women's Institute. She should take up bridge, learn the piano. She should. She should. She should.

Heather swiped her handbag from the worktop and headed out into the garden. Dragging a slimy patio chair out of sight, she took out the little plastic bag of weed she'd bought Esme, the Rizla papers she'd driven fifteen miles out of her way to buy at an anonymous petrol station and rolled her first ever joint.

When she'd finished, the ends looked more like untrimmed pubic hair sticking out from knicker elastic, but when she lit the end with the kitchen gas lighter, and sucked, she saw a tiny flicker of fire before the hot smoke scorched her trachea.

'Happy birthday, my friend.' She coughed and took another draw. She hoped that, somewhere, Esme could see her sneaking out to tick off the first item on her bucket list, the list Heather had come to think of as her own.

'Mum? Where are you?' Sarah shouted from the kitchen.

Heather tried to stifle a coughing fit and at the same time waft away the tell-tale smoke.

'I'll be there in a sec,' she called. Heather stubbed out the smouldering joint and hid the nub in the weeds growing in a cracked plant pot on the patio. She straightened her clothes, used her fingers to spike up her hair and strolled back inside as nonchalantly as she could. Everyone was staring at her. Heather had been warned about paranoia after inhaling marijuana, but here it was, people were talking about her already.

'So, Mum,' said Tilly, scraping her spoon around her empty dish. 'We're still waiting to hear. What *are* you going to do?'

Heather thought of the box that had been delivered the day before yesterday, accompanied by a letter from Esme's solicitor. A niece in Ireland had inherited her estate. However, a handwritten and signed amendment to Esme's will had been found in her flat, which the niece had not disputed. Esme had specified certain items should be given to her dear friend Dr Heather Winterbottom, and that she would know what to do with them.

Inside the box, wrapped in tissue paper, Heather had found the completed baby blanket. She'd brought the soft wool to her cheek and wept over Esme's eternal optimism. The second item was Esme's beloved copy of *The Odyssey*, her bookmark tucked neatly inside the last page. She'd finished it. And now it was Heather's turn to read it. To relive that adventure.

'I have decided to take a gap year,' she told her family now.

'You are?' Alan's seaweed eyebrows forecast stormy weather ahead.

'I haven't finalised my itinerary yet, but I'm starting in Greece.'

'That's brave,' said Sarah.

No, Heather wanted to say, brave would be staying here for the rest of my life.

Alan's eyebrows didn't know what to do. 'Greece? On your own?'

The third item in the box from Esme's solicitor had taken Heather completely by surprise, one from which she was still reeling. In addition to the baby blanket that might never get used, and a thirty-year-old paperback book, she was now the custodian of an eco-friendly, one hundred per cent biodegradable cardboard urn containing Esme's ashes.

'No, as a matter of fact I won't be travelling alone,' said Heather, looking around the faces at the table, each creased with individual expressions of concern, 'I'm taking a friend.'

16

Chicken or beef?

THREE AND A HALF HOURS WAS A LONG TIME TO BE WEDGED between a bull-necked businessman and a tattooed hipster with a bushy beard. The middle seat had been the only one available at such short notice. Even Esme, safely stored in the overhead locker, had more room. But Heather had prepared herself for the inevitable discomforts of budget travel – she'd have hitched a ride on a donkey to get to Greece if she had to.

She remembered the stories her friends told her of their gap years, of sleeping in stations, under seats and on top of luggage racks; tales of lost passports and stolen traveller's cheques; of being harassed by ticket collectors and chased by amorous locals. It was all part and parcel of the gap year experience. But with her brand-new wheelie suitcase, and hiking boots so advanced they could walk themselves to base camp, Heather Winterbottom, née Wilson, was ready for anything.

The businessman in the aisle seat had fallen asleep not long after take-off, he and his rumbling snores blocking Heather's only access to the toilet. On the other side, the hirsute hipster's over-sized headphones obscured any glimpse of the twinkling Ionian Sea she might have hoped for. Until she'd experienced the unrelenting *tshh-tshh-tshh* sound emitted from the headphones, Heather had never truly appreciated the misery of tinnitus.

She tried an in-flight movie in the hope that Chris Hemsworth would distract her from the fact that her man-spreading neighbours had between them claimed both armrests.

When the first whiffs of lunch escaped from the galley, Heather kicked off her new boots and pulled down her tray table, ready. After such an early start, she was starving and, determined to put Alan's penny pinching behind her, prepared to pay the exorbitant price the airline charged for refreshments. Indeed, after a bloody Mary she was feeling much better. She tried not to think about home, about what Alan would be doing. Tilly. Stan. It was way too early to be missing them. The real question was, would they be missing her?

None of her family had hidden their disapproval over her plan to travel solo. She'd heard them talking while they cleared away after the Sunday lunch, insisting that she go into the living room and put her feet up. It would have been nice to think it was their way of showing appreciation for her work preparing a lovely meal. She suspected it was their way of getting her conveniently out of earshot.

She'd heard snippets. Alan was blindsided. Tilly thought her completely irresponsible. Sarah was more compassionate but worried she was acting out of character. Tilly asked if brain tumours caused changes in personality. Alan said they did, especially when they involved the frontal lobe. Only Ravi was vaguely sympathetic, saying his mother had lost her way after going through 'the change'. The only thing they all agreed on was that Heather needed to 'get it out of her system'. Whatever *it* was.

She leafed through the duty-free catalogue and waited for the trolley to make its way down the narrow aisle to her row. She had barely made it past the mini-perfume collections when the captain made an announcement. If there was a doctor on the plane, could they please make themselves known to the cabin crew. She froze. For a moment, she was torn between duty and the Mediterranean chicken panini that was only two rows away. She sighed and pressed the call button.

A female cabin steward appeared, not bothering to hide her irritation at the interruption. 'Yes?'

'I'm letting you know that I'm a doctor.'

'You're a *doctor*?'

'Yes, well, still technically.'

'*You're* a doctor?' This time the emphasis stung. She had qualified at a time when patients expected their doctors to look and sound a certain way, so for over half her career, she'd been considered too young and too female to be taken seriously. Except by Alan, who'd hired her specifically because she was young and female, to make his life easier. Now, with her close-cropped silver hair, did she look too old to be a doctor?

The captain repeated the announcement with a new and unmistakable urgency in his voice. The cabin steward's pencilled eyebrows sketched a frown. 'Follow me, please.'

It was easier said than done. When neither Heather nor the steward could wake the businessman, Heather was forced to clamber over him whereupon her foot became entangled in her seatbelt, and she stumbled into the aisle like a drunk evicted from a bar. She brushed herself off and tried to look as professional as possible. As she followed the steward, second thoughts turned her legs to water. What was she thinking? She'd once delivered a baby in the frozen food aisle at Tesco, and conducted a commendable mental health assessment through a letterbox, but it had been years since she'd treated a genuine medical emergency singlehanded, let alone performed a Good Samaritan act at thirty thousand feet.

Relax, she told herself, someone will have splashed hand soap in their eye, or stubbed their toe on the drinks trolley. If she timed it right, a team of emergency physicians, all travelling on the same flight to a conference, were bound to beat her to it.

At the back of the plane a small crowd had gathered in the aisle. As Heather arrived, they parted like a shoal of startled fish to reveal a pair of feet emerging across the threshold of the toilet cubicle. But instead of the proverbial traveller left robbed and beaten on the road to Jericho, she found a young man, a typical backpacker, slumped altogether less biblically over the pan of the economy class toilet. His bloated face – what she could see of it above the white porcelain bowl – was the colour of a baby beetroot, and his gastrointestinal system was attempting to expel his in-flight meal simultaneously from both ends.

'He had the beef,' the steward added.

'The beef is trying to kill him,' Heather muttered.

'What? Am I going to die?' wheezed the backpacker, terror briefly prising his oedematous eyelids apart.

'Of course not.' Not if Heather could pull herself together and focus.

Anaphylaxis.

A single stowaway sesame seed or peanut butter fingerprint on a door handle was unlikely to cause such a severe reaction, but after forty years of experience, Heather was confident in her diagnosis. Time to go back to basics. *ABC.* Airway, breathing, circulation. Yes, all three were present. A good start. It was easy when you knew how. Like riding a bicycle. Then she remembered Tilly trying to ride her tricycle down the steep staircase at The Elms. It had taken a couple of days, but eventually Heather had noticed her crooked arm.

Heather ignored the anxious glances from the cabin crew as they manoeuvred their trolleys around the makeshift resuscitation area. The young man's body continued to swell, and his fingernails tore at angry welts, leaving trails of blood down his forearms. Heather tried taking his pulse, but all she could feel was the *thud-thud-thud* of her own heart.

The plane's medical kit was reassuringly well-equipped, however. With valuable seconds ticking away, she took a deep breath and identified the adrenaline vial. She broke off the lid and started to draw up the clear liquid into a syringe.

How many millilitres was 0.3 milligrams?

Nerves reminded her of the very worst case scenario if she got this simple calculation wrong. A decimal point could mean the difference between saving a life and a single unclaimed backpack circling the baggage carousel.

Primum non nocere. First, do no harm.

A doctor had once saved a passenger's life on a flight using a coat hanger and a ballpoint pen. She was struggling with the simplest of mental arithmetic. Where was Alan? He was the numbers man. He thought in columns while she thought in rows. That's why they made such a good team; the whole so much greater than the sum of its parts. But Heather was on her own. It was up to her to decide. Wasn't that what she'd wanted?

The part of her brain that didn't overthink everything told her she needed 0.3 millilitres.

She plunged the needle into the backpacker's thigh. Almost immediately, his wheezing subsided, and the rash began to fade. A smile crept into the corners of the young man's swollen lips.

'Thank you, doctor,' he said.

Heather slumped back against the cubicle door. There was a ripple of muted applause from the other passengers, relieved to find another toilet free at last. After thirty minutes, the backpacker was feeling well enough to return to his seat. Heather returned to hers. She would never see him again. When he made it home with a head full of adventures and a pile of dirty laundry, the episode on the plane would be nothing more than an amusing travel anecdote.

She thought about all the lives she'd touched in her career, however briefly. Their stories were part of her own. No one could take away what she was and what she'd done. Once a doctor, always a doctor, Esme had said. But it was time to find another way to define herself, to find out who else she could be.

When Heather reached her seat between the bearded hipster and snoring businessman, she nudged their elbows off her armrests and defiantly spread her knees. It was time to reclaim her personal space, and the part of her she'd sacrificed to be a good daughter, wife, mother and doctor. For the next twelve months she was going to put herself first. If that made her selfish, then so be it. She'd waited long enough.

When the hipster removed his headphones, Heather glimpsed the cobalt blue of the water far below dotted with tiny islands that looked as if they'd been scattered haphazardly into the sea by the gods themselves. She opened Esme's paperback and read the first lines of *The Odyssey*.

Sing to me of the man, Muse, the man of twists and turns
Driven time and again off course, once he had plundered
The hallowed heights of Troy.

At that moment she couldn't think of anything she wanted more than to be driven off course. For way too long, men were the ones who'd had the adventures while the women stayed at home. It was time for Heather and Esme to twist and turn, to do a little plundering of their own.

17

A room with a view

In the hypnagogic moments between her dream and wakefulness, Heather reached for Alan. The sheets where her husband should have been lying were cool and empty. When she opened her eyes, the light was disconcertingly bright, the air warm and unfamiliar. She stared up at the wobbly ceiling fan above her head, ticking with each unbalanced revolution. Behind her ribs, her heart pumped pure excitement to every cell in her body. She'd fallen asleep into one dream and woken in another.

She raised her head from the pillow, taking in her surroundings. White walls made the tiny room seem cavernous, sheer muslin drapes shrouded the floor-to-ceiling French doors. Her new suitcase rested on the low wooden trestle. Her pristine pink and blue hiking boots were a glaring contrast to the soothing neutrality of the decor. She'd been too tired to unpack last night. Hungover from spent adrenaline, she'd taken out only her pyjamas, her wash bag and Esme's book.

Even after the plane landed, her body had stayed on high alert. She'd spotted the young man whose life she'd saved waiting at the carousel for his backpack. He only had eyes for his phone screen and didn't spot her. It was a relief to see him looking perfectly well, bearing no outward scars of the medical emergency that had nearly ended his life. It was always hard to let go, but she had to remember that he wasn't her patient. She wasn't responsible for what happened to him now. Or anyone else. From now on, the only person she was responsible for was herself. And Esme.

She'd waited ages for a taxi which promptly became stranded on the side of the road with a puncture. It would have been quicker to walk the eight kilometres from the airport into Cephalonia's main town. She'd sent a brief text to Alan to let him know she'd arrived safely when she checked into the hotel, and he'd responded with a thumbs up emoji. Time apart might be good for them. Just what the doctor ordered. Or would it be a case of out of sight, out of mind?

The room's tiled floor was cool under Heather's feet. She parted the gauzy curtains and opened the doors onto the narrow balcony. As advertised, the room was clean, comfortable and spacious, and, most importantly, it had a sea view. What she hadn't realised when she'd booked it was that there was a busy road between her and the Ionian Sea. The mosquito-buzz of a moped set her teeth on edge. It was followed by another, and another. It wasn't quite what she'd hoped for, but it was only for a few days. After she'd explored this island, she would board the ferry and hop between the other islands. Having been tied to an appointment schedule for most of her life, Heather was already dizzy with the idea of having time to herself. If she chose to disappear, she could adopt the human equivalent of aeroplane mode.

The Poseidon was a Goldilocks of a hotel – not too expensive, not too cheap – and conveniently located for the airport, the town, ferries and a couple of nice beaches. For once she hadn't overthought every detail of the trip, unlike her meticulous planning for their New Zealand holiday. Weeks of research and forensic examination of every Tripadvisor review had resulted in an itinerary that would have made the D-Day landings look impulsive. With Tilly now back in Netherwood, there seemed no point in her and Alan flying all that way, risking deep vein thrombosis simply to argue whose turn it was to empty the chemical toilet in the four-berth portacabin on wheels, so Heather had cancelled and used the money to fund her Greek escape instead. To be fair, Alan must have had a rare moment of insight because he refrained from pointing out how many jars of baby beetroot they could buy with the refund.

'How about a nice cup of tea on the balcony?'

Heather removed Esme from her hand luggage where she'd spent the night. She carried the recycled cardboard urn decorated with a lovely Tree of Life design out to the little table on the balcony and placed Esme so she had a view of the Ionian Sea before making herself a cup of tea using the miniature kettle and complimentary carton of UHT milk.

At first, Heather luxuriated in the sun's restorative rays. And to think she could do this every day. Soon, however, sweat began to bead her forehead. She moved a fraction into the shade. How lucky that Sarah had volunteered to take her shopping before she left. Her new travelling wardrobe of crease-resistant lightweight fabrics would be perfect for this climate. After the disappointment of Darlingford's time-warp department store, they'd found everything she needed in a camping and hiking shop. It was a lovely gesture on Sarah's part, given that no one in the family completely approved of her plans. Perhaps there was part of the eminently sensible Sarah that wished she'd done the same before settling down with Ravi. She'd even commented on her mother's close-cropped hair too, declaring it to be 'sassy'. Heather liked that word. From now on it would be her touchstone.

A refuse lorry stopped on the road beneath the balcony. Briefly nauseated by the stench from the industrial bins, Heather focused on the water shimmering between the spiky palm trees that lined the promenade. The palms reminded her of a row of carrot tops and therefore of Alan. It was going to be hard not to think about him without avoiding every vegetable in Greece.

After showering and dressing, Heather headed down to the hotel restaurant for breakfast. Several tables were set up in the open, under an awning, separated from the pavement by a low fence of planter boxes. The waiter showed her to a small table for two, and made far too much of clearing away the other place setting. He took her order for a pot of English Breakfast tea and told her to help herself at the buffet. She returned to the table a few minutes later with a bowl of fresh fruit and thick yoghurt, drizzled with delicious local honey. Another couple were now seated at the adjacent table.

Without hearing their accents, Heather could tell they were English. And apparently she was equally easy to read.

The man turned around and, before Heather had enjoyed her first mouthful of breakfast, said, 'You're English.' It sounded more of an accusation than a question. He was leaning so far back on his chair that he was nearly in Heather's lap. He was wearing an *I love Ibiza* t-shirt. His wife was wearing a sleeveless top and first-degree sunburn across her shoulders.

'Yes, that's right,' Heather replied, smiling politely.

'You can always tell,' he said in an Estuary accent.

'Oh, definitely.'

Heather started on her fruit and yoghurt and tried not to think about what Alan would be having for breakfast. Without her there, he could toast stale bread or fry kippers with impunity. Perhaps he was looking forward to her going away as much as she had been looking forward to getting away. She hoped he enjoyed his break from the gentle reminders he called nagging, and the helpful advice he deemed nit-picking.

The Englishman returned from the buffet with a heart attack on his plate. The mountain of eggs, bacon and other cholesterol-rich foods was so high that he would need crampons to scale it. His wife must have seen Heather's face because it was her turn to lean over and interrupt.

'It's important to get your money's worth,' she said. 'At least you know what you're eating in the hotel. If you go to a restaurant, half the time the menus are in Greek! And even when they're in English, the names are unpronounceable.'

'And you have to pay extra for chips,' said the husband.

'I mean, no one in their right mind would come to Greece for the food, would they?'

'People do,' said Heather feeling suddenly defensive. 'The Greeks have some of the best cuisine in Europe. Fresh seafood, tomatoes, olives. Greek olive oil is supposed to be the best in the world.'

'It plays havoc with my gall bladder,' said the woman, indicating the vague anatomical area of the bilious organ. While she went into more detail, Heather zoned out, seeing images on an ultrasound screen of bright white stones in a shiny bag shaped rather like the husband's shiny head.

'And when the waiter brought us a bowl of hummus, I thought he said it was hair mousse.' When Heather failed to show sufficient mirth, the woman repeated the punchline. 'Hair mousse instead of hummus. Get it?'

Heather ha-ha'd politely.

Thankfully Heather's tea arrived and the waiter cleared away her empty bowl. The man took this as an invitation to turn his chair to fully face her.

'Will your husband be joining you?' He was staring at her ring finger.

Heather fidgeted with her wedding ring. After she'd lost her baby weight it had become loose enough to slide easily over her knuckle. She'd deliberately kept it that way, so she could slip it off and pop it into her pocket when she was at work. Now that she wasn't washing her hands every ten minutes, she supposed she should have it tightened. Or take it off completely and keep it somewhere safe.

'No.' She didn't feel like explaining the whole situation to a stranger. Not when she couldn't explain it to herself.

'So, you're here on your own.' The woman shuffled her chair along to create space at their table. She introduced herself as Pat. 'Come and join us. We don't mind do we, Jeffrey?'

'Not at all. We don't want you to be all alone.'

He stood and was about to drag Heather's chair – with Heather still sitting in it – to the other table when Heather said, 'Actually, I'm here with a friend. She's upstairs in the room.'

Not a complete lie.

'Well, you're both welcome to join us here for dinner,' said the woman.

'That's very kind of you, but –'

'And breakfast tomorrow.'

Heather wiped her mouth on the napkin and stood up, leaving her tea. 'Thank you for the offer. Please excuse me, I'm off to explore.'

'No need,' said the man. His outstretched legs were blocking her escape route. 'We can tell you all the best places to go.'

'Do you like the beach?' the woman asked. 'I do. Only Jeffrey's not very good with pebbles.'

'They play havoc with my plantar fasciitis,' Jeffrey confirmed. 'If you're looking for adventure, we've heard there's a water sports centre that hires jet skis up the road. They also have kayaks if that's more your thing.'

'I think I'm just going to have a look round then find a nice quiet spot to read my book.'

'What are you reading?' Pat pointed to the paperback in Heather's hand. The paperback that Heather had optimistically brought to the table so she could avoid talking to well-meaning but very annoying couples like Jeffrey and Pat.

'The Odyssey. By Homer.'

'Homer Simpson wrote a book?'

'Don't be daft, Pat. Homer, he also wrote The Iliad.'

Why was it all men seemed more familiar with *The Iliad*? Was it because it was a story about rescuing a woman, full of heroic types like Achilles and Hector, and gruesome descriptions of deaths on the battlefield, while *The Odyssey* was about a husband returning home to his wife?

Pat chuckled. 'Is *The Iliad* the one with Brad Pitt? I didn't know they'd made it into a book too.'

In the hotel room upstairs, Esme must be turning in her urn.

'Is it any good? I'm looking for a good holiday read,' said Pat. 'Only I'm more of a Jilly Cooper person myself.'

Heather had only managed to read a few pages on the plane, and while the taxi driver was mending the puncture. So far, she gleaned that the story was divided into twenty-four books. Books within a book. The language was a little flowery and repetitive in places, presumably to make it work as a poem. Odysseus hadn't appeared yet, although his son Telemachus had set out in search of his father. Without telling his mother, naughty boy.

'It's not quite what I expected. So far, all the characters seem to be leaving Ithaca rather than returning to it.'

'Isn't Ithaca where we went on that boat trip the other day, Jeffrey?'

'I'm thinking of visiting the island myself,' Heather said. 'What did you think?'

Jeffrey wrinkled his nose as if he'd smelt something unpleasant. 'Not a lot, to be honest. There wasn't much there.'

Apart from three thousand years of history, myth and legend.

'A few hotels and bars. Beaches, the usual. The shops weren't up to much,' said Pat. 'They were much better in Ibiza.'

Jeffrey started in the foothills of his bacon and egg mountain while Pat poked about warily in her breakfast. Heather finally excused herself, certain that whatever she ate for dinner this evening would have an unpronounceable name and be chosen from a menu printed in Greek.

18

Not waving but drowning

KEEN TO GET DOWN TO THE SERIOUS BUSINESS OF SELF-discovery, Heather booked three tours. Unable to decide between horse-riding, water-skiing and wine-tasting, she signed herself up for all of them, to the undisguised delight of the woman in the tour office next to the hotel. The only advice had been to wear flat shoes and bring her own water. Heather had thought this strange for a water-sport activity until she realised the woman was referring to the horse-riding.

The following morning, an air-conditioned minibus picked her up from her hotel. Inside, Heather joined American honeymooners, and an intense, athletic-looking family of four from Germany. Whether it was the contrast from the pleasantly cool interior of the minibus, or the fact that the stables was located away from the cooling breeze on the sea-front, Heather wasn't sure, but when she climbed out, the heat rose from the parched soil beneath her feet and engulfed her in the first hot flush she'd had in more than a decade. The mother-of-the-bride hat she'd bought on impulse before she left proved a very effective fan, and she was grateful for her cropped hair until the stable's owner greeted the party and plonked what looked – and felt – like a padded cannonball on her head.

Felipe was in his seventies, she guessed, and judging by his *genu varum*, born with a horse between his legs. Heather congratulated her retired brain for remembering the Latin for bow legs. Unfortunately, when it came to putting her foot in the stirrup to mount her steed, her retired brain found discerning her *sinister* from her *dextra* more problematic, and had it not been for Felipe's timely intervention, she would have ended up facing backwards in the saddle.

'Here, I help you,' he said, gathering the reins into her left hand, holding the stirrup iron steady for her left foot, and offering her right buttock gentle guidance from his free hand. To be fair, his helping hand, uninvited as it was, saw her shoot up onto the horse's back Cossack style.

Felipe winked at Heather, and when he introduced all his horses, each named after a Greek god or goddess, it came as no surprise that he would be riding a horny-looking stallion called Zeus. Heather's mount was Persephone, a dappled grey mare who the stable staff had nicknamed Hippo. She assumed it was on account of her colour and because she was as wide as she was high, leaving Heather feeling as if she were sitting astride a table.

When they were all mounted, Felipe ran through the basics. Keep the reins short, the heels down, and look straight ahead. Heather already knew the fundamentals, having ridden her cousin's tiny Shetland pony as a child, but her early experience hadn't prepared her to handle a flirty mare that was at least sixteen hands high. And wide. Meanwhile the Germans looked ready to represent their country at the next Olympics.

It all started well, with the horses clearly accustomed to carrying novices in single file down the well-worn track that led out the back of the stable yard and across the series of scrubby-looking fields towards a wooded area. Heather found Persephone's plodding walk comfortable enough and before long she was rocking back and forth with the motion. Soon, she was confident enough to let go of the mare's dark grey mane and feel the contact of the reins with the bit in the horse's mouth.

A large fly had been following Persephone from the stables. She flicked her tail and tossed her head only for the annoying insect to return seconds later. The mare also made her displeasure known when Felipe wheeled Zeus back and rode alongside Heather, asking her where she was from and whether she had a husband. Persephone flattened her ears and, with more tail swishing and head tossing, tried to nip Zeus in the neck.

'Try not to tense up,' Felipe instructed Heather.

'My horse doesn't seem to like your horse,' said Heather, gripping a fistful of mane again.

'These two love each other!' Felipe roared with laughter, which turned into a husky cough. 'They are like an old married couple. Sometimes she, how you say, has the shits with him.'

The implacable Zeus took no notice of Persephone's increasingly vocal snorts and squeals of annoyance. Felipe was in no hurry to take Zeus back to the front of the line as the group meandered through the shade of an olive grove. This should have been the most perfect, idyllic way to explore the island, but the more Persephone played up, the tighter Heather clung on.

'Relax,' said Felipe, his smile gone now.

The more Heather tried to relax, the tighter she gripped with her heels, her knees, her hands. The horse was pure energy beneath her, like a shaken-up bottle of fizzy drink that no one was brave enough to open.

Felipe called to the rest of the group that it was time to trot, and to please keep in order. He assured them that the horses knew what to do, but that it was essential nobody tried to overtake the horse in front.

'Shorten your reins and squeeze with your heels.'

At that, Persephone bucked and strained at the bit, as if a starter's gun had gone off. Heather hung on, a rising scale of '*Oh-oh-oh-oh!*' bursting from her. Persephone took this as encouragement and broke into a gallop. Faster and faster, passing horse by horse in the line, until finally she kicked dirt into Zeus's shiny black face and was off.

Heather assumed she was going to die, and yet she was unusually sanguine about her life ending so dramatically. It beat wasting away in a nursing home. Her sudden demise would probably warrant a write-up in the local paper back home. Alan would eventually read about it. The girls would be devastated of course. Hopefully Alan too. Her only regret would be that she missed the chance to say all the things she wanted to say to each of them, to tell them what they meant to her.

Contrary to what she'd always believed, her life did not flash before her eyes. Olive trees, an abandoned shepherd's hut, and a rusty car, yes. But not the highlights of her childhood, the tender moments of early motherhood, nor the happier times with Alan. She gave up the struggle and surrendered to her fate. As she relaxed she realised that if she stood up a little in the stirrups, leaned forward and balanced her weight, she might literally be able to ride this out. She didn't know how to stop this bolting animal, but she knew the horse would eventually run out of steam. All she had to do was hold on. Wherever Persephone was going, that's where Heather would end up too.

The trees thinned and, ahead, Heather saw the deep blue of the sea. Persephone was breathing hard, frothy sweat making her neck slippery under Heather's hands. The moment the horse's hooves touched sand, she slowed to a canter, then an uncomfortable jog, and finally a plodding walk. Every muscle in Heather's body quivered. Persephone's glistening flanks heaved in and out as she caught her breath. Heather didn't have the energy to dismount. Spent, she clung to the animal, lying her face flat against its neck.

Felipe cantered up behind them, cooing soothing Greek words to Persephone, who'd begun to paw the sand.

'Turn her away from the water,' Felipe called. Unfortunately, by the time the feeling had returned to Heather's fingers and she'd found the reins, Persephone was up to her fetlocks in the water. Helpless, Heather tugged on the reins while the horse paddled deeper and deeper. The rest of the group appeared in the low dunes in time to see Persephone's legs fold beneath her, and Heather enjoy her first taste of the Ionian Sea.

Later, back at the stables, Heather learned why the staff had nicknamed Persephone 'Hippo'.

'Hippopotamus is from the Greek for "river horse",' Felipe explained while she towelled herself off. He insisted on refunding her money, despite her protests that it was 'only water'. Apart from the humiliation, and the mild discomfort of riding the rest of the way in soggy jeans, she told him she'd found the whole thing quite invigorating. At the very least she would have a self-deprecating story to entertain people with.

Heather didn't have to wait long to add another story to her personal anthology. Less than twenty-four hours later, she was zipping herself into a wetsuit at the water sports centre, wondering why this particular suit appeared to have a redundant codpiece of baggy neoprene at the front.

The young Greek instructor did his best to keep a straight face.

'I think you have watched too many James Bond movies,' he said, pointing to the German family who had booked the same trip and were already standing in pristine wetsuits, all correctly zipped up at the back. 'You have it on backwards.'

Heather laughed at her silly mistake.

From the shore she watched the sporty Germans master the art of standing up on two skis behind a speedboat. They made it look effortless, progressing to a single ski after only a couple of circuits of the bay each. Unfortunately, Heather's attempts were less successful, and after half an hour spent mostly underwater, she'd had enough. She had to be hauled back onto the boat, at which point warm salty water sluiced out of orifices she'd considered anatomically impossible to fill.

She'd wanted to do all the things her nineteen-year-old self – fit, fearless and primed for adventure – might have done. Instead, her 66-year-old body was bruised and leaking. If the third tour hadn't been a wine-tasting tour the following day, she would have been tempted to stay in bed for the rest of the week. Tempted to book the next flight home and crawl back to Alan, tail between her legs. But it was wine, maybe a few olives and a seat in the shade. How could that possibly go wrong?

~

Pat and Jeffrey spotted Heather before she had a chance to abort the mission.

'Over here, Heather!' Pat shouted, bouncing up and down on the rustic wooden bench in excitement. Jeffrey moved aside and insisted Heather sit between them.

'This is cosy,' said Jeffrey with a big grin. Lest there be any lingering doubt about his nationality, today he was wearing his best England football shirt.

'You didn't tell us you were going wine-tasting on your own,' said Pat, tapping Heather's wrist.

'You naughty girl, you could have shared our taxi,' Jeffrey chided, bumping Heather's shoulder.

The whole idea of coming to Greece on her own was that she didn't have to be accountable for her actions.

There were half-a-dozen other tourists sitting around the long wooden table in the corner of a cobblestone yard filled with old wine-making equipment and wooden barrels. Thankfully the table was in the shade of a dense vine-covered pergola and Heather was able to remove her hat and fluff up her short hair.

'It must be very liberating when you can finally let yourself go,' said Pat, staring at Heather's head. 'Jeffrey was convinced you were a lesbian when we first saw you at breakfast.'

'I said librarian, Pat. Not lesbian.'

'Actually, I'm a doctor.' It slipped out before Heather had fully thought through the consequences.

For a moment, Pat and Jeffrey were both silent. Was it Heather's imagination or did they both sit up a little taller?

'Are you a specialist, or just a GP?' Pat asked.

'GP,' Heather winced. *'Just a GP.'*

'Pat had to see a specialist last year, didn't you love? Some women's problem. Had a lump removed the size of a melon.'

'Not a melon, a lemon, Jeffrey.'

Here we go, thought Heather. As predicted, her new friends reeled off every medical anecdote in their repertoire. Heather knew what to do. Smile and nod. She'd had plenty of practice. It was easy. Simply smile and nod.

Pat's eyebrows clashed in a confused frown. 'He nearly *died*. They rushed him to hospital, and the doctor said if we'd left it another five minutes, he wouldn't have made it.'

Heather tried to look suitably sombre. Why was it people were always 'rushed' to hospital? She tried to change the subject, wondered out loud when the wine would appear.

Jeffrey finished another anecdote with, 'I don't care what the papers say, I think you doctors and nurses deserve every penny.' He shook his head in silent admiration. 'Especially the nurses.'

Plates of Greek food to share arrived on the table. Hunks of fresh bread, sliced tomatoes, cubes of feta with thyme and preserved lemon. Heather was famished, having consumed nothing but seawater the previous day. She tried to focus on the spiel from the winemaker, an attractive woman of about forty, as she introduced the bottle she would be serving.

In one ear, Heather heard about organic grapes from the semi-mountainous slopes of Cephalonia that produced hints of citrus and chamomile. In the other ear, she heard Pat say she only ever drank wine in spritzers. Something to do with her hiatus hernia, which she pronounced without 'h's.

A small measure was poured into each of their glasses. Pat asked if she could have lemonade in hers, while Jeffrey knocked his back in a single gulp. Heather was pleasantly surprised to find that the wine did indeed taste like lemon and lime, with something herby in the background. She'd never paid much attention to Alan's descriptions of the wines he served. She drank whatever he chose, although she knew what she liked.

By the time they reached the reds, Heather was fully engrossed. She learned that Vostilidi grapes were perfectly adapted to the local climate, and many were grown on ancient vines using traditional techniques.

'So where is your friend, if you don't mind me asking?' Pat enquired, a cold shower on the sensual honey and apricot flavours exploding on Heather's tongue.

'My friend?'

'You said you were here with a friend.'

Heather didn't like the way she said the word, nor the way she was exchanging glances with Jeffrey.

'She's still in the room. She's nearly ninety.'

'It's wonderful that you older women are still able to travel. I hope I'm like you when I get to your age.'

Heather smiled weakly at Pat, who could only be a few years younger than she was, and signalled to the winemaker for a refill.

The final wine was a dessert wine, made from overripe grapes left to sun-dry to concentrate their sweetness. Heather cradled her glass, wanting to savour every sip of sunshine.

'Jeffrey,' said Pat, leaning across Heather and offering an eyeful of the deep crevasse between her unrestrained holiday breasts. 'I might get a bottle of this to put in the trifle at Christmas. What do you think?'

At the mention of Christmas, Heather had a pang of nostalgia. A wreath on the front door at The Elms, holly wrapped around the bannisters, a fire crackling in the living room, and fairy lights twinkling on the tree. She pictured the girls on Christmas Eve when they were young, bubbling with excitement in matching pyjamas, begging to open just one present, their squeals of delight when she gave in.

Where would she even be this Christmas? Would the girls spend the day with Alan? Heather imagined them sitting around the table in the cosy kitchen without her, while she swapped small talk with the likes of Pat and Jeffrey or FaceTimed her family, alone in a hotel room. It would be easy enough to return home, tanned and relaxed after a fortnight's holiday, and resume her old life with Alan. There would be no shame in admitting she'd been overambitious. She would have got 'it' out of her system, and nothing more would be said. But she wasn't ready to go home yet. Not until she and Alan started missing each other.

19

A man called Nobody

FEARING THAT HER SHORT HAIR WOULD OFFER LITTLE protection, Heather decided to don her now misshapen mother-of-the-bride hat and hope for the best. It was barely nine o'clock, but the sun was already hot. She walked in the shadows of the buildings and carrot-top palm trees along the promenade, then around the town square and side streets using a pocket map the hotel concierge had given her. As the sun rose further and the shadows became thinner and sharper, Heather looked for somewhere she could stop for coffee. Preferably somewhere with a padded seat. After her horse-riding tour, her ischial tuberosities were still advising extreme caution on sitting, and her hip adductors were refusing to adduct, leaving her walking as if Persephone were still between her legs.

None of the cafes around the square particularly spoke to her. Most had signs painted in English with pushy owners spruiking to tourists. She continued along the waterfront, where the water was so clear she could see fish darting around a turtle that, according to the concierge, was something of a local celebrity, and headed for a marina marked on the map. She had all the time in the world and nobody to answer to. She'd even managed to avoid Pat and Jeffrey three mornings in a row by ordering breakfast in her room. Earlier, over tea and a flaky croissant, Heather had phoned Alan to let him know she was still okay. Better not to mention that, since she'd arrived, she'd nearly been killed twice.

Alan had been in a hurry, and she could hear Kevin in the background. She told him she'd let him go. He made her promise to phone again that evening. He'd be in. The way he said it struck Heather as odd, as if he might not always be.

The marina wasn't exactly the Monte Carlo waterfront she'd imagined, and she was only a little disappointed. Instead of monstrous gin palaces, she saw row upon row of nearly identical white yachts tied up by the stern and facing out to sea, as if ready to set sail at any moment. The sight of the boats brought back memories of learning to sail in little wooden dinghies as a child. These were some of the happier moments of her otherwise lonely childhood in the shadow of her mother's diagnosis.

Heather found a spare table in a small taverna at the edge of the marina. The waiter, a film-star handsome young man, brought her a cup of coffee and a glass of water. The coffee was very strong, the caffeine livening her aching and sluggish body. She ordered a second cup, employing the dubious principle that if the drug was working, doubling the dose would make it work twice as well.

'Would you like anything to eat?' the waiter asked.

Why not? It was mid-morning, the time when, if she'd been at work, her coffee would already be cold and her biscuit soggy in the saucer. She'd skipped too many meals, poured too many cold coffees down the sink, spent too long chasing the hands around the clock. It was time to slow down, wake up and, yes, smell the coffee. She asked the waiter to bring her something typically Greek. He looked pleased and returned with what he claimed was the best baklava on the island. His mother's speciality.

'*Efcharistó*,' she replied, determined not to be a typical foreigner who expected everyone to speak English.

When Heather bit into the pastry the sweetness of the sticky golden triangle assaulted her tastebuds. She remembered the day she'd shared the village store's version with Esme on the bench. This was next-level delicious. She'd never tasted anything like it. If only Esme was here with her, enjoying this view of the boats, tasting this honeyed piece of paradise. But she was back at the hotel, still hidden away beneath a pile of clothes in her suitcase.

Esme's niece had made it clear she was only interested in disposing of her aunt's inheritance and not her earthly remains. The obvious place to scatter the ashes would be with Aubrey in the cemetery at St Luke's. But eternity was a long time to spend in Netherwood. Bringing Esme along for the ride was the least Heather could do. Her duty of care had ended long ago. Now her duty was *to* care and she owed her old friend a final hoorah.

Heather was in no hurry to leave her seat in the taverna, even after she'd chased the last sweet flakes around the plate with her finger. It was the perfect spot where she could watch the comings and goings: old men in pairs playing backgammon;

young, tanned gap-year staff cleaning and restocking the charter boats, and running through navigation briefings with holidaymakers. A relaxing day after the thrills and spills of the previous days. There were one or two fishermen mending nets on their painted blue and white boats. With their bushy beards and flat black caps, they looked as though they'd been sent by central casting.

She took her book and mobile phone out of her bag. There were no new messages or missed calls. Should she be relieved or disappointed that Alan wasn't checking in on her every hour? The waiter was busy attending to other customers, otherwise she would have asked him to take a photo of her to send to the girls. The first of the 'proof of life' shots she'd promised to send every few days to ease their worry. Never mind that they often went for weeks, or in Tilly's case months, on end without so much as a phone call to their mother.

Heather held the phone up to head height and turned the display onto herself. Good god. Was that really what she looked like? No wonder people of her age didn't post selfies. The hat was ridiculous. She took it off, fiddled with her hair and experimented with a few poses. The light was harsh and cast every wrinkle and contour into sharp relief. She tried smiling. Pouting. Teeth showing. Lips closed. It didn't matter what she did with her features, it was still the same face. Taking pity on her, the waiter came over and offered to take her photo for her. Later, when Heather examined the shot with the aid of her glasses, she noticed that she was slightly blurred in the foreground, and an attractive younger woman was in sharp focus bending over behind her. Oh well, she'd send the photo to Alan instead. He'd appreciate it.

The boarding card she'd used as a bookmark on the flight marked where Penelope, stuck on Ithaca, was still waiting for Odysseus to come home.

When she looked up she caught the eye of a man who was walking past. He smiled back. He could have been a clean-living seventy-year-old, or fifty with interesting stories to tell. She struggled to think of another way to describe his complexion besides swarthy, which made his wavy grey hair appear almost white. And yet, unable to look away from him, she noticed he had curiously dark eyebrows that shaded his eyes, giving him an evolutionary advantage in the Greek sun.

The man shouted '*Kalimera*' to the waiter, who shouted something back in Greek that made them both laugh. He was carrying a coil of rope under one arm and a supermarket bag of groceries in each hand. Heather was struck by his long languid stride. Alan used to walk like that, before decades spent sitting at a desk or leaning over a stethoscope had corrupted his posture. Maybe gardening would succeed in straightening him up again. Annoyed that yet again Alan had popped into her head, Heather returned to her book and tried to concentrate. When she looked up again, the man with the eyebrows was walking back in the opposite direction empty-handed.

'*Kalimera*,' he called over. Heather looked around. The waiter was busy inside. This time he was talking to her. 'It's a beautiful day.'

'It certainly is,' she called back without thinking. 'The sky is so blue.'

The man slowed. Heather's pulse quickened. Had she really said that? For a moment it looked as though he was going to come over to her. She held her breath, not quite sure how to make a conversation out of how beautiful the day was, or the colour of the sky. To her relief, he carried on walking. People were friendly here, she told herself. Sunshine made people friendly.

She read on.

When she looked up some time later, the man was there again, this time walking past with a case of wine. From behind her paperback, she watched him walk towards a boat at the very end of the wharf.

It was lunchtime by now and, not wanting to take up the table any longer, she left a ten euro note and waved goodbye to the waiter. The sun was even hotter than it had been when she'd arrived and she experienced a wave of unexpected drowsiness. The lead-up to the trip, the rush to the airport, the flight, and the inexplicable need to squeeze three activities into her first few days, had caught up with her. She put on her hat and decided to stroll to the end of the marina before heading back to the hotel for a siesta.

The boats in the marina were mostly modern yachts and catamarans, many bearing the name of a charter company on their boom. Others looked as though they never went anywhere, their pristine sails and cockpits protected by bright blue covers, mooring lines tied firmly to shore. There were one or two small and discreet private yachts too, on which good-looking crew wearing matching white shorts and polo shirts bearing the boat's name washed decks and polished already-shiny brass. It was a world away from her old life in Netherwood. A world away from Alan. If Heather had been hoping to absorb the glamour by osmosis, she was disappointed. However close she got to the gleaming white hulls and teak decks, she still felt as if she was looking in at this world from the outside. Perhaps she was only ever going to be at home in a small English village.

At the end of the furthest limb of the marina berths, Heather noticed a boat that looked unlike any of the others. The dark blue wooden hull with its red trim stood out against the row of cookie-cutter plastic yachts, and the sails were made from aged canvas rather than gleaming new nylon like the charter boats. Unlike its neighbours, this well-used and obviously well-loved boat was tied up with its bow facing in towards the jetty, making it difficult to peer into the cockpit. Perhaps the owner preferred their privacy.

When she inched closer to get a better look, a head appeared out of the cockpit. It was the man with the highly evolved eyebrows. Heather didn't trust herself to say anything sensible. As she turned to leave, a gust of wind lifted her hat and carried it off before her hands could save it. The hat landed, naturally, in the water just beyond the wooden boat's stern.

Before she could think what to do, the man leaned out of the boat and hooked the floating hat on the end of a long pole.

'I think this belongs to you.' He handed her the sodden lump of straw, the fake flower on the side now hanging limp on the band.

'Thank you,' she said, then corrected herself. '*Efcharistó.*'

'*Parakaló.* You speak Greek?'

'Oh no.' Heather laughed.

'Ancient Greek?'

'What?'

He pointed to the bag on her shoulder. 'I saw you reading the greatest work by the greatest Greek poet.'

'It's a translation. Although my husband claims he read it in the original Greek when he was at school. He said it was like picking the tiny bones out of a fish. It's all Greek to me!'

A smile creased his face revealing teeth too white to belong to a fisherman. He stepped onto the gunwale and leaned over, hand on his chest.

'Nobody – that's my name. Nobody – so my mother and father call me, all my friends.' Heather's face must have registered her confusion because his smile broadened and he said, 'You obviously haven't reached the part where Odysseus is trapped in the cave of the one-eyed giant Polyphemus. To escape, Odysseus gets the Cyclops drunk and when asked his name replies, "Nobody". Later when Odysseus pokes him in the eye with a hot poker to escape, and the other Cyclopes ask who blinded him, Polyphemus shouts, "Nobody!"'

'Thank you for the spoiler,' said Heather in mock horror.

'I am sorry.'

'It's all right. I know there's a happy ever after coming. It's still interesting to see how they get there.'

'I apologise for my sense of humour. I'm Dion,' the man said, placing his hand on his chest.

'As in Celine?' Oh really, what was wrong with her? That was the kind of joke Alan might make.

'As in Dionysius, the god of wine, fertility and pleasure.' He did a little bow. 'Everyone calls me Dennis.'

'And I am Heather. As in . . . the bush.'

Her cheeks prickled.

'Well, Heather-like-the-bush, I am pleased to meet you.'

20

Calluna vulgaris.
The common heather

WITH ONE FOOT BALANCED ON THE YACHT'S POLISHED gunwale, Dennis regarded her, an elbow resting on his bent knee like a Rodin sculpture. After a few seconds of contemplation, he invited Heather to step aboard. Not waiting for her reply, he extended a hand to help her.

'I wouldn't want to impose.' How British of her.

His eyebrows – Alan's, but darker – registered his disappointment. 'Please,' he said, more an order than a request. 'I have coffee.'

More coffee. Heather's bladder was already bursting from the two she'd drunk at the taverna but, not seeing a public toilet anywhere, she'd resigned to holding on until she got back to the hotel. She hesitated, running through a quick risk analysis in her head. Dennis didn't look like a sex trafficker and although one of Britain's most notorious serial killers had been a Dennis, this Dennis could quote Homer. Heather reached for his hand and climbed onto the boat, ducking under the awning as she lowered herself into the cockpit.

'Welcome aboard *Athena*. As in the goddess of wisdom, not the poster of the tennis player who is not wearing any underwear.'

Heather laughed. He loved epic poetry, *and* he had a sense of humour.

The boat was a beauty with a wide cockpit trimmed in varnished teak, and bench seats that ran around three sides. But, despite her undeniable aesthetic appeal, Heather formed the impression *Athena* was no pleasure boat. She was crammed with extra equipment and gadgetry – coiled ropes, fuel canisters, solar panels – and had an air of functionality about her. She had the fur coat and, unlike the poster girl, the knickers.

'Do you live on here?'

He smiled and shrugged. 'The short answer is yes, but the answer to "why?" is a much longer story. First, coffee. Sit, please.' He gestured to the bench covered by a padded canvas seat cushion, which Heather found surprisingly comfortable. What a shame Persephone hadn't had something similar. Although she managed to lower her buttocks onto the seat without mishap, she couldn't fully relax, still not quite believing that she had stepped onto a strange man's boat with a bursting bladder and barely a second thought. Then she remembered Esme saying that she only regretted the things she hadn't done, rather than the things she had. One way or another, assuming she made it out alive, this encounter would make another excellent story for her collection.

Dennis disappeared, launching himself down through the hatch without touching the polished wooden ladder like a paratrooper exiting an aircraft.

'You've done that before,' Heather said, chastising herself for stating the obvious. When she was nervous, her brain forgot that she was an intelligent and occasionally articulate mature woman with a medical degree, believing instead that she was still fourteen and had just drunk the contents of her parents' drinks cabinet.

'A few times,' he replied, his teeth appearing much whiter now his face was in the dimmer light down below. He returned a few minutes later with a steaming stovetop coffee pot, two white cups with saucers and a sugar bowl.

The coffee was dark and strong. As were Dennis's exposed forearms poking out from the neatly rolled sleeves of his light blue shirt. Where his shorts ended, his knees were the most perfect synovial hinge joints she'd ever seen on a human being, alive or dead. His skin was upholstered in silky dark hair. Greek men were notoriously hairy, yet Dennis had the perfect skin-to-body-hair ratio. It was hard to fault him at all. If she'd ever had a sexual fantasy, her imagination would have conjured up a tall, dark and handsome stranger who looked exactly like Dennis. In her fantasy, he would have had a different name, obviously. Men called Dennis were rarely the subject of lustful thoughts. Neither were many Alans. Now, if he'd been a Thor, a Bear or a Barack, it would have been a different story altogether.

It was perfectly acceptable to look, she told herself. She could look, but under no circumstances was she to touch. Ogling Dennis was no different to admiring a piece of art or a museum artefact. He wasn't real. He couldn't be real.

When the girls were younger, Heather had taken them to the British Museum to see the mummies. Tilly had been going through her Egyptian phase. They'd detoured via Ancient Greece where Heather had been struck by the physical beauty and anatomically perfect proportions of the figures decorating the vases and amphora. She'd never come across anything vaguely resembling these flawless, athletic figures in Netherwood. The Ancient Greeks, she'd read in her guidebook, valued symmetry and balance in the human form. And although Aristotle disagreed with most of what Plato taught, they agreed that objects should be both beautiful and functional.

'I don't want sex,' she said.

Dennis spat his coffee across the cockpit. 'What?'

'Just so we're clear. I'm not looking for a gigolo. I wouldn't want to give you the wrong impression.'

He wiped coffee from his face with the back of his hand and coughed a couple of times.

'Thank you. It is refreshing to hear an English person being so direct.' He poured himself another cup. Offered to refresh hers.

'No thank you, I must be going.' Heather stood, her coffee only half drunk. 'I must phone my husband. I promised I would.'

'He is not here with you in Greece?'

'No, he's in Netherwood. With his vegetables.'

'He is a farmer?'

'Not exactly.' She sat down again. 'I'm sorry. This is all a bit new to me.'

A smile crept back across his face like a rising sun. 'You mean you haven't drunk coffee before?'

A couple walked past, looking at the boats. Dutch, Heather thought, since they were both well over six feet tall. They stopped to admire *Athena*. Dennis waved and shouted, '*Kalimera!*' Followed by, 'It's a beautiful day.' Exactly as he had to Heather.

'Look,' said Heather when the couple had gone. 'Why don't we start again?' This time she would try to act like a normal person.

'Agreed, Heather-like-the-bush.' Dennis clinked his coffee cup against hers. '*Yamas!*'

'Cheers.'

'You must not read too much into the situation. The Greeks are known for their hospitality. It is a custom of ours going back to ancient times when hosts would offer strangers food and wine, even a bath and a bed.'

Heather glanced down the hatch and through the open door of one of the cabins at the corner of a neatly made bed. Exactly how hospitable was Dennis planning to be?

She tried to keep the conversation light. 'In that case I obviously picked the wrong hotel. Mine has four stars and I only have a shower,' she joked.

'Which hotel?'

'The Poseidon,' she said, without thinking. Now he knew where she was staying.

'It is more than politeness, you understand. It is an obligation, like a law. In Ancient Greece it was called *xenía*, meaning guest friendship. The Greeks use the same word *xenos* to mean stranger and guest. We welcome and respect strangers, whatever country they are from.' He kicked at a loose rope with his toe. 'At least that is how it used to be. In modern times, we have less to offer, and more who wish to take it. Of course, you would know all about the rules of hospitality from your book.'

She looked around for her bag which had fallen under the bench. Her sopping straw hat was drying in the sun. A few more minutes and she would be able to wear it again.

'Yes, I wondered why everyone was so generous in helping Odysseus and his men to get home.'

The sun had moved and Heather's left arm was burning. Dennis noticed and invited her to sit on the shaded side of the boat.

'Am I holding you up?' Heather asked.

He checked his body – no, no one was 'holding him up' – and she clarified, 'I meant, am I interrupting you from doing what you were doing?'

He shook his head. 'No, I am here for a few more days. I've been waiting for spare parts to arrive from Athens. The engine is . . . problematic.' He shrugged. 'But I am in no hurry. I have plenty of food and I know the marina owners well, so there is no need for me to leave too soon.'

Heather's relief was unexpected. She examined her contradictory thoughts. Dennis was simply offering her traditional Greek hospitality. Also, Dennis was flirting with her. It was a long time since anyone had flirted with her. A long time since she'd done any flirting of her own.

When Heather first joined the practice, she and Alan had kept to their agreement to pretend the night of drunken passion had never happened. They maintained a professional distance at all times, albeit one fuelled with sexual tension. A few weeks into their working relationship they found themselves alone in the upstairs dispensary. Alan was mixing a pot of Upton's paste for a verruca; she shaking a bottle of

Penicillin V syrup for a toddler with tonsillitis. Their eyes met and, for a second, she thought he might kiss her. Instead, he'd reached for the salicylic acid at the same time she reached for a sticky medicine label, their arms springing apart as if they were the north poles of two magnets. They didn't touch again until the night Alan proposed.

Back in the present, Heather waited for a natural pause in the conversation so she could leave. This time she would stand and thank him again for the coffee, then walk back to the hotel. Only, there was no pause. Her bladder couldn't cope any longer. After she'd swallowed her pride and asked to use the 'head', they chatted easily until the sun moved round and started to burn Heather's other arm.

'So, tell me more,' Dennis said, ushering her to a new shady spot. 'Why Greece? Why Cephalonia? Why alone?'

The Greece part was easy, she told him. She'd always wanted to come. In her imagination, it was the perfect holiday destination – perpetually sunny, with beautiful scenery and crystal-clear sea. The food was amazing and didn't automatically come with chips. There was also the undeniable lure of all that history, the fact that Greece was considered the cradle of Western civilisation, and Ancient Greece the birthplace of democracy and politics, philosophy, literature and theatre, science, mathematics and the Olympic Games. She didn't tell him that many of her compatriots viewed this amazing country on the edge of the Mediterranean as a cheap place to get a suntan and a hangover.

The Cephalonia part was harder to explain without sounding completely ignorant. Instead of telling him the truth, that she'd opened the brochure randomly and booked the first hotel on the page, she said, 'A friend introduced me recently to Homer, and I became fascinated by the story of Penelope and Odysseus. I wanted to see some of the places in the story for myself.' Not a complete lie, but one that was feeling more like the truth the longer she spent on the island.

Dennis tugged at his chin and narrowed his eyes. 'And what do you think, now you're here?'

She took a deep breath, averted her eyes. 'It's very nice.'

He closed one eye. 'Really? Isn't that what the English say about a cup of tea? Is Cephalonia, the place where I was born, like a cup of English tea?'

Sweat trickled down Heather's back and soaked into the conveniently fluid-wicking waistband of her crease-resistant trousers.

'I only arrived a few days ago.'

'Wait, don't say any more. We need wine.' Dennis sprang up again and disappeared down the hatch. He returned with a bottle of wine and two small tumblers. 'I hope you are hungry.' Moments later, the small wooden table in the cockpit was laden with bread, a ripe fig, olives and a simple bowl of olive oil.

'I think you will like this wine. It is a *xinómavro* blend,' Dennis explained, then made her repeat the name phonetically *ehk-see-no-mav-roh*. 'The main grapes are grown on the rocky soil on the slopes of Mount Olympus. A wine for the gods themselves.'

Heather was starting to get the hang of this wine-ponce business. She closed her eyes and identified each distinct flavour: cherry, raspberry, fennel and something else . . . tomato maybe?

'You shouldn't have gone to all this trouble,' she said, meaning exactly the opposite.

'What can I say? I am named after the god of wine.'

'And I am named after a short, squat bush that grows in bogs and on windswept Scottish moors.'

He leaned back against the handrail, stretching out his long legs. 'You know, my daughter is a florist. She would say that heather is a strong and resilient plant because it can survive both in snow and also in the hot Greek sun. It has roots that support the soil and allow other plants to grow.' He studied her, taking his time. 'And when heather flowers, it is not with big, brightly coloured flowers that are all for show. Heather is the kind of plant that does not know how beautiful it is.'

Heather accepted a second glass of red wine. How could she not? She watched Dennis tear off a chunk of bread and dip it into the olive oil. She did the same. It tasted like heaven.

'I could get used to this,' she said.

A crowd of young men in football shirts walked past nursing beer bottles and peeling noses.

'I am glad to hear that. In my experience there are two kinds of tourists who come to Cephalonia.' He was looking at the group that could only have been English. 'Okay, three if you count the packets.'

Heather laughed, then regretted it. 'They're called package holidays. Sorry, please go on.'

'The first kind are the Nicolas Cage fans. They come to this island because they have watched *Captain Corelli's Mandolin.*'

'They heard him do that terrible Italian accent and they still came?'

Dennis laughed. 'Yes, it is hard to believe. They like the scenery, but they are disappointed that the island does not look exactly like it did in the movie. They do not appreciate that the earthquake of 1953 destroyed most of the old buildings.'

'The brochure didn't mention anything about earthquakes.' Heather wondered if he was old enough to have lived through it.

'It was a very big earthquake, magnitude seven point two. Four hundred and fifty people died. Even a troopship in the harbour rolled and was badly damaged.'

'That would explain why the town looks so modern.'

'There are one or two examples of the traditional Venetian architecture the region is known for. Not many. If you want whitewashed churches and windmills, go to Santorini, and good luck with the crowds.' He waved his hand dismissively as if he didn't need to explain further.

'And what is the second kind of tourist?'

'People like you. Homer-philes.'

She grinned. Esme would be proud of her.

They finished the bottle of wine between them. It was well into the afternoon when Heather managed to tear herself away. She offered to wash up the glasses and plates. Dennis wouldn't hear of it. Her hat was almost dry though it had shrunk after its earlier dip, so she shoved it into her bag.

'You didn't answer my last question,' said Dennis as he helped her climb over onto the floating wharf.

'What was that?'

'Why you came alone.'

He must think her a cliché. Another middle-aged woman living out her *Shirley Valentine* fantasy. Women running away from their small lives, hoping to find a new version of themselves under the sun. And yet, wasn't that exactly what she was doing? She didn't owe him an explanation. She didn't owe anybody an explanation. Apart from Alan, who hadn't even asked for one.

'When I asked you if you lived on *Athena*, you told me it was a long story. I also have a long story.'

'I would like to hear it.'

'Another day, perhaps.'

In the movie version of what happened next, she would have backed away, still sharing a meaningful look with this handsome Greek god. In real life, as she turned to leave, she caught her toe in a mooring cleat and windmilled half-a-dozen paces before she regained her balance, narrowly avoiding the same fate as her hat. Thankfully, when she looked back, Dennis had already gone.

21

Keep calm and carry on

BACK IN THE HOTEL ROOM, ESME WAS WAITING UP FOR HER. Heather could have sworn she'd left the urn in her suitcase but there it was, sitting expectantly on the bedside table.

'What?' Heather snapped. If human ashes could cross their arms and tap their foot disapprovingly, then Esme was waiting for an explanation. Demanding to know where she'd been all day.

'Okay, if you must know, I spent all day with a handsome Greek man on his boat.'

Heather's cheeks stung with guilt when she said it out loud. It made Dennis sound like Onassis.

Esme didn't say anything.

'He's a nice friendly local, that's all. Nothing untoward happened.'

She poured herself a glass of water, surprised by how thirsty she was. Then she collapsed onto the bed, luxuriating in the afternoon breeze blowing in through the French doors.

The mopeds must be enjoying a siesta too because the road outside was quiet.

Heather yawned. She tried closing her eyes but, even though she was tired and drowsy, she couldn't relax enough to drop off. Her mind was alive, in spite of the alcohol. When she rolled over to face Esme's Tree of Life urn, her head began to spin. Now that she thought about it, she couldn't remember walking back to the hotel. The wine had been surprisingly good; even better by the third glass.

'I am on holiday,' she said. When this seemed insufficient justification for Esme, she added, 'I was simply respecting an act of traditional Greek hospitality.'

Heather opened her book, read a couple of lines then slammed it shut again.

'Blame Homer. You've read it. He might have been blind but there was nothing wrong with his tastebuds. Every other line mentions wine. Honeyed wine, seasoned wine, heady, mellow, heart-warming, *irresistible wine*. And how many times does he refer to the *wine-dark sea*? I say, when in Greece, do as the Greeks do.'

When Heather looked at the urn again, the Tree of Life motif was facing away from her. Esme was in a huff. Heather was surprised at her friend's disapproval. The time on the boat with Dennis was exactly what she imagined Esme would have done if she'd had half a chance.

'You'll have to spell it out for me. I'm not a mind reader,' Heather muttered. How much easier her job would have been if she'd been able to read minds. How much easier her marriage, especially the last few weeks of it, would have been too.

She must have dropped off because when she woke the light had changed. The sun had already disappeared behind the hotel and all that was left was the apricot glow on the walls of her hotel room.

Her first thought was that she needed to speak to Alan. Only by phoning home could she prove to herself that she'd done nothing wrong today, and by now, her liver enzymes had metabolised enough of the alcohol that she could safely phone her husband and have a coherent conversation without slurring her words.

The first call to the landline went through to the answering machine. Heather imagined the phone ringing in the hall at The Elms, Stan lifting his head from his paws as if to ask if anyone was going to answer it. She hung up without leaving a message. How easy it would be to leave it at that.

She tried Alan's mobile instead. He answered it on the second ring.

'How's your holiday going?' he asked.

Is that how he saw it, nothing more than a nice fortnight away in the sun? She'd tried to talk to him, tried to tell him how stuck she felt in her life. Clearly, he was hoping that a few days on a beach would unstick her. Heather suspected the girls understood her better. But they'd always sided with their father, telling Heather to lighten up, to go easy on Alan. The only person who really understood her was Esme. And she was dead.

She told Alan about horse-riding and water-skiing, and he'd made sympathetic noises that, to his credit, sounded genuine. When she told him about the wine-tasting, he'd made a derisive remark until she reminded him that the Greeks had been making wine for centuries before the French caught on. Then, surprisingly, he backtracked, saying he'd heard good things about Greek wine and hoped she'd enjoyed it.

'What have you been up to, Alan?' Heather asked.

'I've been busy in the garden.' He spent the next five minutes describing exactly how busy he'd been. The carrots were coming along well, and he had high hopes for the cos lettuce and leeks, although he'd gone off script by planting some radishes, which he'd read were good at keeping cucumber beetles away.

'That's great, Alan. It's good to hear how it's all coming together. How are the girls?'

'They're well. Belinda is laying already, and Chantal and Dee are looking promising too. I'm a bit worried about Alice though. Her feet are a lot bigger than the other hens and yesterday I caught her trying to mount Dee. I was prepared to overlook her sexual preferences until I woke up at five am to her *cock-a-doodle-dooing*. I think Alice might be an Alistair.'

'Right,' said Heather, drumming her fingers on the balcony railing. 'Actually, I was enquiring about Tilly and Sarah. Our daughters.'

'I know,' Alan said. 'My pathetic attempt at humour.' He sighed. His voice sounded weary, and she wondered if he was all right. If there was something he wasn't telling her.

'Any news?' She meant about Sarah being pregnant.

'Nothing to report. Nothing has changed here.'

Had she really expected everything to fall into place the moment she jumped onto that plane? For Alan to miss her so much that he'd abandon his vegetables and come chasing after her? His days would carry on regardless of whether she was moping about the house, or off chasing her dream. The distance between her and Alan seemed so much further than 1500 miles. Greece was in a different time zone, two hours feeling like light years ahead of what she'd left behind.

'So, you're having a nice time?' Alan asked.

'Very nice, thank you.'

Like your English cup of tea.

'That's good. I'm glad you're having a nice time.'

Silence. At first Heather thought they'd been cut off. Then she heard a blackbird in the background.

'Is everything all right, Alan?'

'Oh yes. Everything's tickety-boo.'

'How's Stan?'

'Stan's well. I took him for a walk this morning.'

'Good. That's good.'

Heather couldn't think of another thing to say. Everyone was well. Everything was fine without her. Alan was apparently fine without her. It was good to know he wasn't pining or missing her too much. It made it easier for Heather not to miss him too.

'Well, I'll leave you to it,' Heather said.

'Jolly good.'

'Okay, then. Bye, Alan.'

'Hang on a minute, Heather. Don't go. I need to talk to you about something important. It's been on my mind since you left.'

Finally, they were going to talk.

'What is it, Alan?'

'I've been tying myself into a Gordian knot trying to come up with the answer. I need you to decide.'

'Decide what?'

'It's the potatoes. I can't decide which variety to plant. Would you say we're more mashers or bakers?'

22

Slave to love

LATER, AFTER EATING SPIT-ROAST LAMB, FOLLOWED BY A delicious olive oil cake served with creamy Greek yoghurt, in a quiet taverna in the town square where she'd spoken to no one besides the waiter, Heather made a nest out of the pillows and cushions on her bed and sat up reading long into the night.

At first, she'd struggled to get into *The Odyssey*, distracted by Homer's insistence on stretching or squeezing the story to fit the strict lines of poetry. She understood why a youthful Alan might have found the whole thing heavy going, although as the characters came to life and the epic voyage unfolded on the tea-coloured pages, Heather began to forget she was reading poetry at all. Her enjoyment was interrupted only by her frustration with Odysseus as he meandered home. Only time would tell whether Penelope, smart woman that she was, would swallow any of his elaborate but ultimately pathetic excuses when he finally arrived home.

By the time Heather drifted off to sleep in the early hours, Odysseus had encountered a witch called Circe who'd turned his men into pigs; he'd travelled to the Underworld and been passive-aggressively berated by his dead mother for never visiting; tied himself to his mast to avoid the Sirens; and found himself sailing between the six-headed man-eating monster Scylla and the deadly ship-devouring whirlpool Charybdis.

Heather woke in the dark with her glasses balanced on the very tip of her nose and the open paperback still in her hand. She closed the book, removed her spectacles, and placed them next to the urn on the bedside table before going back to sleep. She blamed Esme for the dreams that followed. In one, she was wearing a knitted swimsuit. She was on *Athena* with Dennis, re-enacting the famous boat scene from the *Shirley Valentine* film. Unlike Pauline Collins, Heather, sensible Heather, had insisted on keeping her swimsuit on rather than diving in naked. Unfortunately, when Heather climbed out of the water again, the wet wool sagged then unravelled completely, to the amusement of Alan's fan club who were spying through binoculars from a nearby boat.

What a relief to wake up. Such a relief in fact that she decided to brave the hotel dining room for breakfast. Jeffrey and Pat were lying in wait.

'Here she is!' Pat announced.

'We've saved you a place.' Jeffrey patted the empty chair to his right. His hand lingered on the seat as he watched her approach.

There was no escape. The hotel restaurant was unaccountably busy and the table she'd sat at yesterday was taken up by a man conducting a Zoom meeting on his laptop.

'Did you have a nice day yesterday?' Pat asked.

'We looked for you,' Jeffrey said.

'I had lunch with a hot Greek guy,' Heather told them.

For a moment there was silence. Then Pat play-punched her in the shoulder. 'Oh, you tease!'

'You had us going there,' said Jeffrey.

Heather ordered tea then did a circuit of the buffet before returning to the table. Unfolding her napkin across her lap, she asked, 'So, what did you two do yesterday?'

The couple exchanged glances. 'Jeffrey tried water-skiing. He said, if Heather can do it, so can I.'

Jeffrey didn't respond.

'Oh yes, and how was it?'

'A little painful.' He glanced down at his groin where Heather noticed a wet patch in his shorts.

'Icepack,' whispered Pat. 'I'm going to park him on a sun lounger and take myself off shopping for the day.' She didn't sound particularly disappointed.

'What about you? Is your friend feeling better yet?'

'Much better,' said Heather. 'In fact, I'm taking her out for the day.'

'Where is she?' Pat looked around.

Heather patted the bag hanging over the arm of the chair. 'She's in here.'

She'd eventually worked out what was wrong with Esme, why she'd been so touchy since they'd arrived. It wasn't the fact that Heather had come home tipsy after spending the day with Dennis. Esme didn't disapprove of Heather's actions. She was jealous. As soon as Heather promised to take her along in future, things were back to normal between them.

Pat and Jeffrey made their excuses. Jeffrey walked away like John Wayne, one hand holding the icepack in place.

Heather had seen a few scrotal haematomas in her time, and though she was the proud owner of a well-hidden womb and ovaries, she could only imagine the pain he must be in.

~

Heather avoided the marina that day. She took Esme to the beach where they rented a sun lounger and snoozed in the shade of a yellow beach umbrella, listening to the sounds of families on holiday. A day of doing absolutely nothing should have been just what the doctor ordered. Instead of feeling relaxed and rejuvenated, Heather felt bored and irritable. The whole point of coming to Greece was to have adventures. Even Esme made no attempt to hide her frustration, rolling repeatedly out of Heather's beach bag and onto the warm sand.

The following day, a week after she'd arrived in Cephalonia, Heather was back at the marina. She liked the coffee at the waterside taverna, and the baklava really was the best she'd tasted. The table she'd sat at the other day was vacant and, now that several of the charter yachts had left the marina, offered the perfect view of the finger wharf where *Athena* was berthed. Her heart fibrillated. The dark blue hull and wooden mast were still there.

While she waited for her coffee, she followed Odysseus who, having several books previously washed up on the island of Phaeacia and jumped naked out of the bushes in front of the beautiful young princess Nausicaa, was now accepting her father's generous offer of a new ship and sailors to help reach Ithaca.

When she looked up, Dennis was standing next to her table, smiling.

'*Kaliméra*. It's a beautiful day,' he said.

She couldn't help but smile.

The waiter brought her coffee and clapped Dennis on the back, offering to bring him one too.

Heather invited Dennis to join her.

'I can't make up my mind about Odysseus,' she said, sliding her boarding pass between the pages to mark her place as she closed the book. 'He thinks nothing of exposing himself to young girls, has slept with the nymph Calypso *and* the witch Circe. Talk about having his cake and eating it.'

She'd meant it to be a light-hearted observation.

Dennis shrugged as if in defence of his entire gender. 'What can I say? Life at sea is full of challenges.'

'And opportunities, no doubt.'

'A girl in every port? Not me. I am divorced now but I was married the whole time I was at sea. I had two children, Isabella and Nico.'

Two coffees later, during which Dennis's chair inched closer and closer to hers, he'd told her all about his years in the Hellenic Navy.

'I was a lieutenant commander,' he said. 'In recent years, most of our missions have been in peace-keeping or humanitarian roles. And this was good for me. I joined the navy not because I wanted to go to war, but because I love the sea and I wanted to travel. It is a Greek thing, I think. I always enjoyed my job, apart from the time away from my wife and children.'

Heather thought about Alan, and how they'd begun to live separate lives under the same roof. Could distance be the very thing that brought them back together again? Only time would tell. Meanwhile, she was having coffee and talking Homer with an ex-naval commander with very attractive knees.

'I was planning to take the ferry over to Ithaca, tomorrow,' she said.

'No, you mustn't do that! I will take you on my boat. I will give you a private tour of Odysseus's palace.'

'Really? It's still there?'

'Only ruins, of course. It is situated at the foot of Mount Neriton, just above a small village called Stavros. They call it the School of Homer.'

Why hadn't the tours office mentioned this important tourist attraction? The brochures showed mainly photos of holidaymakers on beaches or ice-cream-coloured buildings around pretty harbours. Perhaps it wasn't true and he planned to rob her, or kidnap her and demand a ransom from Alan. She was curious to know how much she was worth to her husband, but really, the notion was ridiculous. Dennis was a kind, generous and possibly lonely man, who was extending her the ancient principle of hospitality. It would be disingenuous to assume he had an ulterior motive; and delusional to imagine that, if he had, it was sexual.

When his attentive sable-brown eyes fixed on hers, Heather decided to override her concerns. The wild thing was curious.

'I wouldn't want to put you to any trouble, Dennis.'

'I need to test *Athena*'s engines,' he said, as if she was the one doing him a favour. 'It is quite a long sail. We would need to leave before breakfast, but we would return in the early evening. Naturally, I will provide lunch.'

Sail to Ithaca with a handsome Greek? It beat traipsing around Sainsbury's with Alan.

23

Throwing caution to the wind

HAT. SWIMSUIT. SUNSCREEN. TOWEL. HIKING BOOTS. Bottled water. When she was young, Heather had taken the Girl Guide motto to 'be prepared' very seriously. She'd emerged from those Wednesday evenings with skills that were sadly wasted on her metropolitan housing estate upbringing: how to light a campfire, signal SOS in Morse code, and bandage a snakebite. But Guides had made her dependable and sensible. The kind of sensible that had cemented her lifelong role as a 'good influence', and at school invariably seen her sharing a desk with the class disruptor.

Today, being prepared meant setting an alarm for six and requesting an early morning call from reception at six fifteen. Just to be sure. Dennis had been very specific about leaving on time if they were going to sail over to the island and back in a day. The two islands were only two nautical miles apart at the narrowest point on the east coast of Cephalonia, but Heather's hotel – and Dennis's boat – were on the west coast.

Esme insisted she come along too. Heather didn't need a chaperone, especially one she'd have to lug around in her bag, but she felt bad about her friend missing out on the fun.

At the marina, Dennis was waiting for her. *Athena*'s noisy diesel engines were already running, reminding her of the Land Rover idling in the drive at The Elms.

'Good, you are here,' he said, taking her daypack from her and when he nearly dropped it into the water, expressing surprise at its weight.

After stowing the bag under the bench seat, he offered his hand to help her onboard. Dennis's hands were sun-freckled and his fingers grease-stained from tinkering with his engine. She had a sudden flashback to Alan preparing to deliver Rosemary Lawson's baby. Back when even the sight of him washing his hands had been a turn on.

Alan, again. If she was going to enjoy this experience, she was going to have to put her husband out of her mind. She would not waste time ruminating over the past or worrying about their future together. Today, she would live completely in the now, and enjoy every moment as it arrived.

There was no time for niceties. As soon as she was aboard, Dennis sprang into action, untying the mooring ropes before darting to the wheel to carefully reverse *Athena* out of her berth and past the other boats, then swinging round, towards the buoys that marked the entrance to the marina.

'What can I do?' Heather said, looking around helplessly.

Dennis gestured to her to take the wheel.

He couldn't be serious, could he?

'But I don't know how to,' she said, shaking her head.

'It's easy. Come.'

Gingerly, she stepped up to the wheel and grasped where his hands had been. He covered her hands with his and showed her how to steer. There was nothing lascivious about it, he was merely guiding her as he might a young sailor taking the helm for the first time, and yet the heat from his large hands travelled along her arms, through Heather's body to the soles of her feet.

'Keep parallel to the shore,' he instructed, releasing his hands. *Athena* chugged out into the main channel. He pointed to the promenade where tourists were already strolling along the mosaic walkway beside the water. Several turned to watch them motor past. She'd never turned heads before. She'd been invisible for so long. Now she didn't care who saw her. She waved when they passed The Poseidon where Pat and Jeffrey would be enjoying their full English breakfasts.

Athena's rudder began to react to Heather's guidance. It wasn't quite like driving a car. She soon realised that she had to be patient and anticipate several seconds ahead. *Athena* wouldn't be rushed.

'Very good,' said Dennis. Then he disappeared, leaving her alone at the helm.

'Dennis!' she shouted. 'Large cruise ship dead ahead!'

The blue and white ship dominated the tiny harbour. She could see the activity as tiny figures spilled down the gangway, and a tug hovered nearby.

'Steer round it,' Dennis called from somewhere she couldn't see.

Shit.

Dennis returned in the nick of time, a giant white fender in each hand.

'Line the bowsprit up with that headland over there.' He pointed to where the land dipped down towards open water, then vanished down the hatch with the fenders.

Once they were past the cruise ship and the channel widened, Heather relaxed a little. It had been at least fifty years since she'd been on a boat, not counting the memorable-for-all-the-wrong-reasons trip to Spain on the ferry the girls dubbed the Vomit Comet.

What would happen when they reached the headland was anyone's guess, but since Dennis seemed to be quite content to give orders, and she to follow them, she wasn't too worried. Heather gripped the wheel and held her course as if her life depended on it.

'Aim into the wind,' he barked from the main mast where he was busy untying the sail covers.

'Which way?' she asked, feeling pathetic again. How many winds were there?

'Look at the tell-tales.' He pointed to the top of the mast where two tiny strips were flying in the direction of the breeze. The sails were already unfurled and luffing expectantly in the breeze.

'Okay, you can do this,' Heather told herself. They were in open water. What was the worst that could happen?

She yanked the wheel clockwise, turning, turning until she felt the boat change direction. Dennis staggered then found his balance. He attached the winch and began to wind the handle, taming the flapping canvas until it caught the wind and drove the boat forward. The muscles in his upper arms tensed as he wound. Biceps, triceps, deltoid. Heather imagined the arterial blood flooding through the individual myocytes, swelling each muscle compartment beneath his golden skin.

She agreed with Plato and Aristotle about things being at the same time beautiful and functional. Dennis was both.

Esme was already ogling, the urn peeking out of Heather's bag. So why not her? She was a happily married woman – okay, a moderately contented married woman – but she was still a woman.

As Dennis winched in the sheet, the hem of his shirt lifted to reveal his midriff. Heather knew a thirty-two-inch waist when she saw one, and this one was where the anatomy textbooks suggested it should be. She could also tell that, courtesy of all that extra virgin olive oil, his blood pressure would be a perfect 110/70 and his LDL cholesterol a flawless 4.0.

With nothing but open water beyond the bowsprit now, Heather relaxed. She was in charge at the helm. At a time when everything else in her life felt so out of control, this magnificent old boat was obeying her commands. It was easy to believe that every day on the Ionian Sea was this perfect. This blue. From the cobalt of the deepest sea, the azure of the water at *Athena*'s bow and the aquamarine of the shallows nearest shore, to the Wedgewood blue of the sky at the horizon. She thought of Netherwood on the day she left, swaddled by clouds in fifty shades of grey.

When the sails were taut with wind, Dennis cut the engine and took over the wheel. *Athena*'s mainsail strained and Heather felt the boat quicken as a gust tugged at the canvas above her head. She closed her eyes. The breeze lifted the short hair at her scalp. How liberating not to worry about how her hair looked, whether it was tangled, sweaty, whipping in her eyes. Heather ran her fingers through what the hairdresser had left behind.

'Good,' said Dennis. 'I will take this watch. You can sit and relax.' He indicated the bench seat, now in the shadow of the mainsail. She accepted his offer, grateful to rest her legs, and happy to spectate for a while.

He stood so straight, bare feet firmly planted on the immaculate teak deck. Everything about him was precise and efficient and watchful. Every inch a naval officer. This was a very different man to the one who'd opened the bottle of wine the day they met. It was as though he was back on duty. His attention and focus made Heather a little uneasy, but perhaps that was not a bad thing. The last thing she needed was to drop her guard completely and do something she might later regret.

They took turns at the helm. With the consistent wind they stayed mostly on a single tack, making a steady six knots. Dennis trimmed the sails, like an artist making tiny brushstrokes then standing back to admire his work. A quarter turn of the winch handle here, a minor adjustment of the rudder there. Here was a man in tune with the sea and the wind. His skill and passion were elemental.

And yet, she knew almost nothing about him.

'I can tell you love sailing, Dennis,' she said, hoping to open a conversation.

'Yes,' he answered.

If this was a consultation, it would be going nowhere. She tried again. 'What do you love about it?'

'The freedom. It is just the wind and the water out here.'

She noticed that he spent long periods staring wistfully towards the horizon. At times he even seemed to forget Heather was there, leaving her feeling awkward, as if he wished he was alone.

The wind and the movements of the boat demanded his constant attention, and they sailed in silence for two or three hours.

'Shall I make us something to drink?' Heather asked, more for something to do than because she was thirsty.

He told her where to find the coffee pot. The main cabin was immaculate considering Dennis lived in this tiny space. Or so he said. There was always the chance that he had a wife somewhere and his *modus operandi* was selling romantic notions to gullible Englishwomen like her. So far Dennis hadn't tried to seduce her, nor had he asked her for money by making up some sob story about a friend or relative in trouble, or claiming the boat needed some urgent repair he couldn't afford. If anything, his inattention since they'd set off was more of a worry.

She waited for the coffee to percolate in the pot on the gas stove while trying to keep her balance as the boat pitched and rode each wave. She couldn't resist sneaking a look around the cabin, searching for clues about the enigmatic Greek she was quite possibly trusting with her life. In the forward cabin the bed was neatly made with simple white cotton sheets. The galley was clean, and she had a sense that every item had earned its place; from the single saucepan and frying pan to the pair of tumblers and the rack of chef's knives, each well used but also well cared for. Nothing was left to chance.

Back on the deck, they drank the coffee in silence, watching the sails flap then billow as they caught the wind. Heather had started to watch the speedometer and felt a tiny thrill every time a gust saw the boat gain a knot or two. When a brief lull saw the empty sails hanging idly, Heather asked Dennis how long he'd owned the boat.

'Ten years,' he replied. 'I bought her when I retired, to keep me busy. She was in very bad condition. It has taken many hours and many thousands of euros to restore her.'

'You've done a beautiful job. I can tell it was a labour of love.'

He sipped at his coffee. 'These older boats need to be treated with care and respect. They need a gentle touch from someone who has skill and patience and knows what they are doing. The newer boats are okay, but they have no character, no story.' He looked directly at her then. 'Like women. They become rarer and more unique and, in my opinion, more beautiful as they age.'

The coffee evaporated in Heather's mouth. Was this the beginning of the 'seduction'? When the wind came around and fanned her flaming face, she was grateful for the cool breeze.

'And they become much wiser,' she added firmly.

'Exactly. There is no fooling *Athena*.'

Something caught her eye beyond his shoulder. An island, looming straight ahead.

Ithaca.

Dennis ordered her to take the helm while he reefed in the sails. The wind had died, and for the past half an hour they'd been barely making three knots. 'We will motor the rest of the way, otherwise we will not make it back in time. Don't worry, when we return this afternoon, the wind will be much stronger and we will have a good sail.'

It was difficult to have much of a conversation over the din of the engine. Heather stood beside Dennis as he steered. She noticed a small brass plaque above the dashboard bearing the name of the shipwright and the year the boat was built.

Heather and *Athena* were the same age. From then on, Heather couldn't help but watch the way Dennis handled her, the way his strong broad hands stroked the polished wooden wheel, how he caressed her timbers. It was as though he were making love to this boat.

Heather tried to concentrate on the orders he gave her as they approached a small bay on the north-west corner of the island. Unhitch the anchor, pull in the small inflatable dinghy that had trailed behind them, and keep an eye out for swimmers in the water. The pale blue-green sea was so clear she could see the bottom. The depth finder told her there was still ten metres below the keel. Fish darted about the boat. A young woman in a bikini floated by at a safe distance on a pink inflatable li-lo.

Before she knew it, the anchor was down, the engine silent. Dennis held the dinghy close to the boat for her to climb in. Hiking boots in one hand, daypack over the other shoulder and hat – still a little worse for wear after its dunking at the marina – perched on her head, Heather lowered herself into the smaller boat. Dennis joined her, cast off from *Athena*'s gently rounded stern, and took out the oars. Every action was well-practised and performed with frightening efficiency.

'Put your legs between mine,' he instructed as he began to pull on the oars.

The dinghy was tiny and skin to skin contact was unavoidable. She had spent her life touching other people's bodies, probing their most private parts, without a second thought. Now she felt every millimetre of contact between her bare leg and Dennis's.

In his hands, the oars made light work of the short distance to the jetty where he secured the dinghy and helped her out.

Heather swore the jetty was moving even though it was made of solid concrete. If he felt the same motion, it didn't register on his face.

The beach, made of pale pebbles and sand, looked inviting and Heather could easily have been persuaded to eat a leisurely lunch in one of the bougainvillea-covered tavernas that lined the narrow bay, and later collapse onto the warm sand for a nap. She could do that any time in the endless weeks to come if she chose to. As Jeffrey had pointed out, there were sandier beaches elsewhere in the Mediterranean. None of them were overlooked by hills containing so much history, however. It struck her that this might have been the very place that Odysseus set sail from, and eventually returned to. Dennis strode ahead. He stopped outside a small, whitewashed house to talk to an old man who was sitting in a ladder-backed wooden chair watching the world go by.

'Eh, Georgios!' he called to a younger man, Dennis's age, who emerged from inside the house.

After a brief exchange and much macho back-slapping, Dennis took charge of a small motorbike and climbed astride. He started the engine and revved a couple of times until he was satisfied.

'Come on,' he said, wriggling forward on the narrow seat to make room for Heather.

On the back of a motorbike? With no helmet? Doctor Heather was appalled. Gap Year Heather said, 'Hell, yeah!' and clambered on. She barely had time to link her arms around Dennis's waist, Esme nestled safely between them in Heather's bag, before they were off with a skid of dirt. Dennis waved to the old man and Georgios.

Heather had never been on a motorbike before. She'd made her daughters promise never to accept a lift on one. Memories of mashed brains and splintered limbs from her days in casualty had made her wary. Yet here she was, clinging to the muscled torso of a virtual stranger, racing along a foreign road covered in loose stones, leaning into blind bends, with the wind flying through her bad-ass hair.

Winding up from the beach, the road opened into a small town square. Dennis parked the motorbike under the shade of a large tree. He offered his hand and helped her off. Dennis was more of a gentleman than any Englishman. Overhead, sparrows tweeted, and a white butterfly hovered around her head. Heather's arms were aching from holding on. She shook them back to life.

Dennis led the way to a newish-looking grey bust mounted on a stone plinth. 'Meet Odysseus,' he said triumphantly.

Heather regarded the statue sceptically. No one knew what Odysseus looked like, or whether he'd existed at all. Her only frame of reference was a vague memory of Kirk Douglas in the 1954 movie *Ulysses*. Both were equally disappointing, the film too old-fashioned and the sculpture too modern. She preferred the version her imagination had already created from Homer's epithets. Resourceful, cunning, great-hearted Odysseus; tactician, mastermind of war, and a man of many twists and turns.

Registering her flat response to the face of the famous Bronze Age hero, Dennis led her to a wooden shelter that housed a small outdoor exhibition. He pointed to a display case housing a scaled down model of Odysseus's palace. Like the bust, the reconstruction bore little resemblance to the image she'd formed in her mind.

'There is a museum too,' said Dennis, eagerly. 'Some artefacts found in a cave near here. The Cave of the Nymphs. We can visit on the way back if you like.'

Heather nodded. She wondered how many times he'd played tour guide to women like her.

In the town square, they passed a butterscotch-coloured church topped with terracotta domes.

'Saint Sotiris,' said Dennis. 'In August there is a religious festival here. For two days and two nights, the whole island comes to eat, drink and dance.'

The closest thing St Luke's Parish Church could manage was midnight mass on Christmas Eve after The Four Candles kicked the rugby club out. She thought about the jolly bell-ringers and their secret stash of sherry and shortbread in the belltower. If she hadn't decided to come here, she might have been tempted to sign up.

'Come on,' said Dennis, starting the motorbike again. 'A little further up here, then we walk up to the palace.'

This time, as Heather hung on to his back, she shamelessly sniffed his shirt. A brand of washing powder she didn't recognise, a musky aftershave, and a hint of sweat. It was already hot, at least thirty degrees she guessed, and the cotton clung to his damp back. A frisson of excitement travelled through her arms, down her body and this time into the hot saddle of the motorbike between her legs. The motorbike juddered over a pothole in the road and Heather smiled.

24

Ruined

THEY STOPPED AT A SIGN THAT READ, *ARCHAEOLOGICAL SITE*. 'School of Homer'. Heather pondered the use of quotation marks and the inauspicious entrance to a place of such historical significance. Undaunted, Dennis led the way up the steps and along a rough and rocky path. There were a few helpful yellow signs bearing arrows that marked the route. Heather's incongruously new hiking boots were about to get their first real outing.

The climb was hot despite the intermittent relief of shade from wind-twisted olive trees. Esme was heavy in her bag, but this was the one place she wouldn't want to miss out on. Heather was grateful every time Dennis paused to point out the local flora and fauna. A bee, legs heavy with pollen, hovered lazily on a bush while she took a drink from her water bottle. The only sounds to break the ever-present hum of the cicadas were the crunch of their footsteps and the occasional clinking bell of an unseen goat. The air, heavy and scented with wild sage, was sauna hot. By the time they reached the site, Heather's thighs were shaking and her chest burning. Walking Stan around Netherwood hadn't exactly prepared her for this. She only hoped the effort had been worth it and that she was about to find the reality in the ancient myth.

Heather wasn't sure what she'd been expecting. Not an actual palace, obviously. Perhaps something like Pompeii, with carefully excavated ruins, helpful tour guides and plenty of photo opportunities. Not piles of stones, with anything vaguely resembling a building looking as if it dated from three hundred years ago rather than three thousand. Far from the frenetic activity of archaeologists busy uncovering the secrets of the ancient Mycenaean world and the palace that had supposedly stood on this spot, the site was deserted. She and Dennis were apparently the only people foolish enough to venture up here in this heat.

The panoramic view from the top of the site was spectacular, however, spanning three different bays including the one where *Athena* drifted in a leisurely circle around her anchor chain. The rocky hillside was sown with low bushes and long brown grasses, with occasional taller pine or cypress trees stretching up towards the brilliant midday sky. It was a wild and rugged landscape, so different to the lush green hills and wooded areas around Netherwood. And perhaps its beauty lay in its history, in myth and imagination, rather than something to decorate postcards.

'What do you think?' Dennis stood with his hands on his hips, his face animated with boyish enthusiasm.

'It's a very powerful place. You can feel the history, can't you? I mean, there's not much left to see, obviously, but with a little imagination, I could see Penelope gazing out to sea, waiting for her husband. It must have been hard for her, being left alone to raise her son virtually single-handed,' Heather mused, running her fingers through the fine leaves of a gorse bush.

Dennis's grin fell away, and he looked at the ground.

'I'm sorry. I shouldn't have said that.'

'You are only saying what is true,' he said. 'The navy was not very suitable for family life. My wife,' he stopped and corrected himself, 'my ex-wife, did a fantastic job as a parent. Our kids have grown into kind, hard-working adults. I am very proud of them. I am less proud of myself.'

She said simply, 'It must have been very hard for you both.' It was best to let people tell their stories, in their own way, in their own time.

'The hardest part is that my wife waited until I retired to ask for a divorce. I think she was so used to being on her own when I was away at sea. She could not adjust to me being at home all the time. We had to face the problems that we had hidden our whole marriage, the things that it was easy to ignore when I was away working.'

'You're not alone,' said Heather, briefly touching his arm in comfort. 'I've heard there is a big spike in divorce among couples in their sixties, after they retire. For women who have stayed at home to care for children it must be hard to adjust to suddenly having their husband around all the time.'

He shrugged. They walked around the site together, looking at the rubble. They peered down a disused well, inside a tunnel and stared up at an abandoned staircase. Heather took several photos on her phone, making sure that Dennis wasn't in any of them. He offered to take a shot of her standing on a ruined wall, but she declined. She would trust her memory instead.

Dennis told her that the government didn't have the money to fund more excavations. The economic situation in Greece was very dire, he explained, and reasoned that what money they did have was rightly spent on taking care of its citizens in the present day, rather than trying to uncover the mythical story of their ancestors.

'And, of course, Greece is taking in so many refugees and asylum seekers who arrive by boat,' Heather said, offering him her water bottle. 'That must be a burden for the authorities.'

Dennis's whole demeanour changed. He handed the water bottle back without drinking.

'We should be going,' he said coldly. 'It is a long sail back to Argostoli.'

He walked away without waiting for her response. What had she said? What raw nerve had she touched?

'Dennis, wait,' she called after him, stumbling over the uneven ground to keep up with his ranging stride. 'Wait!'

Her water bottle rattled in her bag and Esme was heavier than ever. Sweat dripped down her neck and into her cleavage. At least it was all downhill from here. She only hoped the museum Dennis had talked about was air-conditioned. She ploughed on, Dennis's back retreating further and further down the track.

Later, she recalled the sensation of her foot sliding on a loose stone, followed by the explosion of pain in her ankle as her weight turned it into an unnatural fulcrum. Whether she heard a crack, or felt it viscerally, she wasn't sure. The next thing Heather remembered was the brown dust rising to meet her and the heaviness of her body colliding with the earth. Then, all she could think about was the pain.

Dennis was beside her in seconds, concern written all over his face. He must have heard her fall. Had she screamed? She didn't remember. Hot tears of pain and anger at her own stupidity scorched her eyes. Dennis squatted and helped her remove her hiking boot, as gently as if he was defusing a bomb. Indeed, it looked as if the bomb had already gone off beneath her skin. Her ankle swelled before her eyes, and she could almost see blood seeping from the frayed ends of the ligaments beneath her skin. Her ankle sent unambiguous signals to her brain, demanding she lie still.

'Are you okay?' Dennis asked, holding her foot.

'I think so. Damn ankle.'

'We need to get you to a doctor.'

Heather managed a wry chuckle. 'I am a doctor.'

He studied her intently. The sign of a new respect or, more likely, disbelief that a clumsy clot like her could be responsible for actual human lives.

She palpated the bones around her own ankle and, finding none of them tender, sighed in relief. 'It's a sprain,' she said. 'Anterior talo-fibular ligament most likely. No bones broken.'

'Are you sure?'

She half smiled. 'Would I dare to tell you how to plot a course?'

He raised his hands in surrender, and relief. 'Okay, you know your job.'

They sat for a while, working out what to do. It was another half a kilometre or so back to the road and the motorbike. They dismissed the idea of Dennis fetching the motorbike on the grounds that one accident was enough for today.

'See if you can stand,' he said, helping her up and throwing the strap of her bag over his shoulder. It was then that Heather noticed the small pile of pale grey ash where the bag – and presumably the urn inside – had spilled open. Hopefully, the rest of Esme would stay in the bag, and she could return her to her urn later. She was in too much pain to explain. Part of Esme would remain on this hillside forever. There were worse places.

It was soon obvious that Heather wouldn't be able to walk down the rest of the path; she could hardly put weight on her foot and the ground was so uneven. She felt the wetness of tears turning the dirt on her cheeks to mud. Stupid tears. What must she look like? This was her punishment, her karma. If she didn't believe in the wrath of the vengeful gods before, she certainly did now. They were having a laugh at her expense, and it was no less than she deserved. It served her right for being so reckless, for not thinking through every possible complication and consequence. This was what she got for believing in fairytales, for not overthinking the situation, for being spontaneous.

Dennis turned his back to her and widened his stance. 'Get on,' he instructed, waving his hands at his sides.

'Don't be ridiculous! You can't carry me all the way down.'

'Do you have a better idea?'

She didn't.

It was slow progress on Dennis's back. He wasn't a young man, and even though she'd ridiculously breathed in to make herself lighter, every step he took felt more laboured. When she suggested they take a break and she try to walk the last part of the track, he simply held tighter around her knees, fists clenched against his sides.

'Relax,' he ordered. 'It's easier if you relax your muscles.'

Going against everything her instinct was telling her, she consciously loosened her muscles and leaned into his solid back and broad shoulders. *Trapezius. Latissimus dorsi. Rhomboids.*

'That's better,' he said.

Finally, they reached the road, attracting a quizzical look from a young couple who were just setting out on the track. The couple smiled, as if judging this a romantic gesture, a husband carrying his exhausted wife.

Heather offered Dennis the rest of the water in her bottle, which wasn't much. He refused more than a mouthful and insisted she drink what remained.

'I'm sorry,' she said.

'What for?'

'For being such an idiot.'

He pointed to her ankle. 'That,' he said, 'has nothing to do with intelligence. Some things cannot be helped. I am the one who should be sorry. There isn't time for the museum, and we will have to sail hard to make it back before it gets dark.' He looked out to sea where white caps were forming, the horizon now hazy.

Heather's hip also hurt from the fall and her lower back was starting to stiffen. She climbed gingerly onto the motorbike. Dennis rode slowly down the mountain, through the village and back to the jetty where he delivered her straight to the dinghy before returning the motorbike to Georgios.

'He's a good friend of yours?'

'Georgios? We were at university in Athens together.'

It hadn't crossed her mind that he might have been to university. 'What did you study?'

'Mathematics.'

Why should she be surprised? He looked as much a mathematician as presumably she did a doctor. She let him concentrate on rowing back to the boat. Was he angry at her, or did he not like talking about his past? He was so different to the jovial, hospitable man she'd met the previous day. Something had upset him, and it had happened before she sprained her stupid ankle.

With a comical combination of clambering and shuffling on her backside, Heather managed to scramble back aboard *Athena*. The boat, having waited patiently at anchor in the bay while they explored the ruins, now felt more solid than the ground that had given way under her hiking boots. Dennis insisted she raise her leg on a tower of folded towels and filled a plastic bag with ice from the fridge in the galley. No sooner had the engine started, the anchor was raised and safely stowed in its locker, and they were heading out of the bay into the wind. He was clearly used to handling the boat single-handed. The sails were up in minutes, the mainsail straining to contain the steady north-westerly wind. Soon, Ithaca disappeared from view, and they were in open water, hugging the north coast of Cephalonia.

'Is that a navy emblem?' Heather pointed to a blue and white coat of arms screwed onto the bulkhead at the top of the steps down to the cabin. She hadn't noticed it before. There was very little decoration or ornamentation on the boat, so this must be significant.

'Yes, it is the seal of the Hellenic Navy. If you look you can see an anchor in front of a Christian cross, signifying Greek Orthodoxy, and a trident, symbolising Poseidon, god of the sea. He supported the Greeks against the Trojans in the Trojan War.'

'But he wasn't so kind to Odysseus, was he?'

Dennis laughed. It was good to see the strain leave his face again. 'No, after Odysseus blinded his son Polyphemus, he did everything he could to stop him getting back to Ithaca. Storms, shipwrecks. Yes, he really wanted revenge.'

'And what does the writing across the top of the seal say? Is it a motto?'

Dennis traced the Greek letters with his finger. Μέγα τὸ τῆς θαλάσσης κράτος. 'It comes from Thucydides' account of Pericles's oration on the eve of the Peloponnesian War. It means something like "The rule of the sea is a great matter".'

'Pericles? He of the famous funeral oration?'

'You know him?'

'In a way.'

She thought of Alan's retirement speech, how she'd denied him his valediction. Imagine if Pericles's wife had told him to shut up because he was boring everyone. She felt ashamed now, picturing Alan's crestfallen face. Perhaps she had been too harsh on him. She'd stopped listening to him long before his speech. They'd stopped listening to each other.

25

Based on a true myth

DENNIS CALLED A TAXI TO TAKE HEATHER BACK TO HER hotel. Judging by the backslapping banter, the taxi driver was another of his friends or relatives. The driver, Stavros, who was a good deal older than Dennis, looked as though he'd borrowed his moustache from a 1970s porn star. But he seemed friendly and took great pains to make sure Heather was delivered safely. He refused to accept payment of any kind for the trip, saying in broken English that any friend of Dennis was a friend of his. More Greek hospitality.

After suffering the indignity of hobbling up to her room on the shoulder of the concierge, Heather collapsed onto her bed. Sore, sunburnt and ashamed that she had spoilt the day Dennis had so generously planned, she closed her eyes and moaned self-pityingly for a while. Her ankle had stopped swelling, but the skin was variegated in livid violets and purples. It throbbed in time to the pulsing pain in her head.

Shuffling to the edge of the bed, she reached for her bag. Mumbling an apology for her dereliction of duty, she scooped what was left of Esme back into the urn.

'Go on then,' she said. 'Let's get the I-told-you-so's over with.'

Esme said everything she needed to without uttering a single word.

'You were the one who encouraged me,' said Heather irritably. She tossed and turned on the bed, unable to settle. She traced the Tree of Life motif searching for clues in the cypher.

'Do you think I should phone Alan and tell him everything? Get him to medevac me back to Netherwood?'

What would she be confessing exactly? Nothing untoward had happened between her and Dennis. She'd made it clear she didn't want sex and, slightly disappointingly, he'd respected all her boundaries. It would have been nice to kiss him, having only ever kissed one man in her life. She'd always assumed Alan was a good kisser. What if he was a terrible kisser? She'd never know. There was no evidence to support the theory, none to disprove it. To test the hypothesis that her husband was indeed a good kisser, she'd need to run the gold standard in medical research, a randomised controlled trial. She couldn't do that with a sample size of one. She needed a control group. The problem was that she was unlikely to see her control subject ever again after today. Assuming Dennis hadn't already dropped dead from a heart attack after lugging her down the hill, he would see her for the sad sack she was and avoid her at all costs. Heather would go back to being invisible and the natural order would be restored once more.

It was getting late by the time Heather realised how hungry she was. Room service had finished. Lowering herself to the floor, she commando-crawled over to the minibar and helped herself to a bar of chocolate and a bottle of retsina.

'It's medicinal,' she told Esme. 'I'm self-prescribing a few hours of complete oblivion. And it's another item crossed off my bucket list.'

She could almost hear Esme's reply, that according to William Osler, 'A physician who treats himself has a fool for a patient'.

Heather hobbled back to bed with her glass and checked the messages on her phone.

Three missed calls. One from Alan, two from Sarah.

A text from Tilly, *Dad has news*, accompanied by a cabbage emoji and a laughing face.

She wondered how all those gap year kids and their parents had managed in the pre-mobile days. Was being contactable but unreachable worse than being completely uncontactable in the first place?

She phoned Sarah first, hoping, praying that Alan's news was the news they'd all been waiting for. She wanted to hear it from her daughter first.

'Hi Mum,' Sarah said when she answered her mobile. 'Are you all right?'

Why wouldn't she be?

'I'm fine.' Heather kept her answers brief in case Sarah could tell she'd been drinking.

'I was worried about you.'

In that moment, Heather felt something shift. The river of concern had started to flow back upstream. Sarah was worrying about her for a change, but Heather felt the weight of guilt rather than relief.

'Dad said your horse bolted and tried to drown you.'

'It was quite funny, now I look back,' said Heather.

'You need to be careful at your age, Mum.'

Thank goodness Sarah hadn't seen her mother on the back of that motorbike, without a helmet, hadn't been there to say, 'Wait a minute, who is this bloke?'

'There is no need for you to worry about me, darling, I am perfectly safe here. As you've so kindly pointed out, I am of an age when I can look after myself.'

'I know. You're a strong, independent and frighteningly capable woman,' said Sarah. 'I think that's why I worry about you so much. That's why you need to be careful.'

Heather didn't understand. She steered the conversation back to Sarah. She was fine. Ravi was fine. The whole of England was apparently fine without her.

'Promise me you'll phone Dad,' said Sarah.

'Is he all right?'

There was a pause. 'He's missing you, Mum.'

Not enough to come and join me though, Heather thought. 'I'm surprised he's even noticed I've gone. What with the vegetables and the hens, and Kevin.'

'Sometimes I want to bang both your heads together. You're both as stubborn as each other. Once you get an idea in your head, that's it. Neither of you will give in.'

'Would you prefer I was a Stepford wife? One who'd stayed at home to mind the house and raise the kids while my husband went out and furthered his career?'

Why were they having this conversation now? She had always assumed Sarah was on her side, supported her choices.

But what if this was years of accumulated resentment talking? What if, having been virtually brought up by Mrs Gee, she was unleashing on her mother because, once again, she was off chasing her own selfish desires?

Sarah sighed heavily into the phone. 'I'm not saying that at all. I'm merely pointing out that you are so evenly matched that you are perfect for each other, and also the worst two people to be married to each other.'

Evenly matched. Like Penelope and Odysseus.

'There is nothing for you to worry about, Sarah. Your dad and I are fine. Our marriage is fine. But right now we want different things, that's all. Once we both get this out of our systems, it will be business as usual.'

Heather was eventually able to pacify Sarah. But the words that had come from her own mouth were left lingering in the air, like the fumes from the refuse lorry that had paused below her open window. *Business as usual*. She had no idea how this would all end. One thing she knew for sure was that she could never go back to business as usual with Alan.

He answered the phone straight away.

'Did you get my voice message?' he asked.

'What message?'

'About my spinach.'

'No . . .'

'Kevin says he's never seen a green leafy vegetable like it. He reckons it could win a prize at the show.'

'Netherwood fete?'

'No, at Darlingford Horticultural Show.' He sounded as excited as if his spinach had scored a century at The Oval. 'And, he says my pumpkin seedlings have great potential. You should see them, Heather. They are quite impressive, even if I say it myself. Let's just say, Cinderella will go to the ball!'

Heather poured herself another glass of retsina and limped out onto her balcony. In the distance, away from the lights of the main promenade, she could see stars. Not many, but a few. The same stars would be shining down on Netherwood. She wondered why, surrounded by fields and countryside, she and Alan had never been outside this late and simply marvelled at the spectacular universe above their heads.

'That's amazing.'

'It is. Truly amazing. There's a miracle happening in our garden, Heather. Kevin reckons we'll produce far more than we can ever eat. He suggested going halves on a stall at the farmers' market selling the excess produce, but I'd prefer to do what Dad did and share it, run a fresh foodbank for anyone in the village who needs a little help. Dad always said there was something special about the soil. What a shame he's not here to see how it's thriving.'

His voice was thick with emotion.

'Are you all right, Alan?'

'Yes, I'm a bit choked up, that's all. It's not quite the same when there's nobody to share it with.'

'What about Tilly?'

'She's hardly here. I barely see her. It's just me and Stan.'

'Come on, it sounds as if you've been so busy you won't have had time to miss me.' The phone went silent. 'Do you miss me, Alan?'

She heard him take a deep breath. 'Of course. It goes without saying.'

'It always does.' She sighed.

'I miss you,' said Alan. 'There, I said it.'

'Enough to come and join me?'

He exhaled violently. Heather imagined him ploughing his hair with his fingers.

'Do you miss me enough to come home?'

Heather drained her retsina, grimacing at the taste. At least she knew where she stood in the grand scheme of things. Slightly below the pumpkins.

He hadn't understood her at all. He saw her trip as a nice little holiday. Something he would indulge her in while he got down to the serious business of single-handedly rescuing the village from scurvy. She imagined him bumping into someone he knew at the supermarket, lamenting the fact that his wife had run off to Greece with an urn of ashes. Cue the sympathetic head tilts, the casseroles left by the front door. It wouldn't be long before the 'we hate the thought of you being on your own' dinner invitations turned into invitations to 'meet our newly single friend June, whose husband ran off with his trichologist'.

'What did you do today?' Alan asked.

'I sailed over to the island of Ithaca to look around the ruins of Odysseus's palace.' The ease with which she withheld the whole truth shocked Heather.

'Most unlikely,' he said. She could almost hear Alan's sneer down the phone. 'I think you'll find that the Ithaca Homer refers to is not real, it's a mythical place.'

'But I've been there, Alan. It was real.'

He laughed down the phone. 'No one knows where it really is, or whether Homer as a person even existed at all. Scholars have been arguing about it for years, claiming he is referring to everywhere from Corfu to Sicily. Someone even made a case for Denmark. If you read *The Odyssey* and compare the geographical references to modern-day Ithaca, the place you visited today can't possibly be the island that Odysseus returned to.'

Heather was speechless, her Homeric bubble well and truly burst. And yet she couldn't deny that something hadn't felt quite right about the ruins Dennis had taken her to.

'I saw it with my own eyes, Alan. There were official signs everywhere.'

'Don't be naïve, Heather. The government and the locals want you to believe it. To sell you a fantasy. It's in their interests to keep the tourists coming.'

And yet, there hadn't been any tourists around, as if modern Ithaca wanted to keep its history a secret, to remain unspoilt and uncommercialised. If anything, that was even more reason to accept the unprovable myth. To believe that Dennis could well be descended from the Ancient Greek hero himself. What did she *want* to believe? The romantic illusion or Alan's cold, pragmatic reality?

The call fizzled out, Alan and Heather claiming simultaneously that they had to go. Where either of them had to be that late at night wasn't the issue. How typical of Alan to rain on her parade. How typical of her to dig her heels in. How typical that they had never, ever had a blazing row about anything, that their disagreements always ended like this, unresolved. No wonder the passion had died.

26

The devil and the deep blue sea

Her first thought was how she could get an urgent MRI scan. Not of her ankle, which overnight had defied even her most pessimistic predictions, but of her brain. Headache, nausea and vertigo, severe enough that she could barely raise her head from the pillow. She'd suffered a cerebellar stroke, or had a brain tumour, until proven otherwise. Then she saw the empty bottle of retsina on the table, and the single glass.

She'd slept through breakfast. At least she wouldn't have to face Pat and Jeffrey. Heather wondered if The Poseidon's bar was open yet. Only the pure ethanol in a bloody Mary would counteract the effects of the methanol that her liver was currently breaking down into formaldehyde, the very preservative that had kept her and Alan's student cadaver Fred from decomposing. One call to the local medical school and she could donate her body to science and be done with it.

Heather had never been very good at hangovers. Which was why she'd gone out of her way to avoid them, preaching moderation to her patients, who largely ignored her advice. Today, she had a fool for a patient, indeed.

A quick glance under the sheets told her all she needed to know about her ankle, even before she tried to hobble to the bathroom. She was momentarily distracted from the pain by the memory of being carried down a mountain by Dennis, and the conversation with Alan that had pushed her over the edge and sinking to the bottom of a bottle of what had tasted like turpentine.

After a shower and a handful of paracetamol, Heather felt marginally better. Enough to decide that she couldn't spend all day in this room feeling sorry for herself. If she was going to wallow in self-pity, she might as well do it at the beach, since she was in Greece and only minutes away from some of the world's most picturesque beaches. According to Alan, nursing a hangover on the beach was what gap years were all about.

She changed into her swimsuit, threw a loose dress over the top, grabbed her bag and hat. She was testing her weight on her ankle when there was a knock on the door. Half-a-dozen heavy hops and she'd reached the other side of the room. Leaning against the wall for support, she opened the door.

'Good morning, Mrs Heather,' said a young woman. 'These are for you.'

The woman, wearing the uniform of a receptionist, was holding a large flower arrangement, the colours of which were so vivid they hurt Heather's eyes: indigo blue irises, mauve anemones, magenta gladioli, and a spray of tiny blue star-shaped flowers the colour of the morning sky.

'For me?'

'Yes, they arrived a few minutes ago. A man dropped them off.'

'What kind of a man?'

The receptionist shrugged. 'A Greek man.'

Heather examined the hand-tied bouquet for a card or message. She wanted to ask what the man who'd delivered the flowers had looked like. Had he been a generic courier or an older, ex-navy type with excellent knees? But the woman had already gone. Heather hobbled back inside and searched for anything resembling a vase in her hotel room. The only suitable receptacle, besides Esme's urn, was the water jug. It would have to do.

She untied the string around the stems and arranged the flowers with a swelling unease. Who had sent them? Alan, as a gesture of his affection and, possibly, an apology? Or Dennis?

Alan wasn't known for his generosity on the floral front. They simply weren't part of his repertoire except to acknowledge the hours of agony she'd endured giving birth to each of his two children. He'd also sent a bunch to the attractive midwife who'd delivered Tilly, something he insisted was by way of an apology for the noise Heather had made in labour.

But what if this unexpected gesture was his way of reaching out to her? It was impossible to know without asking him. If they weren't from Alan, he would have a very valid concern that another man was sending flowers to his wife. But what if they were and she didn't thank him?

'Any ideas?' Heather asked Esme.

The Tree of Life was facing the arrangement as if admiring the display. Esme had always loved flowers. After Aubrey died, she had done her best to look after his beloved garden. Heather could still smell the honeysuckle growing around the front door of the Clarks' immaculate cottage that always featured in postcards of the village. She could still picture the masses of lavender, geraniums and hydrangeas that filled the flower beds, and hear the bees that buzzed between them. In the end it had outgrown Esme's valiant efforts. She sold the house and moved into The Willows. The new owners had concreted over the flower beds and now parked their cars on the spot where Aubrey had taken his final breath.

Unable to decide what to do about the flowers, Heather decided to do nothing. She caught a taxi the short distance to the beach, hobbled across the hot sandy pebbles and flopped down onto a spare sun lounger. She was relieved to be horizontal again, and grateful that she still had enough alcohol in her bloodstream to numb the pain from her ankle. After paying the attendant, she slathered herself in factor 50, and settled into her book. Odysseus had finally landed back on Ithaca, disguised as a beggar to test Penelope.

It wasn't long before Heather felt the first twinges of hunger. She looked around for a waiter and caught the eye of a young man. She ushered him over and ordered a virgin Mary, and a toasted cheese and ham sandwich. It was only when he started to laugh that she recognised him, not as a roaming Greek waiter, but as the young backpacker from the flight. He introduced himself as James and was so entertained by the mix-up that he volunteered to go to the bar for her, returning minutes later with her drink, and after a quick trip to the local cafe, her sandwich. They each apologised for not recognising the other at first, then chatted like old friends. He was taking a year off to travel before starting a law degree. He'd been working at a pub and saving up for months. When he asked her if she was enjoying her holiday, Heather admitted that she was doing the same as him, taking a year off.

He thought about it for a moment. 'That is sick,' he said. 'You are sick.'

She gathered that was a good thing.

How much easier it was to meet people away from home. She thought about Alan spending his gap year chasing girls, and how if she was eighteen instead of sixty-seven, she might choose to hang out with James and his friends. They would visit the local bars and clubs, and perhaps travel together for a while, catching the same ferry to the next island, going wherever the whim took her. Heather saw how this year off could change a young person's mind, broaden their horizons, reset their goals and, in some cases, make them question their entire future. It was easy to believe that anything was possible, that the world really was their oyster. Perhaps that's why it was so much easier to do before you gathered responsibilities. When home was so much easier to leave.

After a while, James noticed an attractive young woman sitting alone on another lounger and excused himself saying it was good to 'catch up'. Heather drained the dregs of the spicy tomato juice, crunched through the celery garnish, and devoured the toasted sandwich. Back on Ithaca, Odysseus had bumped into his son Telemachus who he hadn't seen since he was a baby, and between them they hatched a plan to massacre the suitors. It wasn't what usually happened when long-lost family were reunited on shows like *Who Do You Think You Are?* but she wouldn't let that spoil her enjoyment of the story. Every family had its tensions.

Her phone beeped with a message. It was hard to read the screen in the sun's glare. Under the shade of her towel, she saw the message was from a number she didn't recognise. The number began with +30. It was a Greek phone number.

How is your uncle?

She smiled. His English was excellent. Google translate, less so. Before they'd sailed to Ithaca, they'd exchanged numbers in the good old-fashioned way on pieces of paper, in case plans changed and they'd needed to contact each other. Giving her number to a stranger had been a gamble. She'd reassured herself it would be easy enough to block him if he turned weird. Easy enough to remove him from her contacts before she went home.

Heather typed her reply.

My uncle has dementia and lives in a nursing home near Brighton.

The dancing dots indicated he was typing something, then disappeared. She'd lost him.

But I am pleased to report that my ankle is much better today!

A complete lie, but she was English and there was only ever one acceptable answer to a query about her health. Should she ask him about the flowers? He'd told her his daughter was a florist but that didn't prove anything. She typed a flower emoji and *Thank you.* That would do it. A thank you for the flowers if they were from him, and a thank you for asking about her ankle if they weren't. Feeling pleased with her cunning, she waited for a reply. Nothing.

A few moments later, she checked her phone again. Still nothing. And nothing from Alan either. The sun had moved round and was burning her feet. She covered them with her dress and returned to where Argos, the old dog, who had been waiting all this time for his master to return, was lying in a dung heap. Recognising Odysseus when he eventually reached the palace, he licked his master's hand, wagged his tail one last time and promptly died.

Heather slammed the book shut, hand over her mouth. She couldn't read any more. Images of Stan, his spine arched with age, made her chest ache.

Stan.

Neither she nor Alan could have imagined that the cute bundle of fluff they'd brought home in a cardboard box to fill the void after the girls left home would one day grow into Netherwood's tallest dog. Scratched furniture and chewed human footwear aside, what had surprised them most was how the scruffy hound could read the prevailing mood and bring comfort after even the most taxing of days with a simple wag of his wiry tail. Stan was the common language they both spoke, using a special voice that seemed to suit him. He was the glue that bound them, the conversation starter when they were both too weary to speak. Heather missed him. A tiny piece of her wondered if she missed her dog more than her husband.

Ping.

A new message appeared. From the same Greek number. The gist of his broken English was that he wanted to make up for the less than perfect end to the Homer's School visit by taking her to the most beautiful place in the world.

The exchange continued. The catch was that it was on the other side of Ithaca, more than a day trip away. He said he had to move *Athena* anyway because his friend who managed the marina needed the berth, and he was planning to sail her round to Sami, the main port on the east coast of Cephalonia. Dennis proposed that his taxi-driver friend Stavros pick her up from her hotel on Friday morning, by which stage he hoped her uncle would be fully well. In order to make it to the island and back in a day, Stavros would drive her to the harbour at Sami, a forty-minute drive away – thirty minutes if Stavros's wife was angry with him, he added with a gritted teeth emoji. What did she think?

A trip to see the most beautiful place in the world. How could she refuse an offer like that?

The phone screen was smudged with sunscreen and her finger shaking so much that Heather wasn't entirely sure what she'd typed in reply. Dennis responded with a winking emoji.

27

Sun, sea, sand and squid

THE MID-FLIGHT ANAPHYLAXIS, THE BOLTING HORSE, THE near-drowning behind the ski-boat, and the hair-raising ride on the back of the motorbike paled beside the white-knuckle journey to Sami. The seatbelts in Stavros's taxi had seen better days and Heather was glad she chose to sit in the back where she could splint herself into the brace position using the passenger headrest. Stavros insisted, in heavily accented English, that he knew a shortcut that would knock five minutes off the journey. The shortcut, through a field of pigs, knocked five years off Heather's lifespan.

Esme had insisted on coming along. Unfortunately, when Stavros swerved to avoid a goat on a bend, she slipped off the back seat and once again shed her flimsy lid, spilling ash into the footwell. Heather scooped up as much as she could. As well as on a historic hillside above the village of Stavros, part of Esme would be spending eternity riding around in the back of a taxi belonging to another Stavros. Heather had a feeling her friend wouldn't mind keeping this wrinkled but still ruggedly handsome Greek man company. As long as she didn't have a problem with moustaches.

Dennis was waiting at the dockside in blue shorts and a crisp white linen shirt, rolled up to the elbows. He looked as if he'd stepped out of a Ralph Lauren advert. His tanned and weathered skin were the only clues to his life in the outdoors, otherwise a casual observer would think him a wealthy weekend sailor rather than someone who lived all year round on a boat.

Again, Stavros refused to take the crisp euros Heather tried to give him and helped her up the makeshift gangway Dennis had rigged for her. Heather tried not to limp. Although she could now bear some of her bodyweight on the ankle, she was relieved to sit on *Athena*'s padded bench seat while Stavros waited around to cast them off from the dockside.

'Shall I take this?' Dennis asked, picking up her bag. If he wondered why it was always so heavy, he didn't ask. In addition to an urn of ashes that, even after the spill, must still have weighed a couple of kilos, she'd brought a bottle of wine and a box of *loukoumádes*, a kind of delicious-looking deep-fried pastry ball garnished with honey, sesame seeds and dried fruit that the woman in the shop had told her were a traditional winner's reward during the Olympic Games in Ancient Greece.

Athena's engine wheezed and choked when Dennis turned the ignition key. He muttered something encouraging in Greek, then when his gentle coaxing didn't work, he checked under a hatch, flicked a few switches and tried again. She imagined him in command of a ship, speaking to the engine room and issuing orders to his sailors. Here, he was captain, chief engineer and coxswain.

Eventually, the engine sputtered to life and Dennis wasted no time in untying the mooring ropes and tossing them to Stavros who, despite his terrifying haste to get here, appeared in no hurry to leave again. As before, Dennis manoeuvred the boat with precision, avoiding the other yachts and fishing boats in the harbour. He resisted Heather's offers to take the wheel, insisting she must take things easy.

'We will motor to the head of the channel then put up the sail. We will aim to stay midway between the two islands, keeping Cephalonia on our port side and Ithaca on our starboard,' Dennis explained. 'A katabatic wind will arrive around midday. It is going to be strong. Maybe twenty to twenty-five knots. See.' He pointed to a thick blanket of cloud topping and tumbling over the mountains, like icing melting on a cake.

'That means we'll need less sail today, right?' Heather asked, remembering her sailing lessons from years ago.

'Exactly,' He beamed at her. 'Well done. But don't worry, we will miss the worst of the weather. Where we are going, it is very sheltered. Very calm.'

She imagined his crew had loved Dennis. He was patient and methodical. He knew and respected the sea.

He offered her the wheel, setting a wooden crate on its side for her to sit on. At the northern-most tip of the channel between the two islands, with open ocean and a steady north-westerly blowing, Dennis put up the mainsail. At first, *Athena* tossed and bucked against the wheel and Heather battled to keep her on course, refusing his offer to take over.

'Gently, gently. Don't fight the wind,' he said. 'You are not driving a rally car.'

Or a 1958 jalopy without power steering. Heather relaxed her arms. After a while, she was able to steer with the lightest of touches, letting the boat do the work.

'You are a natural sailor,' Dennis said, beaming.

She loved his smile. It was genuine and she had the sense that it had to be earned. He stood with one long leg up on the gunwale, balancing against the backstay that supported the mast. *Athena* was in her element, cutting through the Ionian waters with grace and purpose. Heather glanced down at the tanned hands on the wheel and barely recognised them as her own. The wind whipped her cotton dress around her knees and the sensation of air against her skin was deliciously cool after the oppressive heat on the land.

'Look!' shouted Dennis, clasping her by the shoulder and aiming her body towards the bow where a pod of dolphins was swimming alongside.

Heather's heart thrummed each time one of the sleek, dark bodies broke the surface before arcing back into the water. She counted four or five dolphins, some fully grown, some merely youngsters, leaping and diving under and across the bow of the boat, surfacing on the other side then disappearing again. They were playing, swimming with the boat for the sheer fun of it. Dennis took the wheel and urged her to shuffle forward for a better view. She ducked under the beam with its brimming mainsail, crawling across the deck on hands and knees until she could almost touch the dolphins. Before she even felt them build, tears of sheer joy blurred her vision. She wiped them away with the back of her hand.

'I must get my camera,' said Heather looking around for her bag.

'No,' Dennis said sharply. 'Don't look away, not even for a minute. Enjoy them while they are here. Soon they will be gone.'

She watched. No photo could ever do justice to the real-life experience of laying down a precious memory. She would never forget how she felt at this moment.

'Incredible, yes?' Dennis grinned. 'I never get bored of seeing them.'

There was nowhere else on the earth that Heather wanted to be. If only this could last forever.

'Dolphins are very intelligent and social animals,' Dennis explained. 'They have a brain that is much larger than they need to control their body's functions. And dolphins of all ages play, with toys and each other.'

'I think we sometimes forget how to have fun as we get older,' Heather said.

'Play is part of learning.'

'And it's never too late to learn,' Heather mused.

As quickly as they'd appeared, the dolphins were gone. Dennis fell silent and watchful again, into what Heather now recognised was some more troubled part of his head.

'Do you know that if a dolphin is injured the other dolphins will rescue it and help it swim to the surface rather than let it drown?'

'I didn't know that,' Heather admitted.

He said very little after that, concentrating on the tell-tales at the top of the mast. The soporific pitch and yaw of the boat made Heather drowsy. She lay down on the bench in the shade of the sails, staring at the horizon as it trembled in the heat.

She was almost asleep when Dennis turned *Athena* into the wind, reefed in her luffing sails and motored towards a sheltered bay on the north-east side of the island. She joined him back at the helm, her ankle better after the rest.

'Aim over there,' Dennis said, pointing to three towers now visible on the southern-most tip of the bay.

A gust of wind whipped Heather's dress then died again. The water was flat, changing from deep blue to bright green close to the shore, which was lined with pretty, white buildings with terracotta roofs. A dozen or so boats – charter yachts and fishing boats – were already tied up along the quay. As they came closer, Heather could see people sitting under the awnings at the tavernas along the waterfront.

Dennis didn't take *Athena* alongside as she had expected, but dropped her anchor before the water became too shallow. Heather had been dreading the climb into the dinghy. He already thought she was a clumsy oaf and she didn't want to make a fool of herself yet again. The shorts she'd worn to the School of Homer were filthy after her fall. The long dress was the only clean item of clothing left in her backpack. Very *Mamma Mia!* she'd thought. And, with hindsight, totally impractical for boating. The only way to get into the dinghy would be to hitch the long skirt up around her waist and avoid looking Dennis in the eye. But to her surprise, instead of pulling in the dinghy, Dennis made a call on his mobile, speaking in Greek.

When he'd hung up, he said simply, 'We wait.'

A few minutes later, Heather saw a small rowing boat heading out towards them from the shore. An old man was pushing at the oars, facing forwards rather than backwards. It looked like hard work.

'Why is he rowing backwards?' she asked. Or was it forwards?

Dennis shrugged, as if it was obvious. 'It is better when you are that age to look ahead at where you still have to go rather than to dwell on what is behind you.'

The man's face somehow reflected Dennis's wise words. Finally, alongside *Athena*'s fenders, he threw a rope to Dennis. They conversed in Greek and the old man gave Heather a knowing look, grinning at her with a mouthful of teeth that suggested he'd been chewing rocks. He gave a gravelly laugh and handed Dennis a white polystyrene cool box, followed by a shallow wooden crate containing tomatoes, a bunch of fresh basil and a loaf of bread. Heather nodded goodbye as Dennis cast him off again. The man gave her a final, slightly licentious grin as he floated away and took up the oars once more.

'Another friend of yours?'

'My cousin, Cosimo. He has a fishing boat here.'

'What was he saying about me?' Heather asked.

Dennis paused, the cool box in his hands. 'He said he hoped we enjoy our lunch.'

Heather suspected she wasn't the first woman Dennis had brought here. The whole routine seemed too well rehearsed to be a one-off. Still, as he'd said about the dolphins, enjoy it while it lasts. Rather than overthink the situation, she decided to create a delicious, secret memory that would keep her warm, and put a smile on her face in her old, old age.

When the engine eventually started again, Heather noticed a cloud of grey fumes rising from the boat's exhaust in the hull. The grey plume followed them as they motored out of the bay, heading north again. She didn't say anything but could tell from the expression in his eyebrows that Dennis had seen it too. They didn't travel far, around a headland, coming to a standstill deep into a deserted bay filled with emerald water. On three sides, steep cliffs rose from the rocky shore forming a natural amphitheatre. Finally, when Dennis was happy with the length of heavy anchor chain he'd let out, he disappeared down below to what Heather assumed was the engine bay. After ten minutes he still hadn't emerged. She thought about the Land Rover and how nostalgic Alan had been for a vehicle that would in time prove its liability more than its reliability.

Heather offered to make lunch. It was the least she could do while Dennis tinkered with *Athena*'s smoke-generating internals. She opened the polystyrene box, her eyes not wide enough to take in the spectacular array of seafood lying on a bed of ice. Squid, baby octopus, the largest prawns she'd ever seen, half-a-dozen tiny sardine-like fish, two giant lemons and a small bunch of fresh oregano.

Was all this for the two of them? She glanced around the tiny galley, at the tiny rings of the gas hob, and wondered how she was supposed to cook it all.

Dennis emerged from a hatch below the galley floor, wiping his hands on an oily rag.

'Problems?' Heather asked.

He shrugged. 'It's possible. The engine is original.'

The boat was closer to seventy years old than sixty. Her hull and decks might be immaculately kept, and her sails probably updated every few years, but her engine, her driving force, would be showing its age. How very like humans, Heather thought. Appearances could be deceiving. She'd known many patients who'd looked healthy and youthful, and dropped dead before their time. She'd known far more whose outward signs of decrepitude did not match the pristine internal organs that carried them well into old age.

'What would you like me to do?' Heather gestured to the open box.

'You can set the table,' he said handing her plates, two glasses, knives and forks.

He carried the box to a small barbecue attached to the handrail at the very back of the boat. She hadn't noticed the gas bottle hidden behind the row of perfectly coiled ropes and fenders. Soon, the grill was hot and the squid and octopus sizzling in olive oil. The sardines and prawns joined them, along with chopped garlic, salt and pepper, and a generous squeeze of lemon.

Sweating in the heat from the barbecue, Dennis lifted his shirt over his head and draped it over the railing. Heather tried not to look at his tanned body, tried to think about Alan instead. Alan's lovely smile, his kind eyes. Alan's revolting old dressing gown, the smell of kippers, and that tiny dribble of oil running into the cleft of his chin. She tried not to follow the trail of silvery hair from Dennis's chest, down his abdomen and beneath the waistband of his shorts. She tried not to imagine what was below.

But Heather didn't try hard enough. Instead, she thought about sex.

The thoughts collided inside Heather's brain. Unwelcome, inappropriate and naughty thoughts. What if Dennis was thinking about sex too? Why else would he have gone to so much trouble to create the perfect seduction scenario? To her embarrassment, Heather realised that she wanted sex. Really, *really* wanted sex. Not a cricket commentator fumble beneath John Lewis pyjamas, but proper hot, steamy, toe-curling, making-noises kind of sex, garnished with garlic, salt and pepper and a squeeze of lemon. She'd wondered if Greek couples found garlic breath off-putting. Was she about to find out for herself?

'I'm married,' she blurted, unable to contain her incontinent thoughts.

He gave her a lopsided smile. 'Congratulations,' he said, followed by, 'lunch is ready.'

Dennis flipped the octopus with a spatula and squeezed more lemon over it. The smell was extraordinary, and Heather hadn't realised how hungry she was. He'd lined up his prawns all facing the same way, like uniformed seamen at attention. He opened the wine and poured a glass each. At that moment, Dennis was the most perfect specimen of manhood on the entire planet. He was handsome, educated, charming and attentive. She was no Aphrodite. No Helen of Troy. He could easily attract a beautiful younger woman. Why had he brought her all the way here, to what she had to agree was quite possibly the most beautiful place in the world?

Perhaps he was channelling the notoriously unfaithful Zeus, a horny old goat who would have sex with anything and everything, including a size twelve mortal Englishwoman with lumpy thighs and bingo-wings, once he'd run out of nymphs and goddesses to ravish. *Athena* was the only boat in this private little bay. Heather realised that if she screamed, in pleasure or for help, nobody would hear her.

'Heather-like-the-bush?' Dennis frowned. He was holding a plate piled high with delicious seafood, garnished with sprigs of oregano. 'Is everything okay?'

'Yes. Everything is tickety-boo,' she replied, coining one of Alan's stock phrases. She refused to let guilt spoil this perfect moment. After all, he'd chosen his vegetables over her. She clinked Dennis's glass with hers. '*Yamas!*'

'Well-remembered.' Dennis held her gaze as he brought his glass to his lips.

If I only drink the one glass, then nothing bad will happen, Heather told herself. One glass and she could keep her wits about her. She'd been in far more dangerous situations than this in her career. Years ago, she'd thought nothing of driving alone to remote properties carrying diamorphine, essentially pharmaceutical heroin, in her medical bag. Once, while she was working on a psychiatric ward, she'd been attacked by a psychotic patient with a pool cue. She'd been groped and leered at; spat on and threatened by angry patients. She'd even had a stalker, an infatuated patient who'd sat in his parked car outside her house and declared his undying love for her in a series of ever more disturbing letters. When he'd signed the last one in his own blood, she'd called the police.

Okay, two glasses. No more than two. This was so idyllic; she couldn't let it end. The scented air was still but not oppressive. The water licking *Athena*'s hull was as clear as a bath. Swallows with tails shaped like scissors cut through the air above the rocky cliffs where the cicadas were engaging in a full-on chorus. She wouldn't feel guilty for enjoying this moment. Surely everyone was allowed one perfect day.

'This is delicious, Dennis.' Heather peeled another prawn, discarded the empty shell and head into a bowl. Tried not to think about the last time she and Alan had made love. 'Where did you learn to cook like this?'

'My father and his brother owned a restaurant. My mother used to do the cooking. I spent a lot of time in the kitchen, watching.'

'So, your father wasn't a navy man?'

Dennis shook his head. 'I think he expected me to take over the restaurant. I went away to sea instead. He never said it to my face, but I think he was disappointed. So many people left these islands after the earthquake in 1953. It was only the old people left behind, and tourists of course.'

'But you are back now.'

'Not for long. I will leave again soon.'

'Where will you go?'

'Not far unless I can fix the engine.' He laughed. 'Don't worry, we have wind and sail so I will return you safely before dark,' he added, as if able to read her thoughts.

'Where would you *like* to go?'

He gazed past her, out to sea. 'Where the wind takes me. There is nowhere I need to be. No one to answer to. I can please myself.'

'It sounds perfect,' she said, the thought turning into words before she had time to stop it.

'Come with me,' he said, sitting up straight.

'What?'

'Exactly what I said. Come with me.'

'I can't,' said Heather, aghast.

'Why not?'

'I'm married.'

He tilted his head as if to say, 'And yet here you are'.

She put her knife and fork together on the plate and stood up. Sensible Heather was impatient to clear the table and return to normality. To safety.

'I'm sorry,' he said, looking pained.

'No, I'm sorry,' Heather countered. 'I am sorry if I have given you the wrong impression. I am not looking for a holiday fling. I am old enough to know better.'

'Wait, Heather-like-the-bush.' He stood too. 'Please, let us enjoy this day. Forgive me for wanting to spend more time with you. I am a lonely man.' He placed his hand on his chest.

'I doubt that.'

'You misunderstand me,' he said. 'At my age, I prefer the company of a woman who has a beautiful mind rather than a beautiful body.'

'Thanks a lot,' said Heather, crossing her arms defensively.

She blamed menopause. Although her overall weight had not changed, her body had subsided, settled like an old building into something still functional and solid, but barely recognisable from the original plans.

Dennis leaned towards her over the wooden table in the cockpit, looking mortified. 'Please do not take that the wrong way. You have a beautiful body, but that belongs to your husband, of course. But does this belong to him too?' He stroked her forehead, running a finger across the side of her temple.

Did her mind still belong to her husband? Hadn't she already been unfaithful to Alan by being here, by imagining this man's naked body pressed against hers?

Dennis's hand left her temple. Her face tried to follow it.

'Come,' he said. 'Let us swim.'

The relief from the intensity of the moment was instant. He'd broken the spell she could so easily have fallen under forever. She could breathe again.

'A swim? So soon after lunch?' Sensible Heather was appalled, reminding her that a sudden shift of blood away from her muscles to her gastric arteries could potentially cause her to drown. In mirror-flat water. The wild thing told Sensible Heather to get stuffed.

Dennis showed her to the main cabin and shut the door, leaving her to change into her swimsuit in private. So far, he was being the perfect gentleman. Heather didn't know whether to be relieved or disappointed as she stuffed her underwear into her beach bag. She explained to Esme that if she wanted to come along stowaway, she would simply have to put up with the proximity to Heather's intimates. She carried her bag, and Esme, back up onto the deck.

Dennis dived in, his straight limbs creating barely a splash. Moments later, after attempting to cover as much flesh as possible with her swimming costume, Heather hobbled to the boat ladder and lowered herself gingerly down into the water. The sea was so warm that her skin barely registered she was submerged.

'Come on,' Dennis called, already heading towards the shore. His powerful arms pumped and scooped the water, making light work of the fifty metres or so between *Athena* and the beach. He climbed out, water dripping from his golden skin. The way he flicked his hair out of his face reminded Heather of Stan, shaking after a dip in the stream. No, she couldn't think about Stan, or Alan. Whatever happened she must detach herself from her old life, and pretend she was an actor in someone else's story. None of this was real. None of this would matter when she returned home. If she returned.

When her feet touched the bottom, she limped across the smooth pebbles to join Dennis in the shade of an overhanging olive tree. It took several minutes for her breathing to return to normal after the exertion of the swim. Then, the only sounds to break the blissful silence were of nature going about its business as it had in this tiny bay since Homer's time. How fleeting was a human life. How inconsequential. What a shame to waste a single moment of this precious time on earth.

Dennis sat very still, staring out at *Athena* anchored where the water turned from aquamarine to emerald. Side by side on the smooth stones, Heather was so aware of him. It was as though their bodies were communicating, without sound, without touch. Lately, she could have a complete conversation with Alan and get the impression he scarcely registered her presence, let alone heard her. Here, without a single word passing between them, she knew she had Dennis's full attention. This was connection. The kind of connection that she had once had with Alan. What had happened? Would they – could they – ever find that connection again?

She touched her sun-tanned ring finger, searching for the symbol of the bond she thought would last forever. Instead of a smooth gold, she found only a pale band of skin. The ring had gone.

28

Between a rock and a hard place

'MY RING!' HEATHER RAN HER FINGER BACKWARDS AND forwards over the shallow groove in her skin, not wanting to believe her eyes. 'It's gone.'

Dennis caught on quickly, searching the stones around them.

'You were not wearing it at lunch,' he said. He must have been looking at it, consciously or unconsciously, when he asked her to sail away with him. 'I thought perhaps it was a sign.' He lowered his eyes, all brows again. 'I hoped it was.'

In the irrationality of panic, Heather searched her bare finger again, the folds in her swimsuit, her wet footprints up the beach.

'I have to find it,' she said, holding the sides of her head as if the words hurt.

'Let us go back and search the boat. Perhaps you removed it when you undressed.'

If she hadn't been so preoccupied with ripping her clothes off, she would have remembered.

The boat was only about fifty metres from the shore yet it may as well have been in Athens. The water that only minutes ago had looked clear now seemed dark and cold. If the ring wasn't on board, they would never find it on the seabed.

Dennis helped her up onto the swim platform, then to climb over the transom into the cockpit. Heather emptied her bag, then performed a fingertip search of the deck, while Dennis looked down below in the cabin where she'd changed. There was no sign of the ring.

Heather sighed and threw up her hands in defeat. Dennis wanted to keep looking.

'It's no good,' she said. 'It's gone. It must have slipped off in the water. Let's just forget it.'

'No!' Dennis spoke sharply. 'We must not give up.' He disappeared down the hatch and emerged with a mask and snorkel. 'Trust me. I will find it.'

He looped the clear plastic snorkel strap behind his head, adjusted the mask and clenched the snorkel mouthpiece between his teeth. A second later he was gone, disappearing into the shadowy water below. Heather leaned on the safety wires but couldn't see him until he surfaced again, water spouting from his snorkel like from a whale's blowhole. Then he was gone again, the tips of his toes disappearing beneath the surface.

She watched him dive and surface. Dive and surface. Again, and again, until he swam to the platform for a breather.

'Let me have a go,' she said. She reached for the mask and snorkel.

'There is a spare mask in the locker in the main cabin.'

She clambered down below, hitting her head on the low door frame as she stumbled into the cabin. She paused at the sight of his pristine bed; the corners tucked so precisely forming sharp triangles. An hour ago, she had imagined slipping naked beneath those cool, white sheets. Now all she could think about was finding her wedding ring. The ring placed on the third finger of her left hand at the altar in St Luke's church, Netherwood, with a vow to forsake all others.

Heather had never snorkelled before. She and Alan had generally holidayed in Wales or Scotland, places not known for their spectacular coral reefs. As a final year medical student, she'd learned to intubate and ventilate an unconscious patient. It involved considerable skill to pass the endotracheal tube down into the trachea, before attaching the tube to a self-inflating bag, and squeezing oxygen directly into the lungs. And yet she'd mastered it easily, earning praise from her seniors for her calm approach. So, how hard could it be to place a rubber mouthpiece between her own lips and simply breathe?

The answer was, harder than it looked. Her first attempt had the mask upside down and the attached snorkel sticking up like a periscope. On the second attempt she at least positioned the equipment correctly only to find that Dennis must have a much larger head than she did because when she jumped into the water, the mask came off and floated away. Dennis came to her rescue and on the third attempt, the mask and snorkel were ready for action, even if she wasn't. Inhaling half a lungful of Ionian seawater, she learned that snorkelling wasn't the same as scuba diving, and it wasn't possible to breathe underwater.

Eventually, Heather got the hang of holding her breath while she dived underwater and joined Dennis in the hunt for the missing ring. However, her natural buoyancy meant that, having kicked her way to the sandy bottom, she invariably shot up again like a champagne cork. Seeing her predicament, Dennis took her hand and towed her down to the seabed, allowing her several seconds to search before her cellulite carried her back to the surface. Between them, they searched under the boat for nearly an hour.

'It's no good,' said Heather when they were both resting on the swim platform. 'It's getting late, we should head back.' Her ankle was furious, but the pain in her ankle was nothing compared to the ache in her heart.

'Are you certain?' The imprint of the mask had formed an oval around Dennis's forehead and cheeks. His eyes were red from the salt and sun. He offered his hand. This time Heather climbed the swim ladder herself and stood dripping on the deck. Dennis released a freshwater shower hose from a compartment in the side of the boat and they washed the saltwater off each other.

While Heather towelled herself dry, Dennis prepared the boat to leave. He pulled up the swim ladder and tried to start the engine. The sounds of the struggling engine made Heather think about Lolly. And home. Still dripping wet, Dennis tried again. And again. He disappeared down to the engine bay, cursing in Greek. When he emerged, the sun had already dipped behind the rocky cliff on the western side of the bay.

'It's no good,' he said, pushing his wet hair away from his face. 'The engine is kaput.'

Heather wasn't sure whether kaput was derived from the Latin or Greek, but it translated well.

'Can't we sail back? You said the wind was going to be strong today. Do we even need the engine?'

He explained why this was not possible. Somehow, they needed to get *Athena* out of this sheltered bay. If he raised the anchor the current would carry them onto the rocks before they reached the wind. Then there was also the small issue of manoeuvring back into the harbour at Sami, impossible in the dark, under sail.

'How did Odysseus manage it?'

'His men rowed. He had the equivalent of fifty Olympic oarsmen powering each of his ships.'

Alan had been a rower, the long limbs and broad shoulders he'd acquired during his gap year earning him a place in the university squad. Heather had noticed him sneaking late into lectures after an early start on the river. She used to watch him when he fell asleep on his folded arms in his half-written notes. And yet he'd still managed to come away with a first, and a hand-painted Head of the River oar bearing the names and weights of his crew. The oar had been mounted on the wall of the entrance hall at The Elms since she'd known him. But not even Alan could row them out of this.

'What do we do?' The seriousness of the situation began to dawn on her.

'I will call my cousin Andreas to bring a spare part.'

'How soon could he get it to us?'

'It wouldn't be until tomorrow morning.'

'So, we're stuck here overnight?'

'Unless you want to climb up that cliff and walk back.'

The situation called for some serious overthinking. Cast in late afternoon shadow, the cliffs looked even steeper and more perilous than when they'd arrived. There was no way she could scale them with her ankle and it would be dark soon. Staying overnight would mean sleeping here, and there was only one bed. Could she trust Dennis? Could she trust herself?

'Can I ask you something?' Heather asked.

'Of course.'

'Did you send flowers to my hotel?'

His eyebrows dipped like courting caterpillars. 'Yes. To say sorry.'

'Sorry for what?'

'Sorry that the trip to the ruins was not perfect.'

Would a lying, cheating conman really send flowers anonymously? Would he have even bothered with her again after carrying her down a mountainside?

'I didn't plan this,' said Dennis. 'You must believe me.'

'I know you didn't.' Heather's gestalt agreed.

As dusk cast more of the bay into shadow, Dennis swam ashore with a rope he tied to an old olive tree.

'The wind can get up in the night. It might drag the anchor. It is best to have a stern line too.'

Heather eyed the sharp rocks at the base of the cliffs warily, picturing the boat smashed to pieces in a howling gale. She thought about Odysseus trying to navigate between Scylla and Charybdis. Lose a few of his men to Scylla, or his entire ship to Charybdis. He wasn't the only one to find himself between a rock and a hard place.

29

All adrift on the wine-dark sea

AFTER A SUPPER OF LEFTOVER BREAD, SLICED TOMATOES drizzled in olive oil and sprinkled with torn basil leaves, and another bottle of wine, Heather climbed into Dennis's bed in her underwear. Alone. Dennis insisted she sleep in the main cabin, telling her he would be quite comfortable up on the deck. She stared up through the open hatch at the stars. So many stars. So close.

She listened to the lap of water against the hull of the boat and tried to imagine she was being rocked in a cradle as the boat swayed gently from side to side. She thought about Alan, how he claimed she always stole the duvet, gradually rolling herself into a pig-in-a-blanket by morning. About how he simply put up with it, shivering in the early hours rather than waking her to steal it back. Because he loved her.

So much for the wind that might blow them onto the rocks. There was barely a breeze. The stuffy cabin was too hot for her to fall asleep. Heather heard footsteps above her head.

Dennis must still be awake too. Then there was a splash. At first, she thought he must have jumped in for a dip, to cool off. But the splash was followed by more footsteps and stumbling about. What was he doing? She stilled every muscle in her body, listening for clues. Nothing. All was quiet again. She had almost dropped off to sleep when she heard what sounded like someone crying. Sitting up, she listened. There it was again. Stifled sobs.

Dressing quickly, Heather unlocked the cabin door and tiptoed out. She stood in the galley at the bottom of the ladder from where, in the moonlight, she could just make out Dennis sitting on the transom. She climbed a couple of steps until she had a better view. His bare shoulders jerked as he sobbed, his face buried in something she couldn't see. Beside him she could just make out an empty wine bottle. He didn't react as Heather climbed the rest of the ladder and crept across the cockpit towards him.

'Dennis. Are you all right?' she said softly as she approached.

The moonlight caught the wet streaks down his cheeks as he looked up, turning towards her voice. She sat next to him. Waited without saying a word. Then she touched his hand. He turned away.

'What is it?'

Then she saw what he was hugging to his chest. An orange lifejacket. Small enough for a child. He cradled it to his body and wept. Whatever had caused such pain was far worse than anything a physical weapon could inflict. It was the hidden wounds that hurt the most.

For what seemed like hours, Dennis was unreachable. When he eventually fell silent, all cried out, Heather tried touching his arm again. Softly. This time he didn't flinch. She stroked his bare skin until she felt the muscles release.

'Do you want to talk about it?' Heather asked.

He reached for the wine bottle, swigged at it. Finding it empty he threw it into the water. He must have been reading Heather's copy of *The Odyssey* because it was open, face down on the deck beside him. Dennis picked it up, held the page up to the silvery light of the moon and read aloud.

'And if a god will wreck me yet again
On the wine-dark sea,
I can bear that too, with a spirit tempered to endure
Much have I suffered, laboured long and hard by now
In the waves and wars.'

Heather waited, sitting with him through his discomfort. Not wanting to rush him. Her job had needed her to be so much more than a physician. At different times she'd been a psychologist, a social worker and a priest. Wearing many hats, she'd heard many stories. Whatever Dennis's story was, it would not shock her.

'I saw something,' he said. 'I thought maybe it was the branch of a tree. I shone the torch onto the water, and I saw this.' He held the lifejacket up by the shoulders. 'I thought it was a body.'

'It's all right.' Heather wiped away a fresh tear from his cheek with her thumb. He sniffed and took a deep breath. 'It's just an empty lifejacket.'

He held the lifejacket by the shoulders, running the woven straps between his fingers.

'I used to be in command of a patrol vessel in home waters. It was around 2006 when the coastguard started to find more and more boats carrying refugees and asylum seekers. Some of the boats sank and they had to rescue people from the water. The boats were coming from Libya carrying Somalis, then later Syrians, all escaping war. Greece is the entry point to Northern Europe for refugees. Did you know it is less than five miles from Turkey to the nearest European soil on the island of Kos? People came from Iran and Iraq, mostly Kurdish, also from Pakistan, Bangladesh, Sri Lanka. Many had travelled great distances to find a safer place to live.'

Heather had read about the migrant crisis in the papers, heard reports on the evening news. Inevitably the news cycle moved on and the plight of the thousands of refugees slipped from front page to little more than a footnote. But that didn't mean it had gone away.

'So many boats came,' Dennis continued, 'especially in the summer. The Greek Navy began to take part in the rescues. The navy was originally created to fight wars. To win wars. And we were at war. But this was a war against the people smugglers who make money out of putting human beings into boats that can barely float and then abandoning them at sea to fend for themselves. They don't care if the passengers live or die. They only care about money. Things can go wrong at sea, as you saw today. Hundreds have died making that crossing, thousands more across the Mediterranean. This is a war that we can never win.'

'I remember that photo of the little Syrian boy's body washing up on the beach.' Heather felt her own tears building. 'Poor little mite.'

'After that incident the boats stopped for a few days, then they started again. Worse than before. At the beach

265

where they found his body, the local people hung a sign in Turkish saying "Shame on humanity".'

Dennis fell silent, his head resting in his hands now. Without looking up he told her about the night he was on patrol near the island of Lesbos when one of his crew spotted something in the water. As they drew closer, they saw it was a capsized boat, little more than an inflatable dinghy. Around the boat, the water was littered with bodies, some wearing lifejackets, some floating face down in the water. There had been a storm a few hours earlier and the boat had capsized. The people in the water must have clung to the overturned hull, but many were children who, despite wearing lifejackets, had drowned. The handful who were still alive were too traumatised to speak. His words were strangled as he tried to explain what he'd seen.

'We tried to rescue them.' He broke down again.

'You did what you could,' Heather said, stroking his back.

'I lifted a boy out of the water. He was about the same age as my grandson was at the time. He even looked like him. The boy had drowned. He was wearing a lifejacket like this one.'

Realising there were no words to comfort him, Heather took Dennis in her arms. He yielded to the comforting gesture.

'After that I couldn't sleep. Every time I closed my eyes, I saw the boy's face. It got worse as we rescued more and more people, and I saw many more dead children. Greeks are supposed to help people, to offer safety and shelter to travellers, and yet all we could do was put them into body bags. The beaches are piled high with discarded lifejackets and broken boats, and still, they keep coming.'

'You couldn't save everybody,' she said, holding his face in her hands. 'You did your job, and you cared, that's what's important.'

She thought of all the patients she hadn't been able to save, of the diagnoses made too late, of the sudden collapses she was too many minutes away to bring back to life, and those for whom life simply wasn't fair. She thought about Alan, too, how his inability to resuscitate Esme's husband Aubrey must have stayed with him. Then there were the lives they had saved. The tiny dark freckle that she'd noticed when examining her patient after a fall, that had turned out to be a melanoma. The easily missed warning signs on a routine ECG. Rosemary Lawson's breech baby.

'When I left the navy, I couldn't really settle back into civilian life again. Everything seemed so, how you say . . .' he seemed to struggle to find the right English word. 'Pointless. I had nightmares and I would wake up screaming to my crew to hurry, help them, and to the people in the water to swim, swim! It was very frightening for my wife. The only thing that helped was alcohol.'

Like so many returned heroes. *Home, but not quite home.*

It must have been hard to be the one left behind with the memories after a trauma like that. To carry on, to survive year after year.

'Did you get help?'

He sat up straight, stuck out his chest. 'No, because I am a man. Descendent of great heroes. A stupid, proud, Greek man.'

'You're not the first stupid, proud, Greek man. Why do you think your ancestors drank so much wine while they talked about the battles they'd fought and the friends they'd lost?'

In the moonlight she saw Dennis smile.

'It's not too late, Dennis. All you have to do is to ask for help. But that means opening up and making yourself vulnerable.'

'It is easier to be alone.'

'You can't sail a ship without a crew.'

'This is true.' Dennis dropped the lifejacket onto the deck and took both Heather's hands in his. 'When I met you, it was different. I felt it here.' He pressed his fingers into his epigastrium. 'I knew I could trust you. I knew you would understand me. I felt safe with you. You are a doctor.'

'But I'm not *your* doctor, Dennis. I can't heal you. You need to heal yourself, and for that, you need to stop running away to sea.'

The next thing she knew they were kissing. Warm, tender, forbidden lips on hers. He tasted salty, like tears. Like the sea.

They pulled apart at the same time, as if by some unseen signal. Dennis's face had relaxed even if it hadn't yet found a smile.

'Thank you,' Dennis said.

For the kiss or for listening?

'Thank *you*,' she wanted to say.

Dennis was only the second man she'd ever kissed in her sheltered life. The control subject in her randomised trial. It hadn't been a sensual kiss, nor a completely chaste one either. They had both needed that moment of intimacy and connection. It didn't mean everything, but it didn't mean nothing either. It was simply a kiss. Not better than kissing Alan. Not worse. Just different.

Heather lay back on the deck, the teak boards still warm from the day's sun. Dennis lay beside her, not touching but close enough that she could feel the heat from his body.

'Why did you really bring me here?' she asked.

'To this bay? I know it looks like I have planned this whole thing, the engine breaking down, but no. That is not the truth. This place is very special to me. I used to come here as a boy with my father. It is the place where I feel most like myself. I feel calm here. Like the sheltered water.'

'So why bring me?'

'I don't know. It sounds stupid but I saw you had pain inside you too. That you needed this healing place.'

'What makes you think I need healing?' Heather asked, turning on her side to face him now.

'I don't know. I feel it. That is all I can say.'

'You asked me why I came to Greece on my own. I didn't answer your question because I didn't know the reason myself. I suppose I was testing my husband and, if I'm honest, testing myself. We have come to an important crossroads in our lives, and discovered we want to head in different directions. I think we are both afraid of growing old. Well, according to my daughters we are already old, but I think we are both afraid of running out of time. The truth is that we both have more than enough years left to do everything he wants to do *and* everything I want to do. The problem is that we are both obstinate and neither of us wants to compromise.'

'Like Penelope and Odysseus. Testing one another, playing games, each not fully trusting the other. It is natural to protect your heart from pain.'

'No one likes to feel vulnerable.' And yet here she was, in what was possibly the most risky, dangerous situation she had ever put herself in. Why was she willing to make herself physically vulnerable to a stranger, but not emotionally vulnerable to a man she loved and trusted? Was it normal to want two different things? She couldn't have both, even if they made her equally happy, equally fulfilled. She couldn't have Dennis and Alan. Adventure and security.

Dennis rolled onto his side. It could easily have turned into another kiss, and more. Instead, he asked, 'Do you love your husband enough to meet him halfway? You don't have to answer me right away, Heather-like-the-bush. I want you to think about it.'

Halfway would mean her sharing his passion for sustainable gardening, or at least sharing fifty per cent of his passion. Love his broccoli but not his beans? Rave about his pumpkins but remain lukewarm about his beetroot? She could do that. The real question was whether Alan could share half her passion for discovering Ancient Greece. Halfway between Netherwood and Ithaca would be over the Alps somewhere, Slovenia maybe, and halfway between the eighth century BC and today would leave them bang in the middle of the Dark Ages. Was each getting half what they wanted better than one of them getting nothing?

Out of nowhere, the moonlight caught the silvery back of a single wave as it rolled into the bay. The wash from a long-departed ferry, or a freak of the elements. The wave hit *Athena*'s hull side on. She rolled from side to side. Something slid across the deck and before Heather could stop it, whatever it was had landed in the water with a splash.

Dennis jumped to his feet and found a flashlight, the beam picking up a trail of what looked like sand, shell and coral strewn across the deck and down into the silky black water. Then Heather saw the recycled, biodegradable cardboard canister floating away.

'Oh no!'

'What is it?'

'My friend Esme. I brought her ashes with me.' Heather slumped in defeat.

'Do you want me to rescue her?'

'No, leave her in peace. I was looking for the perfect place to scatter her ashes. It looks as if she chose here. I hope you won't mind sharing your special bay. I can assure you she's very good company.'

Somewhere in the dark, an owl hooted.

'Listen,' Dennis said. 'I've never heard an owl in this bay before.'

Heather held her breath and listened for the bird's eerie call. She must have shivered because Dennis asked her what was wrong.

'I've always been a little wary of owls. I suppose it's because they only come out at night and, as a child, I was afraid of the dark. And reading too many books about witches.'

'Owls are my favourite birds. You only have to look at those big bright eyes to believe that owls have a light inside them. They are very intelligent birds too, which is why they have always been associated with Athena, goddess of wisdom.'

'Esme was my wise old owl. She was the one who introduced me to Homer, so in a way, she's the reason I'm here in the first place. The reason we met.'

The owl hooted again. This time it was answered by another owl on the opposite side of the bay. They hooted a duet; the loveliest thing Heather had ever heard.

There was no point going back to bed now. Dennis rigged up a hammock on the open deck and she lay in it, reading by torchlight while he snoozed on the bench cushion.

Heather closed her book. The stars were beginning to disappear overhead, the first light appearing out to sea on the horizon. Homer's *rosy-fingered Dawn*. She was going to miss her old friend and confidante, sharing sweet treats while she whinged about Alan's shortcomings and bemoaned her lack of purpose. Perhaps it was time to take Esme's advice before it was too late, to stop complaining and start taking action. And that included trying to understand Alan rather than assuming everything he did was done deliberately to antagonise her. Meeting him halfway.

She'd come to a decision. Tomorrow, when she returned to the hotel, she would phone Alan and tell him she was coming home.

30

Little white lies

As promised, Dennis's network of friends and cousins came to the rescue. The spare solenoid arrived by speedboat before it was fully light, and *Athena* was soon on her way, sailing back to port where Stavros was already waiting with his taxi.

Heather had seen many dawns break; as a junior doctor after a busy night on call, as a mother with a newborn baby. There was always something comforting about the return of the day. The light after the dark. As they drove back to the hotel, she watched people going about their daily business as usual. Today, even wearing the heavy fog of missed sleep, she felt re-energised. She waved to the receptionist as she limped through reception, then waved to Pat and Jeffrey in the restaurant. This was no walk of shame, skulking in after a night on the tiles. This was a new beginning.

It took several attempts to open the door to her room; she simply couldn't get the hang of these electronic keys. Inside the air-conditioning was pleasantly cool after the humid night on the boat. The room was tidy, though not exactly as she'd left it. Heather couldn't put her finger on what was different. She pulled the loose dress over her head and threw it onto the bed, followed by her underwear. Catching a glance of her naked body in the full-length mirror, she paused.

Her one-piece had stencilled an odd tan. Her arms, chest and legs were brown, the rest of her lily-white. Dennis had told her she was beautiful. Just to hear those words was enough for her to cast aside every insecurity she carried about her ageing body. She ran her hands over her pale breasts, her abdomen, her thighs. For the first time in many years, she felt beautiful again. Desirable.

'Hello, Heather.'

The shock squeezed a scream from inside her chest. Her hand rushed to her chest to catch her heart before it leapt out of her rib cage. No wonder people of her age dropped dead from shock.

She turned to see a man sitting in the armchair behind her.

'*Alan!* What are you doing here?' In seconds, a dam wall of adrenaline had given way, inundating every cell in her body. Fingers twitching, she pulled her dress over her naked body. How ridiculous. She'd been married to this man for forty years. He had watched her give birth. Twice.

'I came. Like you asked me to,' said Alan from the armchair, where he sat like a James Bond villain. All he needed was a white cat on his lap.

'Why didn't you let me know?'

'I wanted to surprise you.'

He'd certainly done that. The first completely spontaneous thing he'd done in their entire marriage.

'How long are you planning to stay?'

'I've only just arrived and you're already trying to get rid of me,' Alan replied. Typical, he could have added, but didn't.

He looked different somehow. If she'd bumped into him in the foyer, she might not have even recognised him as her husband. He was wearing a pair of smart blue chinos, a white short-sleeved shirt, and a pair of trendy canvas shoes. And unless she was very much mistaken, he was wearing new glasses and had visited the barber. She was looking at an upgraded version of her husband. *Alan Winterbottom 2.0.*

He stood up. Heather cowered behind her scrunched-up sundress. Should they hug, kiss? She leaned towards him and pecked him on the lips. Instead of grabbing her playfully and lifting her onto the bed, he didn't react, standing stiffly with his hands in his brand-new pockets.

'Let me have a quick shower. Then we can talk,' said Heather lightly. 'Make yourself a cup of tea. I won't be long.'

She hurried into the bathroom and shut the door behind her. Leaned against it and gazed up at the extractor fan on the ceiling while she caught her breath. His washbag was open on the vanity, toothbrush already in the glass next to the sink. She touched the bristles. They were wet.

Shit. He'd been here long enough to clean his teeth.

She showered and wrapped her wet hair in a towel turban. Pre-prepared a nonchalant smile.

Alan was sitting at the little table out on the balcony.

'Where have you been all night?' He didn't look up. 'I caught the late flight and arrived here yesterday evening. I told reception I was your husband and that I was here to surprise you. I was worried, Heather. You didn't answer your phone. I didn't know where you were.'

'I went on a boat trip to Ithaca. It was supposed to be a lunch cruise only the boat broke down and we had to stay the night. My phone battery died. We got in first thing this morning and I caught a taxi back from Sami.'

Not one word a lie and yet the truth must be written all over her face.

She sat at the table next to him. He stood up and walked back into the room. When she followed him inside, she found him staring at the bouquet in the water jug.

'Who gave you the flowers?' He stroked the petal of a pink lily, releasing a shower of yellow pollen onto his finger.

Should she confess? But confess what exactly? How could she explain what had happened and make it sound as though she hadn't betrayed him? That only by conducting her own independent research could she confirm what she already knew. That Alan was the only man she'd ever love. That while her perineum had briefly tempted her with Dennis, her epigastrium had been right all along.

'Nobody,' Heather replied, remembering how Dennis had first introduced himself. '*Nobody* gave me flowers.' Then, when more explanation seemed required. 'They were from the hotel. I slipped and twisted my ankle. A woman from reception brought them up to my room, presumably to make sure I don't sue them.'

Not exactly true. But then again, perhaps all marriages were built on little white lies.

'I'm sorry I wasn't here when you arrived. I'm sorry you were worried. What can I say? These things happen at sea. Now that you're here, can we start again?'

'I tell you what,' Alan said. 'Why don't you get dressed and we can discuss it over lunch? I went looking for you this morning and came across a lovely little taverna down at the marina. The waiter told me they serve the best baklava in all Cephalonia.'

'I didn't know you liked baklava.'

'I'm glad I can still surprise you, Heather. I think it's time we got to know one another again, don't you?'

She dressed quickly, finding a pair of cleanish white ankle-length trousers at the bottom of her backpack, and a blue and white striped top that just about passed muster.

'We both look like the Greek flag,' Alan remarked. They burst out laughing.

This is going to be all right. Everything is going to work out fine.

Then, at the door, Alan stopped. He was staring at her hand. 'I noticed you're not wearing your wedding ring.'

'My ring. Yes. Now that's a funny story. You'll laugh when you hear it.'

She searched for another white lie.

'Here it is.' Alan produced her ring from his pocket and, taking her hand, slid it onto her third finger. 'It was in the bathroom, next to the sink. You really should be more careful in future, Heather. One day you might lose it for good.'

She knew then that he was never going to ask her for the truth. He was a doctor and knew the old medical adage as well as she did. *If you don't want to find a fever, don't take a temperature.* There was something in that.

31

Relevance deprivation disorder

ALAN LED THE WAY TO THE LOVELY WATERSIDE TAVERNA he'd discovered on his walk. The same taverna where Heather had read pages from Esme's paperback, where she'd first struck up a conversation with Dennis. The taverna with the best baklava in Cephalonia.

While they waited for their coffees, at Heather's favourite table, they chatted easily about all the usual things: the girls, the dog, the chickens. Things were almost back to normal between them. Almost. The wind had shifted, and the tell-tales were pointing in a new direction. All she had to do was change course and sail into it.

'I'm sorry I ran away,' she said. 'You know what I'm like. I've always been impatient, and after all the rushing around, it's hard to change pace. I've always wanted to come here, you know that. I was scared that if I didn't do it right away, it would be too late, that something might happen, and I'd miss out again. Like I did when Mum was dying.'

'And I'm sorry I drove you away, Heather. I can be a stubborn old fool sometimes.'

'Sometimes?'

They laughed.

The whole situation was ridiculous when she thought about it. Alan was a good man, as loved and respected as his father was. He wasn't a drinker, or a gambler or a gas-lighting narcissist. He'd done things she wished he hadn't, and not done things she wished he had. He would probably say the same about her.

Determined to start afresh, Heather asked him about his garden.

'It's your garden too, Heather.'

Alan didn't look up. He had stirred his coffee so many times that a woman on the next table tutted and muttered in Greek at the incessant *clink, clink, clink* of his spoon inside the cup.

'I should have been more supportive about the self-sufficiency thing. I thought maybe it was a passing phase. I didn't realise you were so serious about it. And, if I'm honest, when Kevin came on the scene, I felt a bit left out. Your friendship with him only emphasised how lonely I was. All I could see was that we were growing apart. If you'll excuse the pun.'

'Nothing could be further from the truth, Heather.' The muscles in Alan's hand twitched but he must have thought better of reaching for hers. He ripped open another sachet of sugar and stirred it into his coffee. Tasted it. Grimaced. Stirred in yet another. 'I know I've been a bit distant these last few weeks. There was a lot to process up here.' He stirred the side of his head with his teaspoon.

'They do say that retirement is a major life event,' said Heather, thinking out loud. 'It's up there with the death of a spouse and divorce for causing stress.'

'I can't deny I've been feeling a little lost without the practice,' Alan said.

'Me too, if I'm honest.'

'And I think I've been suffering from Relevance Deprivation Disorder.'

'That's only natural after you've held such an important job in the community.'

'I'm talking about our marriage,' said Alan. He looked at her with his kind North Sea eyes. The luscious eyelashes were pale with age. If anything, they made his eyes seem larger, brighter. Lit from within by the quiet wisdom she'd fallen in love with. 'You're so strong and full of vitality, Heather. So independent. You always have been, that's why I fell in love with you. Only now, you don't seem to need me anymore. I'm worried I've become irrelevant and that I might lose you.'

If it hadn't all been true, she might have told him he was being ridiculous. She might not need Alan, but she wanted him. And that was an even better reason to try to make things work.

Heather sat up straight and pressed back her shoulders. 'I beg to differ, Dr Winterbottom. If you refer to the latest edition of the *Diagnostic and Statistical Manual of Mental Disorders*, you won't find Relevance Deprivation Disorder described.' Alan smiled at the professorial voice she'd adopted. 'But speaking of our marriage, I would like to postulate an alternative diagnosis. The symptoms and signs suggest that our marriage is suffering from Adjustment Disorder.'

Alan tapped the cleft in his chin with his thinking finger.

'That is an interesting theory, Dr Winterbottom. Would you care to elaborate on your hypothesis?'

'To fit the DSM-5 criteria for Adjustment Disorder, the patient must have experienced the development of emotional or behavioural symptoms in response to an identifiable stressor occurring within three months of the onset of the stressor.'

Alan fidgeted on his chair. She imagined him as a little boy who already knew the answer before the teacher had finished the question. 'The condition may manifest in symptoms such as anxiety or excessive worry –'

'Irritability.'

'Lack of libido.'

'Impairment of the performance of daily functions.'

How much easier it was to intellectualise the situation. It helped them both maintain a professional distance from the pain. Their own pain. But they were back on familiar ground again, discussing patient histories, brainstorming diagnoses and treatment options. It was as though, after listening to the static between radio stations, their brains had tuned into the same frequency again.

'And the good news is –'

'The condition usually resolves itself within six months.'

'So, Dr Winterbottom,' said Alan, 'what would you pre-scribe our patient in the meantime?'

'How about a bit of TLC?'

Heather leaned over and stroked his chin. A smile wiped a decade from his face.

Taking a bite of Cephalonia's best baklava, his eyes widened. 'Oh goodness me. I think I'll have to start dropping hints to the fan club about this stuff. It's delicious.'

'How are the fan club?'

'Rather as I expected. They've moved on,' said Alan sadly. 'That handsome bastard of a new senior partner let it slip that he's a Lemon Drizzle man, and within twenty-four hours, Sainsbury's in Darlingford had run out of lemons. I'm old news, Heather.'

She slid her hand across the table. He met her halfway.

'Anyway, enough about Netherwood,' said Alan. 'I want to hear more about Ithaca.'

Heather flinched, hearing 'Ithaca' in inverted commas.

'What can I say? It is a beautiful island, of course. I don't know what I'd imagined. The reality is never quite the same, is it? In a way, it was too obvious, too convenient. The archaeological site was perfectly situated. And, yes, they found a few fragments of Mycenaean pottery, and some bronze tripods in a nearby cave but the stones could have been from any building in the past two thousand years.'

Alan waved his A-ha finger. He could barely contain himself. She hadn't seen him this excited to tell her anything since he'd proved her wrong about the lump on Mrs Maddock's arm. He'd been insufferable for weeks after Heather had diagnosed a squamous cell carcinoma and referred Mrs Maddock to a surgeon, only for Alan to intercept the referral letter and remove a perfectly harmless keratoacanthoma under local anaesthetic.

'Kevin has an interesting theory about Ithaca.'

'Don't tell me our chief NOGGIN is a closet Homer enthusiast too.'

'It turns out he's no amateur enthusiast. As well as knowing his brassicas from his alliums, he also happens to have a degree in Ancient History and Classics.' Alan waited for Heather to make an 'I'm impressed' face before continuing.

'We were discussing parsnips in the greenhouse one morning. I said I wasn't happy with my germination rate and when I mentioned that I'd been transplanting the few seedlings I had managed to produce, he pointed out that this was a rookie error since parsnips have a tap root, and one thing led to another and the next we were drinking his rhubarb wine and discussing Homer.'

'Hang on a minute,' Heather interjected. 'You drank home-brew?' She covered her mouth stifling her incredulous laugh.

'As I was saying –'

'No, wait, tell me what you thought of the rhubarb wine. Honestly.'

'Between you and me it was revolting. Put it this way, you could taste the well-rotted horse manure. Whatever you do, don't tell Ravi or I'll never hear the last of it.'

They were both laughing now. It felt good to be laughing. Everything with Dennis had been exciting and a little dangerous, and laced with an undeniable sexual chemistry. But he hadn't made her laugh like Alan could.

Sensing there was more to come, that Alan was only getting started, Heather caught the waiter's eye and mimed the international gesture for 'Two more coffees, please'. In the minutes that followed, Alan laid out the evidence for why Heather was wrong, and he, naturally, was right.

He went on to explain Kevin's theory. According to a book Kevin had read, written by an amateur enthusiast, the real Ithaca was in fact Cephalonia, or specifically the north-west corner of the island. So the theory went, this part of Cephalonia had once been an island in its own right. Three thousand years ago, a narrow channel separated Ancient Ithaca from the rest of the island. The channel, known nowadays as Strabo's channel, had been filled in over the years due to earthquakes and landslides.

She barely followed the rest of the evidence he produced, but it sounded very logical and convincing. Very Alan.

Suddenly, everything Heather thought she'd understood fell apart, like a jigsaw puzzle knocked to the ground. In her irritation, Heather scalded her lip on the hot coffee. 'Are you saying you have come all this way to prove that you're right and I'm wrong?'

Alan leaned so far back in his chair he nearly fell off it. 'No. Quite the opposite. I thought I'd finally found something we could have a proper conversation about. Something we're both interested in.'

'You've never shown the slightest interest in Greek mythology. You once told me you'd vowed never to touch Homer again with a ten-foot barge pole after your prep-school experience. Something about fish bones.'

Alan raised his well-that's-where-you're-wrong finger. 'I said translating it from the original Greek was particularly tedious. Like picking tiny bones out of a fish. Kevin lent me his copy of *The Odyssey*. I have to admit it makes a lot more sense in English. In fact, I'd forgotten what a great adventure story it was.'

'I still don't understand why you're here, Alan.'

'Patience, my dearest. All will be revealed.' He wriggled on his chair like an overexcited boy. 'I have a surprise for you.'

32

Love Island

HEATHER ALWAYS FELT EMOTIONAL IN AIRPORTS. AS SOON as she walked into the terminal later that afternoon, she felt an inexplicable urge to cry. Farewells and reunions, even between complete strangers, had a profound effect on her. As she and Alan stood waiting in the arrivals hall, Heather observed the comings and goings around her.

She watched a well-dressed man pace nervously with a bunch of flowers only to accidentally headbutt the woman he was waiting for in his eagerness to kiss her. He led her away, nose bleeding, the flowers squashed on the luggage trolley beneath her oversized suitcase. She saw a young family embrace an older woman; an older man embrace a younger woman; and two women squeal and run towards each other. Heather could only guess at all their stories. When a vaguely familiar man wearing a Panama hat and dark sunglasses strode confidently up to Alan and embraced him like a long-lost friend, it was their turn to leave others wondering. It took a moment for her to recognise Kevin. A surprisingly tidy, presentable and clean-shaven version of Netherwood's chief NOGGIN. What was he doing here in Cephalonia?

Before Heather could articulate her confusion, Alan compounded it.

'Is she here?' he asked, looking over Kevin's shoulder.

'She's coming,' said Kevin. 'But you know what she's like.'

They shared a knowing laugh, leaving Heather none the wiser. Then a woman who looked exactly like Tilly appeared through the doors, studying every detail of her surroundings as if she'd landed at the Temple of Apollo rather than international arrivals.

'Tilly!' Heather rushed towards her daughter and hugged her without restraint. To give Tilly credit, she didn't try to wriggle away as she had done since she was little. 'What are you doing here?'

Tilly shrugged as if it was obvious. Maths had never been Heather's strongest suit and she was still struggling to put two and two together until she saw Kevin throw Tilly's bag over his shoulder before taking her by the hand. Tilly and Kevin were together? Heather had been gone barely a fortnight. There was clearly a lot of catching up to do.

Back at the hotel, Heather and Alan hung around reception while Kevin and Tilly checked into their room. A double room. Together.

'Stop gawping and leave them to it,' said Alan, leading Heather away from the reception desk.

When she and Alan were back in the room, Heather said, 'You could have warned me.'

'I thought it would be a nice surprise.'

'I'm not sure I can take many more surprises. How long have they been . . . an item?'

'Not long,' said Alan. 'I think it was the day he popped in to pinch out my bell peppers. It turns out that Kevin wasn't only interested in my vegetables. Tilly was in the kitchen when we came in for a cup of tea. The two of them struck up a conversation about soil erosion. I went out to use the bathroom and when I came back they were sitting at the kitchen table gazing into each other's eyes like a pair of lovestruck teenagers. They're infatuated with each other.'

'Tilly, infatuated?'

'I know. Hard to believe, isn't it? Just shows you there's somebody for everyone.'

'I'm having a hard time processing it all. Our daughter has never shown the slightest interest in anyone of either sex.'

'They're practically inseparable. It transpires she's a bit of a late-onset Homer fan too. Claims she's been wanting to come here for years.'

Perhaps Homer was a common meeting ground for a scientist like Tilly and a classicist like Kevin. But it still didn't explain why they were here now. Why Alan was here.

She had a sudden thought. 'Who's looking after Stan while you're away? The Gees?'

Alan's face turned grave. He led her to the bed and made her sit down. 'There's something I need to tell you about the Gees.'

'What?'

'The Gees are no longer with us.'

A surprising 'No!' came from Heather.

'I thought that's what you wanted,' he said. 'You told me to get rid of them.'

'I know. I didn't think you'd actually do it. I can't believe they've gone.'

Alan tried to comfort her, stroking her shoulder. 'In the end, they didn't put up much of a fight. Mrs Gee said she could see we didn't need her anymore but that she'd promised my father she'd stay on to look after the family. And a promise –'

'Is a promise.' Heather smiled. 'So, they were okay about it?'

'They were more relieved. Mrs Gee said she hadn't wanted to let us down but that she and Mr Gee had been talking about retiring for a while now. Did you know she is eighty-two and he's eighty-four?'

'Good god, really? It's about time they put their feet up then.'

'Not much chance of that. They're moving to Devon to open a bed and breakfast.'

It was just possible that working until such a ripe age had kept them both sprightly. She'd read that having a sense of purpose, a reason to get up each morning, and something to look forward to, all contributed to longevity. She still needed to find her purpose. She was beginning to accept that this trip to Greece hadn't been it. It was only the beginning. A reset. Like unplugging her life at the wall and plugging it back in again.

They lay down together on the bed, Heather's cheek against Alan's shoulder, resting perfectly in the hollow between his anterior deltoid and pectoralis major.

'I hope the Gees get a holiday before they start their new enterprise,' said Heather. 'Running a B&B can be hard work.'

'Don't you worry about that. I gave them a nice little bonus before they left. They managed to get a last-minute deal on a cruise. It's all worked out well. The cruise doesn't leave for a couple of weeks so in the meantime they're house-, hen- and Stan-sitting.'

Two weeks. That's how long Alan was planning to stay.

33

Captain Corelli's other mandolin

HEATHER COULDN'T TAKE HER EYES OFF TILLY AND KEVIN at breakfast the following morning. At one stage, Alan mouthed 'stop staring' at her across the buffet. They were all over each other. The more she got to know Kevin, the more Heather realised how perfect he was for her daughter.

The conversation over the breakfast table mainly involved their plans for the day. Alan was insistent they must be back at the hotel no later than six. Various activities were motioned, then dismissed. The one thing they all agreed on was that no one was particularly keen to waste time lying on the beach. Sightseeing it was.

The hotel concierge ordered them a taxi and, slathered in sunscreen, they waited on the pavement clutching hats and water bottles. They were still arguing about the best places to visit when the taxi arrived.

No, it couldn't be. Heather hid behind Alan.

Yes, it was.

Behind the wheel was none other than Stavros.

After agreeing to a daily rate and promising to return them to The Poseidon by six o'clock, he watched on, faintly amused by his passengers' game of musical chairs. In the end, Alan, as the tallest, was nominated for the front seat. Kevin, Tilly and Heather squeezed together in the back, where part of Esme was still hiding in the footwell.

'Where you want to go?' Stavros asked.

'We'll leave that to you,' said Alan. 'Show us the best of what Cephalonia has to offer.'

'*Endáxi*,' said Stavros, which Heather understood to mean 'okay'. He grinned at her in the rear-view mirror as he said it, his porn-star moustache twitching at the corners of his mouth.

She was the first to fasten her seatbelt and urged the others to do the same. When Stavros set off at a speed that suggested he was once again in the doghouse, the others soon followed suit. His driving hadn't improved, but unlike the other passengers, Heather was prepared for his tuneless singing along to Greek cover versions of ABBA's greatest hits, and his general disregard for traffic signs of any kind.

Their first stop was to board a car ferry. Stavros explained this was the quickest way to Paliki, the north-western part of the island, and coincidentally the theoretical location of ancient Ithaca, now joined to the mainland. Alan embraced the unexpected detour, and as the ferry passed the lighthouse at the northern end of the peninsula and headed out across the wide bay, he pointed out Homer's supposed landmarks to Kevin and Tilly.

Heather was finding it hard to raise the same level of enthusiasm, however. Whether it was the heat, or the accumulation of events from the past few days, she wasn't sure, but she found herself searching for Stavros in his rear-view mirror, seeing in him her time with Dennis.

In the two days since they'd parted at the harbour in Sami, Dennis had sent her several messages, asking if she was okay. She'd changed his contact details to 'Denise' in her phone, the name of an old school friend who still sent Christmas cards. It would be easy to say they'd got in touch again if Alan became suspicious. Her ankle, having shown early promise for a rapid recovery, had swollen up once more in the heat.

They arrived at a beach on the north coast, where, after what had felt like hours of uneven roads and rocky landscape, there were mercifully signs of modern civilisation. No one objected to a late lunch at a beachside taverna, although Stavros declined to join them. While his four passengers tucked into a mezze plate with olives and warm pita bread, dolmades, grilled haloumi and taramasalata, followed by souvlaki served with lemon potatoes and green beans, he sat in the shade of an old olive tree and smoked a cigarette. Alan and Kevin drank cold Mythos beer, while Tilly, who'd uncharacteristically eaten everything without interrogating its ethics, drank something fizzy from a can. Heather didn't have much of an appetite, and only nibbled on the warm pita, blaming the heat.

After they'd paid the bill, Alan, Kevin and Tilly headed off up the beach with great excitement to inspect a site where winter waves had exposed part of an ancient stone wall. The significance of the wall was lost to Heather in a tsunami of geo-technical language from Tilly that both Alan and Kevin pretended to follow. Heather had never seen her daughter speak so passionately or with such authority. Rocks were her world. This was what she did. While Heather had invested years worrying about Tilly not having a proper job or a stable relationship, all along she had been doing just fine. Better than fine. As her parents were descending from the height of their careers, Dr Matilda Winterbottom PhD was still ascending to hers.

Alan and Kevin were so engrossed in Tilly's explanations of ground-penetrating radar and the difference between radiocarbon and optically stimulated luminescence dating, that no one remarked when Heather stayed behind at the table and ordered a gin and tonic. While she waited for her drink to arrive, she basked in the shade, closing her eyes and imagining she was back on the boat, being rocked to sleep in the hammock.

'How is your uncle?'

Her eyes snapped open. At first, she thought she must have been dreaming.

'Dennis?'

'Heather-like-the-bush.' He didn't seem in the least surprised to see her.

'What are you doing here?'

He pointed to a yacht anchored far out in the bay. *Athena*. 'The wind brought me.'

Stavros waved from the open door of his taxi, parked in the shade of a large olive tree.

'Stavros told you I was here?' Or, as was more likely, had the cunning taxi-driver seen an opportunity and manufactured the whole thing?

'He might have mentioned it. The island might not have changed much physically since ancient times, but we do have 4G.'

'I'm here with my husband and my daughter, Tilly. And a classical scholar called Kevin who is also an expert on parsnips.'

'I know,' he said, smiling playfully.

'You've been stalking me?'

'What is stalking?'

It sounded like something Alan would do in the garden. 'It means following.'

'Can you blame me? I wanted to see you again, possibly one last time. Your husband is here. He has left his vegetables for you. That proves he loves you very much.'

She would always keep the memory of her time with Dennis. It didn't matter whether he'd taken her to the real Ithaca or a place of local legend. Part of her wanted to believe the epic poet was a woman, that women could have their own odysseys, and that however long the journey, however many adventures they had on the way, they would always find their way home.

'It's good to see you again, Dennis.' Oh, how she wanted to kiss him one last time. In the distance, three figures were already walking back along the beach towards them.

'Forgive me for planting my stalks in you,' he said. 'I wanted to tell you something, and to say goodbye in person.'

'I'm glad you did plant your stalks, Dennis. On behalf of Esme and myself, I wanted to thank you for your kindness and your perfect Greek hospitality. Your *xenía*. It made me realise something about my own country and how we treat the people who arrive on our shores.'

'That is interesting,' said Dennis, nodding thoughtfully, 'because I came here to tell you that I have decided to go back to Lesbos, to volunteer in a migrant camp. My cousin's daughter is a social worker who specialises in humanitarian aid. I talked to her yesterday, and she thinks that with my background, and my, shall we say ... *maturity*, that I will be very welcome, and I can do a lot of good work in refugee welfare.'

Help those who survived the journey instead of punishing himself over those who did not.

'That's wonderful news. I think you'd be perfect for the job.'

And the job would be perfect for you.

He picked up her hand, rotated the ring on her third finger.

'It turns out I'd left it back at the hotel. I'm sorry to have caused so much trouble.'

'So, it was never really lost?'

'Only temporarily.'

Alan, Kevin and Tilly were almost upon them now but, at the last moment, before spotting her, they detoured towards the toilets at the back of the taverna.

Heather conjured a smile. 'I suppose this is goodbye, then. How do I say that in Greek?'

'There are many ways to say goodbye. Let us use *Is to epanidín*. It means, until we meet again.'

'*Ish-to-ban-ee-vin?*'

'That will do,' said Dennis, laughing. 'Live a happy life, Heather.'

'You too, Dion,' Heather called after him as he strode away, the sun turning his bare calves to pure gold.

34

The second-greatest speech in history

THE RETURN FERRY WAS RUNNING LATE AND, AFTER SOME cryptic texting on his phone, Alan ordered Stavros to drop them off at the taverna rather than the hotel.

'I'm tired,' Heather said. 'Why don't we all have an early night and do dinner at the marina tomorrow night instead?'

Alan raised his trust-me-on-this-one finger. Neither Tilly nor Kevin questioned the decision. After a generous tip, they waved Stavros off. Heather briefly caught his eye and mouthed 'thank you'.

The waiter showed them to a table with a perfect view of the water and removed the reserved sign. 'This table is laid for six,' said Heather to the waiter. 'There are only four of us.'

'Sit down, Mum,' said Tilly.

Heather urged the confused waiter to remove the extra place settings, despite seeing their name, spelled 'Winnerbottoms', written on the back of the reserved sign.

'Where are *we* going to sit, Mum?'

Heather's stomach leapt into her mouth when she turned to see the two extra guests standing behind her.

'We thought we'd surprise you,' said Sarah. Ravi grinned beside her.

Before Heather could co-ordinate her mouth and her words, Ravi leaned in and kissed her on the cheek. 'Wow, Heather, you're looking *really* well,' he said, as if he meant it.

'I can't believe it,' said Heather. 'What are you two doing here?' She looked around at everyone's smiling faces. 'Wait a minute. What's going on?'

Her gestalt was beating bongos.

'Let's sit down and I'll order us some wine,' Alan said. He didn't seem in the least surprised to see Sarah and Ravi standing there.

Ravi looked nervous. 'As long as it's not retsina. Not sure I want to drink turpentine with my seafood. If there's one ingredient not meant for wine, it's pine resin.'

'Did you know the Greeks only added that to the barrels to stop the Romans drinking all their wine?' Alan added. The last word on the subject, as always, belonged to Alan.

When the waiter brought the wine list, Heather snatched it from Alan's hands.

'A bottle of this, please,' she said when she found the wine she and Dennis had shared. Then she turned to her husband and her son-in-law. 'Did you know the *xinómavro* grape is a classic Greek grape grown in Northern and Central Greece, Macedonia and neighbouring Thessaly? It's a fickle grape but worth the effort since it produces a robust wine with high acidity and tannins, and a long aftertaste. It's perfect with lamb.' Seeing their astonished faces, she added, 'See if you can taste the tomato.'

If she ended up flying home tomorrow, the entire trip would have been worth it for that moment alone.

There was silence around the table as everyone stared at their menus.

'So,' said Heather when everyone was seated. 'Does somebody want to tell me what's going on? If you've all come here to stage an intervention, then you've wasted your time. I miss you all terribly, but I'll decide when it's time to go home.'

'You've missed all of us?' Alan asked. 'Including me?'

'Yes, Alan, I've even missed you.'

Everyone laughed.

'So let me get this straight. You miss me, but you want to continue your trip.' He tapped his thinking chin. 'If only there was a solution.'

Sarah and Tilly were grinning at each other across the table. Then all eyes were on Heather.

She understood now. This was the rosy-fingered dawn of realisation.

'You'd really come with me, Alan? Around the rest of the Greek islands?'

'Why stop there?'

She paused to take it all in.

'But you've done all this before. You had your gap year. You've already seen all the sights, hopped all the islands, chased all the girls. You've done Greece. Why would you want to do all that again now?'

'Because I want to do it with you. And I don't want to sleep in train stations or cheap hostels and live on bread and takeaway gyros every day. And, to be honest, I was drunk or hungover most of the last time. The experience was totally wasted on me. What was it George Bernard Shaw said about youth being wasted on the young? Besides, where is it written that a person is only ever allowed one gap year?'

'But what about your vegetables? What about your promising spinach? Who's going to look after your potentially record-breaking marrow while you're away?'

All eyes were on Kevin now.

Tilly took Kevin's hand. 'If it's all right with you, Mum, Kevin and I would like to move into The Elms together. As a couple.'

'Already? Are you sure?'

'Yes, we're sure.'

They did seem perfect for each other. Two academics who were clearly in love. It would be an interesting and no doubt slightly chaotic relationship, but Tilly seemed very happy. It had taken her a long, long time to find a whirlwind romance.

'It's the perfect arrangement,' said Alan. 'Tilly and Kevin can take over from the Gees when they go off on their cruise. They can look after the house, the dog and the garden at the same time.'

'By the time you two come home, we will have finished the renovations on the cottage,' said Kevin. 'My sister's husband is a builder.'

'Hang on,' said Heather. 'Which cottage?'

'Fox Cottage,' said Tilly.

'That tiny, thatched cottage next to the pub? Edith Russell is finally moving house?'

'She died, Heather.'

'She did?'

'It was in the paper.' Alan looked smug.

Tilly linked arms with Kevin. 'We put in an offer, and it was accepted.'

'*We?*'

'Yes, Kevin and me. Not all academics are penniless you know.'

'You're growing up so fast, Tilly.' Tears obscured Heather's view of the daughter who, it only seemed like yesterday, had been her little girl.

'Mum, I'm thirty-five.' Tilly rolled her eyes. 'And I've accepted a teaching post at Southampton University.'

All grown up at last.

Ravi, who so far hadn't said a word, piped up, 'So Alan, Heather, how long do you think you'll be away?'

They looked at each other. Heather spoke. 'I don't know.'

'It depends,' said Alan.

'Depends on what?'

'Where the wind takes us.'

'The wind?'

'Yes,' said Alan. He was bursting to deliver the punchline. 'I've bought you a boat.'

'*You bought me a boat?*' Heather was so shocked it was hard to know where the emphasis should go. Alan had bought a boat. For her. Alan who didn't sail. Alan who didn't like spending money.

All eyes were on her now, everyone waiting for her response, collective breath held.

'Why?'

Frowns now. It wasn't the response everyone had been expecting, or hoping for.

'To say sorry about your car. I shouldn't have done it. I've been wanting to make it up to you but didn't know how. And then you left, and it was too late.'

She tried to stay cross about the car, but the statute of limitations on that particular grudge had long passed.

'Will you forgive me?'

'I might.' Her very own boat! A smile stretched every muscle on her face.

Alan's relief was palpable. Breaths were exhaled and everyone relaxed again.

'It means we won't be at the behest of the Greek ferries,' he said. 'And I thought what better way for us to see the islands and the Mediterranean than from the sea?'

Us. We. The two most hopeful words she'd heard in a long time.

'And . . . ?' Heather sensed there was more. This leopard was still wearing the same spots, whatever came out of his mouth.

'Naturally, I calculated how much everything would cost and if we take into account the flights, ferry tickets and hotel costs, it works out much cheaper to buy a boat and sail it where we want to go. If we sell it again when we've finished, we'll break even.'

'Oh, Alan,' Heather said. 'You're a tight old git, but I do love you.'

'And there she is,' he announced triumphantly, pointing to a blue-hulled timber yacht at the very end of the wharf. 'She's a real beauty. She's got a few years on her but she's immaculate inside. I couldn't believe my luck. I thought it would take weeks to find a suitable boat. This one only came on the market yesterday. I spoke to the owner this morning and made him an offer over the phone. Nice guy. Ex-navy commander. He's off to Lesbos and wanted a quick sale. Got a good price actually. The whole thing is almost too good to be true.'

Almost too good to be true.

It was all Heather could do to keep herself from dissolving at the table. She and Alan, and possibly a little bit of Esme, would be sailing off across the wine-dark sea, heading where the wind took them.

Heather looked around the table. 'You all knew about this?'

They all nodded.

'We came to say goodbye,' said Tilly. 'To wish you bon voyage. And to make sure you two don't kill each other before you set off.'

Then something unexpected happened. Tears spilled down Tilly's cheeks and, before Heather could ask her what was wrong, she jumped up and threw her arms around her mother.

'I'm going to miss you, Mum,' she said. 'I know it's something you have to do, but I'll miss you. You must promise to keep in touch, let me know you're safe. I want pictures and letters and phone calls from every port. You hear me?'

Heather hung on to Tilly, inhaling the scent of strawberries from her hair. It was always harder to be left behind than heading off on the adventure. She knew only too well. Until now, she'd always been the one who was left behind. Her time had come, and it was all the more precious because she'd waited so long for it.

Ravi cleared his throat. 'There's a reason I asked how long you were planning to be away. Sarah and I were wondering if there was any chance you could be back in England by, say, next spring?'

'Why spring?' Heather was puzzled. 'What's going on then?'

Ravi, with a grin from ear to ear, cradled Sarah's belly.

'Because that's when your grandchild is due,' said Sarah.

This was as much a surprise to Alan as it was to Heather. She'd never forget the moment his expression changed as the news sank in. For once he had something to look forward to rather than something to look back on.

'We wanted to tell you in person,' said Sarah. 'It's still early days, but we have a good feeling about this one, don't we, Ravi?'

'Yes, I don't know what it is, but after all the failures and disappointments, something feels different this time. I feel it here.' He pointed to where his chest met his abdomen. The same place Heather felt her own gestalt.

'This calls for a celebration,' she said, gesturing to a waiter. She pointed to the wine list and the waiter returned with an ice bucket and a bottle of Greek sparkling wine.

As the waiter poured, Heather pointed out the silvery bubbles dancing in the golden wine and told them to expect apples, honey and a hint of beeswax.

Ravi raised his eyebrows. Alan sucked in his cheeks.

'Alan, why don't you say a few words?' Heather urged.

'I wouldn't want to bore everybody.' He gave her a meaningful look.

'I owe you an apology,' she said. 'I may have deprived a previous audience of one of the greatest speeches in history.'

'I can't remember it now.'

'Rubbish, you'd been working on it for weeks.' Heather indicated the small crowd gathered at the tables at the taverna under the blue and white awning. 'You have your audience. Off you go. Don't be shy.'

'All right then.' To her amazement, and the collective amusement of his impromptu audience, Alan stood and recited the rest of his speech from the farewell party. Although his words were largely irrelevant to the occasion, he delivered them with aplomb. Like an elder statesman.

He finished with, 'As the great man himself once said, "But the bravest are surely those who have the clearest vision of what is before them, glory and danger alike, and yet notwithstanding go out to meet it."'

This was greeted with a round of applause, principally, Heather imagined, because he'd finished.

Pericles would be proud.

Alan finished with a toast.

'To Tilly and Kevin, congratulations on your first home and welcome to the family, Kevin. To Sarah and Ravi, congratulations and we cannot wait to meet our first grandchild. And lastly, to my darling wife Heather, let's start again. Here's to the rest of our golden gap year.'

Five glasses of Greek sparkling wine and one of orange juice clinked in the middle of the table with a resounding '*Yamas*!'

35

Talk Homer to me

SHE WOKE WITH HER HEAD NESTLED INTO THAT SPECIAL place on Alan's shoulder. While he slept, she caressed the soft paunch that hung over his thirty-six-inch waistband and traced the outline of a clutch of brown, waxy sunspots on his chest that looked like a map of the Greek Isles. A part of Greece that would be forever hers.

Heather slipped out of bed to open the French doors. The curtains billowed like sails in the breeze. Today was the day they set sail. The financial transaction had cleared, and *Athena* now officially belonged to her. *Them.* The girls had helped her with the provisioning, while the boys had conducted a navigation brief over a final bottle of Greek red.

As she gazed out at the diamonds twinkling in the sea, Heather felt several contradictory emotions at once. She would miss Sarah and Tilly, and naturally worry every day about her unborn grandchild, but there was the excitement at starting a new adventure with Alan. Surprisingly, she wasn't apprehensive about spending the coming months with Alan in such confined quarters. Somehow, she knew it would be all right, that the sea would give them all the space they needed.

Alan's copy of *The Odyssey* was resting on top of his open bag. It was a different translation to the one Esme had given her and, having finished reading her own, she brought it back to bed, flicking through the familiar pages as she slipped between the sheets next to Alan. When she looked at his face, his eyes were open, watching her.

Alan sat up and arranged the pillows behind him. He took the book from her, examined it.

'What did you think,' she asked, 'second time around?'

Alan tapped his chin cleft. She waited for his insightful interpretation of its themes – the pain of separation and longing for home, of loyalty and perseverance. Instead, he said, 'You have to feel sorry for Odysseus.'

Heather propped herself up on one elbow. 'How so?'

'The poor bugger has been away for twenty years, and when he gets home, only the dog greets him.'

She laughed at an image of Stan lying in the manure. Alan could always make her laugh. Even when he was being a pain in the backside, he was funny.

'But I must say, I think history has misunderstood Homer. For all his brave and, at times, foolhardy endeavours, I think the real hero of this story is not Odysseus, but Penelope. For putting up with him.'

Heather kissed his shoulder.

But Alan wasn't smiling. If anything, it looked as though tears might not be far away.

'What is it?'

He opened the book to a page he'd marked with an old black-and-white photo. It was of him as a small boy holding his father's hand with a smaller boy sitting on his father's shoulders.

'I haven't seen this before,' said Heather.

'I came across it in a pile of papers when I was looking for my passport.' He propped it up against the lamp on the bedside table.

She was beginning to understand.

'It says here . . .' He scanned the page, holding his glasses like binoculars until he found the passage he was looking for. *'Few sons are like their fathers – most are worse, few better.'*

'Tell me about Ambrose,' said Heather. 'It's time we talked about him, Alan. You know as well as I do that you have to incise the abscess and drain the pus before the antibiotics will work.'

Heather held him while he told her what had happened when he was ten years old, his brother only five. It was in the days before the dual carriageway between Netherwood and Darlingford. The old road crossed the stream at a ford, and Alan's father used to love entertaining his two sons by driving his Land Rover through the slow running water at speed, causing the kind of splash that always put a smile on young boys' faces. One winter, after weeks of rain, the stream was full and the water much higher than normal. A local family, patients at the practice, had tried to drive through the flooded ford in their Morris Minor only to be swept away. On discovering the submerged vehicle, Alan's father had leapt out of the Land Rover, telling Alan to stay behind with Ambrose, and dived into the water to rescue the family.

Sensing the tension building in Alan's muscles, Heather held him tighter, squeezing the pain from his body.

'All I had to do was look after my brother,' said Alan. 'But I wanted to be part of the action. I wanted to follow Dad, help him rescue the family, not stay behind with my little brother, so I climbed out of the Land Rover and waded into the water to get a better view. My father saved the parents and their three children by breaking the window of the car and pulling them out one by one. His arms were cut to ribbons. He was hailed a hero, of course. He'd saved five lives.'

Alan's lips continued to tell the story, but his words were almost inaudible. Heather rested her head on his chest and heard the rest of the tale straight from his heart.

'In all the confusion afterwards, we couldn't find Ambrose. He must have snuck out of the back of the Land Rover while I was watching Dad. There was no sign of him. He'd vanished in a matter of minutes. His body was found the next day, caught up in some tree roots a little way downstream. The coroner found that he'd had an epileptic seizure and drowned in water barely more than ankle deep.'

'And you blamed yourself?'

'I was responsible for him. I should have been watching him. I'd let everybody down.'

'You were a little boy yourself.'

'For a long time afterwards, Dad couldn't even look at me. He abandoned his garden, let the weeds take over. I offered to help him, but he wouldn't let me. It was as though he couldn't bear to set foot out there again, couldn't cope with the memories. Eventually the wooden beds rotted away and there was nothing left. He worked himself into the ground, to escape the pain, I suppose. It was the only way he knew how to cope.'

'And how did you cope?'

'Not very well. Boarding school has a way of discouraging any signs of emotional vulnerability. I managed to keep it buried deep inside. It surfaced, in my gap year, and I tried to process Ambrose's death through booze, drugs and sex. But by the end of that year, I was pretty sick of myself. My father wasn't impressed, I can tell you, and he let me know in no uncertain terms what a disappointment I was. So I decided to pull myself together and pay my penance by becoming a doctor. I thought that if I could become a doctor like him, he'd be proud of me again. And in training as a neurologist, maybe I was making it up to Ambrose too. I was about to publish my first research paper on epilepsy management when Dad died.'

They talked it through, trying to reframe the events as nothing more than a tragic accident. After a while, Alan's body relaxed again. The pain was written across his age-softened features, his wrinkles a relief map of his buried emotions, the peaks and troughs so familiar that Heather had never guessed what lay beneath them. But she could also see the first signs of forgiveness. He'd been punishing himself by holding onto this guilt for so long. Whether it was alcohol, like Dennis, or organic gardening like Alan, every survivor needed a crutch.

'Some men *are* better, Alan,' said Heather stroking his chin. 'Because you've stuck around. You helped so many people in your career, and you're still here. For your family.'

Heroes came in all shapes and waist sizes.

He turned towards her, pulled their pillows together until their noses were almost touching.

She told Alan she was proud of him. What he'd told her took just as much courage as jumping into flooded water and smashing a car window. For Heather, the pieces had finally fallen into place. Buying the Land Rover might have been a sentimental act but resurrecting his father's vegetable garden was a way of reconnecting with his dead brother; what the Ancient Greeks would have called nostalgia. From the words *nostos*, meaning to return from an epic journey, and *algia*, meaning pain.

Alan turned to face her. 'Tell me, what did you think about Homer's ending?'

Heather gazed wistfully into his thoughts. 'I don't know what I was expecting. Not a Hollywood sunset or a last-minute dash to the airport, obviously. The story doesn't so much end as stop.'

Heather lifted her head from Alan's chest, partly to see his face, and partly because his wiry chest hairs were beginning to irritate her cheek. 'Do you think Penelope and Odysseus lived happily ever after?'

'I expect they had their ups and downs, like all couples,' Alan replied. 'You have to wonder if Odysseus ever regretted not staying on as Calypso's sex slave when Penelope nagged him about the prawn heads in the bin.'

A frown felt unfamiliar on Heather's face. 'And I'm sure there were times when Penelope wished she'd bagged a hunky toyboy from her many suitors instead of hanging around for the King of Ithaca whenever he felt the urge to dress like a beggar.'

'I imagine that it took a while to return to normal after living separate lives for so long.'

Alan stroked her neck. 'There was another passage that struck me, one I hadn't appreciated when I was eight years old.'

'Which passage was that?'

'No *finer, greater gift than that . . . when man and woman possess their home, two minds, two hearts that work as one . . .*'

'Ooh, I do like it when you talk Homer to me,' she breathed.

Deep inside, a pilot light flickered and burst into flames, sending hot blood rushing to unfamiliar and long-neglected places. In the end, it hadn't been the hot Greek guy who'd reignited the passion, but a blind bard and a two-thousand-year-old epic poem. And there was no doubt in her mind that one of the greatest stories ever told was a romance between a husband and a wife. The most beautiful love story of all time.

⁓

After a session of proper hot, steamy, toe-curling, making-noises kind of lovemaking, Alan disappeared into the bathroom for a shower. When he emerged, bare-chested, towel wrapped around his waist, silhouetted in steam, he looked like a gladiator in a movie trailer. The illusion soon faded, when after drilling each ear with the corner of the bath towel, he examined the results of his aural excavation with a look of triumph.

'Shower's all yours,' he said. 'I'll make you tea while you're getting ready.'

The bathroom was still steamy, the mirror obscured by condensation from Alan's recent shower. At home she was always telling him to open the window after he'd finished. Either that or, on the day hell froze over, mend the broken extractor fan in the ensuite bathroom. As usual, he'd left water all over the floor, and a soapy foam of iron filings in the sink next to his razor. And yet, rather than irritation, Heather found herself consoled by these small familiarities.

She cleared a window in the condensation with a hand towel and looked at herself. Her face was tanned, eyes much bluer than before. Never one for wasting too much time being disappointed by her reflection, Heather examined herself in the bright bathroom light. Even without her glasses, the change was striking. She barely recognised the woman staring back at her. The lines around her mouth now mapped the contours of a smile. Even the worry creases in the middle of her forehead, lines that she'd considered a tool of her trade, had smoothed, as if a wave had washed away a footprint in the sand.

Heather showered and dried herself off, then helped herself to one of the 'his' and 'hers' hotel bathrobes hanging on the back of the bathroom door. Alan was already sitting out on the balcony looking through the room service menu.

'I thought we'd eat breakfast alfresco this morning,' he said. A cheeky smile hijacked his face. 'I don't know why we haven't done this before.'

Heather went to play-punch his shoulder but stopped. He was wearing a white waffle bathrobe, just like the one she'd tried to get him to wear on that first morning.

'Is that . . . ?'

'Yes,' he replied. 'I rather like it. Can't think why I kept my old one so long.'

Epilogue

At first, Stan didn't react when they walked into
the kitchen. Even when Heather filled the kettle and set it
to boil, the old dog's eyes stayed firmly shut. When he was
a puppy, he'd rush to the front door at the merest sound,
skidding across the polished chessboard tiles in the hall to
greet any and every arrival.

Alan crouched beside the dog basket. Heather leaned over
his shoulder, looking for signs of life. Stan's leather button
nose twitched as he caught a familiar scent. He opened
his cloudy, unseeing eyes. Another wriggle of his nose as his
grey-flecked muzzle explored Alan's hand. Finally, Stan's tail
thumped against the wicker.

The old dog struggled to his feet, arched his back in a
stretch and showered his humans with fishy kisses. He soon
lost interest, circling his bed and slumping onto Alan's old
dressing gown once more.

'It's the same greeting whether we've been gone five minutes or a year,' Heather said.

'At least he remembers us.'

And waited for us, Heather thought, remembering Argos.

Heather made a pot of tea while Alan carried their luggage upstairs. The transformation from the Alan who, only months ago, had huffed and puffed with Tilly's suitcases was striking. If he'd bothered to have his fasting bloods done back then, he would have been well and truly in the pre-diabetic range. Now he was slimmer and fitter than she'd seen him in years, courtesy of all that sail trimming and deck scrubbing. Not quite the athletic rower she'd met at medical school, but a very respectable senior version of him. His skin was tanned, and he'd grown a salt and pepper beard that suited him.

Heather wasn't the woman she'd been a few months ago either. Hers was more than a physical remodelling, however. She'd learned to slow down, to let things go. In the months since they'd been away, she hadn't apologised once. Except to herself.

Towards the end, they'd both been ready to come home. The boat broker already had a keen buyer lined up for *Athena*, and they were looking forward to seeing their family again. Alan was particularly excited about seeing his garden, especially after Kevin had planted the first of the vines.

'Your tea is ready,' said Heather, handing Alan his favourite mug.

'Aah,' he said after his first sip. 'I've missed a decent cup of tea.'

Heather traced the words 'Living the Dream' on hers. This time a year ago she wouldn't have been seen dead in a caravan, and yet she and Alan had essentially spent their gap year living in a floating caravan.

In the middle of the kitchen table, propped up against a vase of fresh garden flowers, was a card from Tilly and Kevin, welcoming them home. With the renovations on Fox Cottage complete, they'd finally moved in. Having travelled halfway across the world to find what she'd been searching for, Tilly had found it barely a mile down the road from where she'd started.

As Heather wandered around the house, reacquainting herself with each familiar room, she was struck by how little had changed. The furniture and all their belongings were more or less as they'd left them. How cluttered her home looked, she thought, seeing it through new eyes. On the boat, she and Alan had survived, thrived even, on surprisingly little; not much more than the clothes they'd arrived with and the food they picked up fresh at each port. They'd collected one or two mementoes along the way – an embroidered tablecloth in Dubrovnik, a ceramic bowl in Palermo and a small hand-painted tray in Rimini – but hadn't missed most of the things they'd previously owned. Alan hadn't read a single newspaper.

While Kevin had kept the vegetable garden and the greenhouse immaculate, the house itself was looking rather tired and in desperate need of maintenance. The wisteria was now so overgrown she wouldn't have been surprised to find Sleeping Beauty tucked up in one of the bedrooms, and the bay window really did need cleaning. The mirror that Alan had been meaning to hang was still resting against the wall, and the extractor fan in the bathroom still broken. The detritus in the dining room obscured the table as always.

The difference was that none of these things mattered anymore to Heather. The job list was like an old-fashioned roller towel dispenser. It would never end. Somehow, there was always a dry bit to wipe your hands on.

The Gees had sent Alan and Heather a postcard from every port on their cruise of Greece and the Adriatic. As a huge Nicolas Cage fan, Mrs Gee had particularly enjoyed the *Captain Corelli's Mandolin* tour of Cephalonia, though a card sent days later from Corfu had been equally impressed by a tour of locations where *The Durrells* had been filmed.

The best part was that each card had been addressed to 'Alan and Heather' and signed from 'Norman and Kaye'. After all these years, they were finally on first name terms.

Heather put the postcards to one side, on top of the pile of unopened letters, medical journals and magazines that would need to be sorted. Tilly had intercepted anything that looked urgent, and they had answered emails whenever they were in port, surprised by how few matters demanded urgent attention. It was tempting to throw the whole lot straight into the bin. But then something caught her eye. A single word on the front of a medical journal.

Refugee.

She tore open the plastic wrapper and flicked through until she found the article in the magazine. As she did, something awoke inside her.

Volunteer GPs sought to mentor refugee and asylum seeker doctors.

She read on. There was a tingling, churning, fluttering sensation in her epigastrium. Heather moved a box of old medical textbooks and sank into the sofa, clutching the article to her chest. She thought of Dennis, as she still did from time to time. At first it had been hard living aboard his boat, sleeping in his bed, without remembering their few days together. She didn't regret a single second she'd spent with him. As wise Esme had once told her, the grass may always appear greener on the other side of the fence. But if you water your own grass, it can grow just as green.

As the weeks passed, however, her thoughts of Dennis began to disappear into the wake behind the boat. She would never forget his tear-streaked face as he told the story about the boy he'd found in the water and the people he'd managed to rescue. And though she would never know for sure, Heather wondered if there had been a doctor in that unlucky boat, maybe even a GP. She pictured those who had survived the journey on other boats, locked up in camps waiting to be processed, afraid, traumatised and facing years of uncertainty.

What if she could help even one doctor who'd escaped a terrible life to start again in a country she loved, doing a job she had loved? She'd made a career out of making a difference to the life of one person at a time. What if this time, the person she helped was someone who could go on to improve the lives of many more?

The idea hit her in a rush. Heather rummaged through the remaining mail until she found an envelope addressed to her, bearing the General Medical Council logo. She tore it open, eyes scanning for dates and key words. She'd forgotten to cancel her registration before she'd left for Greece and the direct debit for her annual renewal fee had been automatically processed. That meant she was still officially able to practise as a doctor. And, more importantly, she could mentor another doctor. A quick check of a bank statement confirmed that Alan had remembered to cancel his own direct debit, and therefore his registration, before he flew out to join her.

It was only fair to tell him what she'd decided to do. While they were away, they'd talked at length about how different things would be when they returned. Heather had agreed to feed the hens, collect the eggs, and help set up a foodbank of fresh produce. In return, Alan had promised to support her in whatever challenge she decided on next.

She found him in the kitchen looking for second-hand breadmakers on eBay. They hadn't even unpacked yet.

'I've worked out that if we made two loaves per week, the machine would pay for itself in less than six months.'

Heather didn't want to burst his bubble, pointing out that the very fact there were so many barely used breadmakers for resale was because the novelty usually wore off long before anyone broke even.

'Where are all the newspapers, Alan?' She had a stack of correspondence to add to his pile. It might be the only way to get him to deal with it.

'I put them all in the recycling bin.'

'You did?'

He leaned back in his chair, hands clasped at the back of his head. 'I decided that life is too short to read old news, Heather. Besides, I didn't much care for the way the world was heading.'

She kissed him on the top of his head. His hair no longer smelt of sea and salt. He smelt like Alan again. And home.

'There's something I want to talk to you about,' she said. 'There's a project I'd like to take part in. It's the perfect job for me. It's part-time, so I wouldn't become too stressed or overwhelmed, and it would leave plenty of time for us to do things together.'

The phone rang in the hall before she had the chance to tell him any more. It was strange to hear that sound again.

'I'll get it,' said Heather.

Her gestalt was calling. So was Alan's.

'No, I'll answer it!' In his haste to beat her to the phone, his chair toppled over behind him.

They arrived at the receiver at the same time.

Alan picked it up. Heather tried to snatch it from him. He lifted it up high out of her reach.

'Switch it to loudspeaker, Alan.'

'Hello?' they said at the same time.

'Heather, Alan. It's Ravi,' said the voice on the other end. This time it wasn't Ravishing Ravi but Rattled Ravi. 'I'm at the hospital. It all happened so quickly; this is the first opportunity I've had to call you.' A pause the length of a deep breath. 'Congratulations. You have a grandson.'

Alan and Heather watched the joy bloom across each other's faces as the news sank in. Then the questions tumbled out. 'How's Sarah? Did she have an epidural? How's the baby? What were his Apgar scores? Has he had his vitamin K?'

'They're both doing really well, considering.'

'Can we speak to her?'

A few muffled sounds later, they heard Sarah's weary but elated voice.

'Congratulations, darling,' Alan and Heather said in unison. 'We are so happy for you.'

'He's gorgeous. You're going to love him. And, if it's all right with you, Dad, we'd like to call him Ambrose.'

Life would never be the same again. They'd returned from one journey just in time to begin a brand-new one. They wouldn't be travelling anywhere for a while, and Heather couldn't be happier. She'd had her adventure and proved to herself what Esme had once told her when Tilly had first moved to New Zealand and Heather feared she was gone for good: that you needed to leave home to miss home.

Acknowledgements

FIRSTLY, MY THANKS TO THE ENTIRE TEAM AT HACHETTE Australia, all of whom go above and beyond. To my publisher Rebecca Saunders, thank you for your vision and your passion for this book. Your instincts were spot on, as always. Thanks also to Holly Jeffery and Kirstin Corcoran in Australia, and to Olivia Barber and Amy Batley at Hodder & Stoughton in the UK. Christa Moffitt from Christabella Designs: thank you for another wonderful cover.

It is always a privilege to work with talented editors who do so much more than dot the i's and cross the t's. Thank you to Karen Ward and Deonie Fiford for your intelligent and insightful suggestions.

Knowing that I was in such good hands with my agents at Curtis Brown freed up much needed creative headspace. Thank you, Tara Wynne in Sydney and Lucy Morris in London.

To the wise and witty women of The Ink Well, namely Pamela Cook, Penelope Janu, Rae Cairns, Laura Boon, Terri Green, Michelle Barraclough, and Angella Whitton: thank you for the love, laughter and endless support. I still maintain our WhatsApp group chat would be an instant bestseller. I would also like to thank the other fabulous women of the broader writing community for their generosity, not only to me personally, but in consistently encouraging and nurturing each other's work. A special thank you to writing friend Claudine Tinellis and her husband Steven, for casting a modern Greek eye over the manuscript. *Efcharistó!* The name Kaye Gee appears in the book courtesy of author Poppy Gee who generously bid to 'name a character' during fundraising for the inaugural Northern Beaches Readers Festival.

I am grateful to the following friends for sharing everything from memories of medical school to the names of gentlemen's raincoat manufacturers: Katharine Hartington, Newton Astbury, Nikki Jackson, Gareth Turner, Will and Kate McConnell, Lucy Guest, and Fiona Hoar. Elly Brimacombe, thank you for answering my many questions about migrant camps.

Thanks to my parents John and Diane Spain, I was lucky enough to write an entire draft of this book in the splendid isolation of the Snowdonia National Park in Wales. Thanks also to Newton for use of another perfect writing space overlooking the picturesque Northumbrian coast.

This novel may never have left the fictional village of Netherwood had my daughter not introduced me to Homer. Charlotte, thank you for the excellent crash course in Greek mythology. To my husband and nautical fact-checker, John,

I will never forget that first Ionian sailing holiday twenty-six years ago. Thank you for being both the wind in my sails and the rudder that keeps me on course. And no John, you are not Alan. To William, my not-so-little adventurer: our long-distance mother–son chats are always a welcome break from writing.

In researching this novel, I read far more widely than I strictly needed to, including both fiction and non-fiction, ancient and modern. The following two books were particularly influential, however. The Ithaca storyline was inspired by the account of an amateur Homer enthusiast who, with the help of a geologist and a professor of Greek and Latin, set out to solve the mystery surrounding the true location of ancient Ithaca. *Odysseus Unbound: The Search for Homer's Ithaca* by Robert Bittlestone, with James Diggle and John Underhill, is published by Cambridge University Press, 2005. *In Search of Homeric Ithaca* by Jonathan Brown, published by Parrot Press, 2020, provided further reading on the subject.

I would like to acknowledge the use of lines from E V Rieu's 1946 translation of *The Odyssey* by Homer, published by Penguin Books. I also acknowledge that Alan's apt description of studying *The Odyssey* as a boy as akin to 'picking bones from fish', was borrowed from Adam Nicholson's excellent book *The Mighty Dead: Why Homer Matters*, published by William Collins Books, 2014.

If you enjoyed

Mrs Winterbottom Takes a Gap Year

you'll love Joanna Nell's other gorgeous books about growing old disgracefully . . .

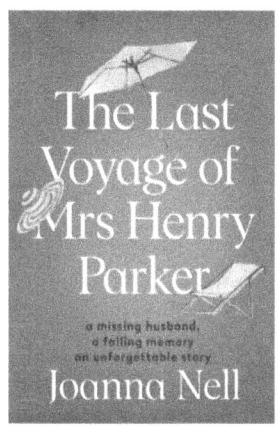

Available in paperback and eBook

HODDER &
STOUGHTON

An invitation from the publisher

Join us at www.hodder.co.uk, or follow us
on Twitter @hodderbooks to be a part of
our community of people who love the very
best in books and reading.

Whether you want to discover more about a book
or an author, watch trailers and interviews, have the
chance to win early limited editions, or simply browse
our expert readers' selection of the very best books,
we think you'll find what you're looking for.

And if you don't, that's the place to tell us what's missing.

We love what we do, and we'd love you to be a part of it.

www.hodder.co.uk

@hodderbooks

HodderBooks

HodderBooks